MAIDEN OF MIDDLEHAM

To dear Rosanna, with love
and Best wishes
Bridget N. Beauchamp.
xx.

1st Edition

Published in 2021 by

Woodfield Publishing Ltd
Bognor Regis PO21 5EL England
www.woodfieldpublishing.co.uk

Cataloguing in Publication Data is available from the British Library

ISBN 978-1-84683-199-7

Printed and bound in England

Typesetting & page design: Nic Pastorius
Cover design: Klaus Schaffer
Cover illustration: P.J. Lynch

Source document:
Maiden of Middleham (final-2).ppp

Maiden of Middleham

A Ricardian Romance

BRIDGET M. BEAUCHAMP

woodfieldpublishing.co.uk

Publishing Ltd

WOODFIELD

independent book publishers

Woodfield Publishing Ltd

West Sussex ~ England

Interesting & informative books on a wide variety of subjects

For full details about all our books, visit our website
www.woodfieldpublishing.co.uk

To my children and grandchildren,
in the hope they will one day come to understand
my obsession with Richard III.

⚜ ⚜ ⚜

This is a story of love and loss set in the turbulent times of late 15th Century England at the end of the Wars of the Roses between the houses of York & Lancaster.

Although some of the central characters are fictional, the story also features real people and events from the time of Richard III, last of the Plantagenet kings.

After his death Richard was demonised by the Tudors in order to destroy his reputation, a character assassination so successful that to this day he exists in the popular imagination as a hunchbacked villain.

This narrative aims to counter this misinformation by portraying Richard as a loving and loyal family man who was popular in his lifetime and would, without doubt, have gone on to become one of the greatest English monarchs.

⚜ ⚜ ⚜

Neville & York Family Trees

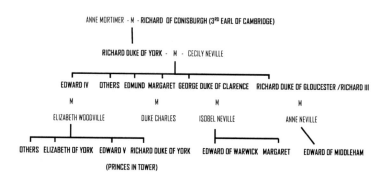

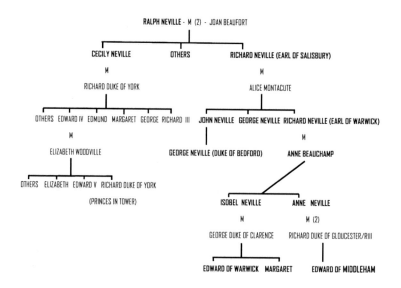

Main Fictional Characters

Eleanor Wildman, *the Maiden of Middleham*
Elizabeth, *her daughter*
Edward & **James,** *Eleanor's brothers*
Marguerite, *ladies' maid* | **Philippa ~ Isabella**
Ralph, *soldier* | **Aunt Mabel** | **Agnes,** *kitchen maid*
Will Metcalfe, *huntsman* | **William,** *Eleanor's son*
Phillipe, *bowman* | **Jane,** *milkmaid* | **John,** *ploughman*

Main Historical Characters

Richard Duke of Gloucester/ King Richard III
King Edward IV | **George,** Duke of Clarence
Richard Neville, *Earl of Warwick*
Anne Beauchamp, *Countess of Warwick* | **Isobel Neville**
Anne Neville | **Edward** of Middleham | **Cecily,** Duchess of
York | **Margaret of York,** Duchess of Burgundy
Charles Duke of Burgundy | **Queen Elizabeth** (Woodville)
Elizabeth of York | **Henry VI**
Marguerite of Anjou | **Eduard** of Lancaster
Edward & **Richard,** *sons of Edward IV*
Henry Stafford, Duke of Buckingham | **Francis Lovell**
Louis XI of France | **William Hastings** | **Anthony Earl Rivers**
Thomas Stanley | **William Stanley** | **Margaret Beaufort**
Henry Tudor | **Bishop Stillington** | **Bishop Morton**

~ About The Author ~

RIDGET BEAUCHAMP IS A RETIRED house-
wife, mother, and grandmother who lives
in Cumbria near the North Yorkshire
border. The author, a dedicated member of the
Richard III Society, has a lifelong interest in British
history, particularly the Plantagenet kings and the
Wars of the Roses. She has been fascinated by Richard
III's life since the discovery of his remains in Leicester
in 2012.

The author wrote this novel in the hopes of portraying a more sympathetic image of this tragic and most
courageous king, driven by a desire to exonerate
Richard from the crimes attributed to him and restore
his rightful standing in the annals of history.

Let valour end my life.

SIR WALTER RALEGH

Middleham Castle.

Chapter One

T WAS LATE MAY IN the year 1468. Across the wide vale of Wensleydale the dawn light invaded the gloom and chased the night across undulating pastures and slowly the stone walls, solitary barns and clusters of cottages crowding round solid stone churches, emerged like ghosts out of the darkness. Resounding across the Rivers Ure and Cover, meandering lazily through this tranquil valley, its lush meadows awakening with the blooms of Spring, the prime bell of Middleham church rang out, proclaiming the new day. The sun's first rays burst over the horizon, lighting the bleak upland crags that defined the skyline, creeping down the steep hillsides, across swathes of dark woodland, in a race with the retreating shadows, illuminating the topmost tower of the great castle keep before unhurriedly revealing the solid outer walls of this Northern fortress which stood guard above the sleepy market town that bore its name.

Farther down the valley, in a Yorkshire farmhouse, a teenage girl stirred in her bed, birdsong permeating her dream, the melodic notes, first distant and wavering, becoming loud and lucid as her attention focused. As the old rooster crowed in the yard, sunbeams filtered shafts of lucent gold through the cracked casement, spotlighting dust particles floating in the warm air of the tiny bedchamber. It was one of those dreams that, upon waking, still lingered, blurring the realms of fantasy and reality; the clamour and shouts from a visionary battle falling away, a flower-filled meadow emerging beneath the dreamer's feet, oozing blood that soaked into her shoes, turning them a rich mulberry red, her voiceless scream metamorphosing into the cockerel's clarion call as actuality crystallised.

Eleanor opened her eyes, slowly adapting to the light, allowing her thoughts to clear in the confusion of sounds and images, so vivid in the world of sleep, now falling away to oblivion.

Saints be praised that was not real! She exhaled with relief as vestiges of the nightmare endured in her mind's eye. The balmy atmosphere pervading her low-beamed room, the reassuring hum as a bee buzzed determinedly around the straws of thatch shading the low-slung window without, foretold of a fine day to come.

Reluctant to leave the comforting warmth of her bed, Eleanor indulged in a few moments to adjust.

'Why do I feel different today, as if my life were about to change?' she pondered, resting on her elbows before sitting up with an involuntary shudder, as if to shake herself free from the demons of the night. Swinging her bare legs over the side of the bed and splashing her face with cold water from the jug on the table before hurriedly pulling a white linen tunic over her head, Eleanor reached for her plain woollen kirtle and milkmaids' apron, girdling the sash tightly around her slender waist. Brushing her long waves of luxuriant auburn hair, pushing stray strands under her bonnet, she slipped into her calfskin shoes before quietly lifting the latch on the bedroom door and crept downstairs so as not to alert the ploughman, asleep outside the pantry. John had been drinking heavily the night before. Eleanor had heard him crashing about in the kitchen, cursing, before collapsing onto the settle in a stupor. He would soon, no doubt, be leering at her as he passed the cowshed on his way to the stables.

Eleanor, now 15, fair-skinned, pretty and innocent, her long lashes shading big green eyes and a smattering of pale freckles dancing over her nose, had been working at the manor farm since she was 11. Her mother had died shortly after giving birth to Eleanor, leaving her in the care of her Aunt Mabel at the farm, a God-fearing spinster, plain and dour in looks but educated and pragmatic in outlook. Eleanor's father John, a retainer of the Earl of Warwick, had been killed fighting for the Yorkist cause at the battle of Towton, seven years previously. Her older brothers, Edward and James, were in service for the Earl and part of the castle retinue, being prepared to ride, hunt and fight when they came of age. They had been away from home since they were 11 and 12 years old and Eleanor had missed their company, despite the frequent fights and relentless teasing she had endured. When she last saw them,

Edward had promised to put in a good word for his sister with the Earl when suitable employment arose in his household.

Eleanor enjoyed her work on the farm, tending the chickens, geese and pigs, milking the cows, often being permitted to ride the big shire horses up on the moors and occasionally the fell ponies, once they were rounded up and broken in. She had a natural seat for riding and as a child, was oft known to don her brother's tunic and leggings enabling her to ride astride, until her aunt forbade such unladylike behaviour. Eleanor would spend hours watching the farrier with his anvil, rasp and hammer, trimming hooves, shaping the horseshoes, knocking nails into the hoof wall, to secure the shoes onto the animal's huge feet. Initially aghast at what looked barbaric to a child, Eleanor had soon learned from the blacksmith which part of the hoof was insensate nerveless tissue. Brushing out tangled manes and long tails, stroking soft noses, offering carrots or apples she had saved for these gentle giants, Eleanor was mindful to keep her fingers away from their eager bite. She loved the creatures she cared for; conscious that kindness cost nothing and would be rewarded with trust.

Her aunt had made sure she was literate, enabling her to enjoy the poetry and chivalric tales lovingly read to her by her father, fuelling her vivid imagination with romantic ideals – Arthurian tales of dashing young men, virile, strong and skilful, loyal and brave, yet tender and compassionate to their womenfolk, risking all for King and country. How often Eleanor's mind's eye had conjured up innocent fantasies of courtly love, visualising herself waving off her knight as he mounted his charger, riding off to prove himself on the field of battle, before returning victorious, to sweep up his lady love in an embrace of unbridled passion.

Sighing wistfully, Eleanor made her way across the farmyard, glancing up to the limestone escarpment above the forest, where the sound of a distant hunting horn echoed across the wide valley from the moorland above. Somewhere up there the Earl and his huntsmen were out scouring the woods and heath for deer and the elusive wild boar, destined for the spits of the castle kitchens. Entering the pungent warmth of the cowshed, she pulled the milking stool beneath her, sat down beside the first cow's extended udder and began to ease the milk from its teats. The rhythmic splash of the creamy liquid hitting the pail, the warmth of the barn and the drone of flies lulled her into a daydream and her mind wandered to the young men riding out on the moor, following the hounds, laughing and urging their steeds forward in the thrill of the chase. She wondered if Edward and James were with the hunting party, envying their escape to the wide open spaces and fresh upland air on this cloudless morning.

This awkward stage of adolescence and the onset of puberty had awakened untapped feelings of desire and longing in Eleanor as she gradually became aware of her femininity and attraction to the opposite sex, her burgeoning womanhood now softening her awkward childhood frame into fetching curves. She had begun to admire from afar, good looking young men, full of promise and potential, ready to grab life by the horns and fulfil the destinies mapped out for them. She had seen the Earl's men riding through the town, her pulse quickening at the sight of their youthful physiques and taut thighs gripping the flanks of their steeds as they rode by, exuding latent power and harnessed energy, striving to excel and assert their masculine prowess. Eleanor delighted in her new-found feminine allure and looked forward to the day a young man would succumb to her charms and call her his own.

Eleanor did not make friends easily, her shyness forcing her to withdraw into self-reflection, keeping her thoughts private and unspoken, as being the best way to shield herself from hurt or her own naivety. Accustomed to ignoring the other village children, who would run off together and hide from her, saying she had ideas above her station, Eleanor was indifferent to their taunts. "Here comes 'Lady' Eleanor," they would chant mockingly, mistaking her reserve for haughtiness, but she was happy in her own company and quite used to seeking her own amusement without the need for the approval of her peers. Her old aunt had brought her up to be well-mannered and conscientious in her work, but having no children of her own was aloof and strict with her niece. Aunt Mabel, straight-laced and pious, made sure Eleanor adhered faithfully to her Catholic upbringing, attending regular mass and confession. Having never known her mother's love, Eleanor missed her father, who had been frequently away in the service of the Earl. After he died, the love and affection she craved came only from her brothers. Since they too had left for the castle, Eleanor was compelled to rely on nobody but herself.

She had always been a thin, pale, delicate-limbed child, but with an inner strength not apparent in her appearance. Her natural elegance meant she held herself well, poised and graceful, longing to dance, envying the ladies of the castle, picturing them in their fine dresses, sparkling jewels and fashionable headdresses, stepping daintily in time to the minstrels' lutes, and fiddles, covertly eyeing up the young courtiers. Smiling inwardly at her romantic notions, Eleanor decided at the end of the day she would walk out onto the heathland path and watch the huntsmen return, perchance to see her brothers too, she told herself.

The pail full, Eleanor got up and carefully poured the warm liquid into a large churn. As she did so, a shadow fell across the wall and she flinched, splashing dribbles of milk down her apron as two fleshy hands grabbed her waist and a lungful of thick ale-tainted breath caressed her neck. John, now awakened from his torpor but still under the influence of last night's indulgence, had crept up behind her and now roughly twisted her body towards him and thrust his face into hers.

"Come on now Miss Ellie, where's me morning kiss then?" he leered in his thick Yorkshire accent, trapping her between his raised arms. Pressing her back against the shippon wall she pushed him as hard as she could but his six foot hefty bulk proved too solid for her slight frame, so instead she nimbly ducked under his arm, a malodorous waft of stale sweat invading her nostrils as she did so.

"Get off me, you stink of ale. You'd better not let Mister Turner catch you in here!" Eleanor retorted, in the vain hope the plough-man would desist in his advances, but as always he ignored her protests, grinning lecherously and undressing her with his eyes while her cheeks reddened as she imagined her garments melting away under his scrutiny.

Just then, to her relief, a voice boomed across the yard.

"John boy, where are you lad? Get those horses harnessed, we need to get the hay in by sundown!"

John stomped off, smirking with satisfaction at the virtuous maid's discomfort. He had laboured at the farm since he was a lad, his stocky build and brute strength his main redeeming features, compensating well enough for his rudimentary intellect. He had long lusted after Eleanor and indeed any other young female he encountered, who all soon learned to forestall his advances.

Jane, three years younger than Eleanor, was busy milking in the adjoining stall but had heard the ploughman come in. She stopped milking and waited for his footsteps to confirm his departure before tentatively popping her freckled face, with its mop of unruly red hair, round the partition.

"Has he gone? Ugly brute! You should get your brothers onto him. If he came near me, I'd knee him where it would hurt most!"

"Hah!" Eleanor laughed. "I doubt he would heed it at all, he's so dense! Anyway, give it a couple of years and *you* may be the focus of his attentions once he tires of me."

"Eugh! Saints forfend!" Jane grimaced.

The hunting horn sounded again, more distant now, and Eleanor looked up dreamily, picturing the riders with the wind in their hair, the thud of hooves on the turf, the jangle of harness, the baying of hounds, the smell of leather and horse sweat.

"They're out early today." Her companion's face lit up.

"Ellie, have you seen the Earl's new ward? I wouldn't mind *his* hands around my waist!"

One of Jane's cousins worked in the castle kitchen and kept her eye out for any new pages arriving on the scene who might be of interest, had pointed him out. Eleanor's brothers had spoken of the likeable youth with boyish looks, who had attracted the attention of the serving girls.

"Do you mean Francis? Edward and James say he's really friendly. I've only seen him from a distance. I was thinking of walking up to see them return from the hunt later, so I will look out for him."

"I'll come too," Jane declared, before remembering her manners and the fact she knew of her friend's preference for solitude. "May I, Ellie?" she entreated hopefully. Jane's enthusiasm was such that Eleanor felt it churlish to refuse, despite her wish to be alone.

"Of course Jane," she conceded reluctantly, "if you've finished your work. But they mustn't see us. I do not wish to embarrass my brothers."

Being the elder of the two, Eleanor sometimes found her companion annoyingly unrestrained and immature, but her honesty was refreshing and Jane had proved herself a loyal friend, despite the age difference, who could be relied upon to spring to Eleanor's defence when needed. Jane was from peasant stock and, as their eldest child, she had been sent to earn her keep from a young age while her parents struggled to provide for their brood. Unschooled but honest and cheerful, Jane was willing and uncomplaining of her position in life and Eleanor appreciated her natural openness and lack of guile.

The day was long and unseasonably warm. The girls worked hard, first in the cowshed, then in the dairy churning butter, and lastly in the farmhouse kitchen kneading dough and chopping vegetables for cook to make into pies and stews for the farmhands toiling in the fields. Eleanor could see them, bent over their scythes, slicing to and fro through the grass, allowing it to dry in the sun before gathering and loading it onto carts to be taken to the barns; their back-breaking day's work broken only by the sext bell at midday, when they would stop for some bread and cheese washed down with warm, watery ale. A Spring heatwave meant haymaking had come early this year and Eleanor was thankful that she could retreat to the shade of the farmyard and the cool of the dairy as she went about her tasks.

Later that afternoon, their day's chores complete, the girls set out for Middleham Moor. The sun was still high in the sky and a welcome breeze fanned the heathland grasses as Eleanor and Jane made their way along the well-worn rutted track, pitted with many hoofprints, now baked hard, which impeded their progress. Rabbits bolted into burrows at the sound of their footsteps, a kestrel hovered overhead and Jane squealed, narrowly avoiding stepping on an adder basking in the sun's warmth, before it slithered silently under a gorse bush, the winged hunter's chance of a tasty meal thwarted by the girls' approach. The sweet heady perfume of the abundant yellow florets permeated the air and in the coppice below them, a carpet of misty bluebells stretched down to the river's edge. Cowslips on the banks nodded their pretty yellow bell-heads and clumps of primroses dotted the fields alongside puddled tracks shaded by May trees, groaning under dense cascades of white blossom, winding their way through the valley. This was Eleanor's favourite time of year, fresh, green, bursting with colour and just warm enough with the promise of summer for the girls to discard their thick woollen cloaks.

As they climbed, Eleanor surveyed the scene, casting her eye across the wide, wild uplands, sweeping down to rolling pastures, verdant and lush, home to many a shepherd's flock with its quota of new Spring lambs, leaping and bleating with the joys of life. Below them the farmstead and beyond the turrets of Middleham castle, ancestral seat of the Nevilles, rising high up above the river Ure, the Earl of Warwick's standard, emblazoned with the bear and ragged staff, atop the battlements, snapping in the breeze. Beyond, the bleak limestone outcrops rigid and unforgiving, rose up in sharp relief outlined against a clear blue sky; a pair of buzzards cruised on the thermals, scanning the fields where far below flocks of lapwings and red-beaked oystercatchers gathered to guard their nests hidden in the grass. Eleanor loved this valley, her home, the only world she knew, fresh and clean, far from the crowds of York, the narrow dirt filled streets, the stifling smells and the clamour of city life.

Settling themselves down by the path, kicking off their shoes and warming the soles of their bare feet on the moss-speckled rocks, the girls chatted together quietly. They talked of handsome princes, dashing knights, gorgeous gowns and fabulous jewels, the men they would marry and children they would have, smiling together in girlish fantasies, exploring the blessings life may hold in the years to come, certain it would be thrilling.

Before long, the sound of the returning hunt reached their ears. Eleanor ducked down in the heather, pulling Jane down beside her. Leading the party and riding a large black courser, Earl Richard Neville appeared, a proud, richly-dressed, middle-aged man with a tanned, bearded face, closely followed by several huntsmen with a pack of unruly hounds running along beside them, before the youths came into view. Among them were an angelic lad with shoulder-length wavy blonde hair, a rather arrogant looking dark-haired thick-set man, Eleanor's brothers Edward and James and several other young men, laughing and chatting excitedly about the day's exploits.

Eleanor's gaze was drawn to a striking, fine-featured youth dressed in forest green, with a serious, pale, chiselled face, collar-length straight light brown hair and soft grey/blue eyes, riding slightly apart from the others, his sleek, splendidly harnessed chestnut thoroughbred stallion tossing its head spiritedly. Eleanor noticed the rider's slim but muscular frame, his clothes of the finest quality embellished by a large, bejewelled brooch fastening his cloak.

He had an air of detachment and quiet contemplation and there was something about him, she thought, that marked him out from the rest. As he neared, a gleaming cabochon cluster adorning his hat caught the sun's rays, casting a blinding shaft of light into Eleanor's eyes and forcing her to raise her hand to shade her face.

Just then one of the horses abruptly shied and reared, as a sudden gust of wind caught Eleanor's bonnet and wafted it into the air, her hair falling loose in a tangle of autumn hues around her shoulders. Eleanor jumped up as one of the huntsmen deftly caught the cap, leant down from his mount and handed it to the red-faced girl. She mumbled a quick 'thank you sir' as the Earl turned in his saddle at the commotion and the party stopped, their chatter dwindling to silence.

"What have we here then?" he chuckled. "Two pretty maids for the price of one! A good catch to add to our quarry!" he quipped, as the men laughed. Jane giggled and hid behind her companion, while several hunting dogs bounded over eagerly, only to be halted by a sharp command from the master of hounds.

Flustered, Eleanor bobbed a curtsey, her cheeks crimson as the huntsmen all turned to stare at the comely maiden with the youthful figure and flowing locks. One of them made a crude remark, evoking further mirth from the group. Eleanor stared defiantly but noticed that the quiet one had fixed his gaze on her, not in jest but intently studying her face. As their eyes met she abruptly cast hers downwards, her stomach turning a somersault, as she sensed a mutual attraction. She looked up again as the Earl spoke, forcing herself to focus on the older man, despite stealing a further furtive glance at the beguiling rider.

"What is your name girl? Where are you from?"

"Eleanor Wildman, my lord, and this is Jane. We come from the manor farm." Jane showed herself and bent her knee politely.

"I beg pardon, my lord," Edward interrupted, moving his mount forward closer to the Earl, "this is my younger sister Eleanor I spoke to you about." The Earl nodded.

"John Wildman's daughter?" Eleanor inclined her head in attestation. "Your father fought with us at Towton; we are indebted. How old are you Eleanor?"

"Fifteen years my Lord."

"Very well Eleanor, come to the castle tomorrow and see the Countess, we may have employment for you. We cannot have you roaming the byways alarming my horses and diverting my huntsmen, now can we!" he chuckled, grinning and eyeing up the bonny teenager admiringly.

"Nay sir," Eleanor replied, abashed, before remembering to thank him.

"Oh aye, sir... thank you my Lord." Eleanor bent her knee courteously as the Earl spurred his horse into action and the troupe moved off again down the hill.

As James passed the girls he turned in his saddle and smirked at his sister, mocking her with a derisory gesture as if to say *you're dead!* Eleanor laughed and stuck out her tongue defiantly. He trotted his mount away with a two-fingered wave that could be mistaken for a vulgar salute.

"My brother!" Eleanor chuckled, rolling her eyes and with a sideways glance at her curious companion. Jane tittered bashfully, amused at the ungracious exchange between brother and sister.

As the quiet young man rode past, he flashed Eleanor a friendly wink and a smile. She smiled back, standing transfixed as the rest of the retinue followed, some with hawks fastened to their wrists, some with game birds hanging limp and lifeless from their saddles, some on foot, lagging behind the main party, bearing a huge dead boar suspended from a pole. Eleanor turned away not wanting to look at the bloodied corpse with its sharp tusks and gaping jaw. Jane was tugging at her skirt.

"Did you see him Ellie? The fair haired one?" I'll wager that's Francis. He's handsome, don't you think?"

Eleanor did not reply. Jane's words had failed to register. She was lost in thought about the mysterious youth who had met her gaze with those solemn grey-blue eyes that seemed to pierce into her very soul. She felt something stir in her breast, the nerves in her stomach fluttered and her skin tingled with anticipation. She just knew she had to see him again.

A swift realisation of the Earl's words hit home. *If I am working up at the castle...?* Eleanor hardly dared allow her mind to race ahead before a stab of fear gripped her at the prospect of leaving her familiar, safe life on the farm. Comforting herself with the thought her brothers would be there too, she smiled at James's departing gesture. She longed to laugh with them again and it would be good to be living in close proximity, even if it did mean a relentless teasing, although now she was older it would be more of an even match and she could respond in kind.

The girls slipped on their shoes and turned back along the track as the hunting party retreated down the hill.

I knew something would happen today! Eleanor thought dreamily. *Aunt Mabel will be pleased I am going to join my brothers, though no doubt Jane will miss me.* Looking across at the younger girl, trotting along happily, talking of Francis Lovell, Eleanor was not listening to her friend's patter. Her thoughts were of another young man, a man she wanted so much to see again, if only for a moment.

Chapter Two

EAVING THE FARM THE NEXT day, on a cool cloudy afternoon, a blanket of grey gloom dampening the colours in the vale along with her mood, Eleanor trudged along the uneven path bordering the river, picking her way between the freshly filled puddles. A welcome spell of overnight rain had cooled the air and swept an oppressive ceiling of low cloud into the dale. Her mind racing, her head full of questions, possibilities and uncertainties, the knot in her stomach becoming ever tighter the nearer she got to the castle, Eleanor slowed her pace in an effort to postpone the inevitable. *What will this new life hold for me? Will I prove myself able? Will they like me?* She had bade farewell to her aunt, who was satisfied that her niece would join her brothers in the Earl's service and considered it long overdue. Working at the farm had been a good grounding for her ward, but was not the life her dear departed sister would have wished for her daughter. Eleanor had hugged her guardian and thanked her for her kindness, promising to visit when she could, for despite her aunt's rigid manner she had grown fond of her ageing relative. Eleanor was surprised to see a tear welling up in the old lady's eye, as Mabel handed over her mother's rosary beads and prayer book, cautioning her niece to observe her Christian education and not neglect her prayers. Eleanor's affirmation was sincere and as she neared the castle, she offered a quick prayer for God's guidance and protection.

Middleham Castle, the 200-year-old stronghold of the illustrious Northern aristocratic Neville family, stood on raised ground above the town, the great central Keep and Inner Bailey encircled by high walls, towering above a wide ditch and moat defending it on three sides, dwarfing the cottages nestled below. The original outer walls had been heightened by Ralph Neville and a second storey added to the structure to provide additional chambers. On the south-west corner a D shaped tower formed the sole rounded feature of this right-angled fortification. This ancestral bastion was not designed to be beautiful on the outside, no embellishments nor fancy ornamentation, just great, sturdy, safe walls, held fast by thick buttresses, punctuated by small windows, apart from the arched stained glass of the chapel and the large newly installed Solar windows, curving high up over the Great Hall and Great Chamber. Beneath these vast chambers were housed the kitchens, wine cellars, wells, fish pools and cool barrel-vaulted storerooms. Ranged around the curtain wall the accommodation included the guardhouse, guest rooms, laundry, mill and bakehouse with nursery above, the Earl's private apartments and, along the Eastern wall, the garderobe tower. To the West an enclosed Outer Courtyard housed a tilt yard, stables, smithy and slaughterhouse, as well as accommodation for servants and retainers. To the Southwest, the castle gardens occupied a sheltered spot beside the moat, beyond which open ground rose gradually on a gentle incline up towards the crumbled ruins of the old Norman fortification, now partly grassed over, and beyond that the high expanse of wild moorland. The walls on the North side loomed high and intimidating as Eleanor nervously approached the barbican, watched from above by sentries posted at intervals on the battlements, one of whom whistled indelicately as she walked by. Resisting the urge to look up, Eleanor composed herself with a measured breath to calm her nerves.

"I've been summoned to attend the Countess," Eleanor told the guard, who ushered her through the arched gateway over the moat, past the guardhouse and into the inner bailey.

As she entered the courtyard, the walls of the imposing Keep uprose intimidatingly before her, dominating the yard below full of noise and activity. A safeguarded stone staircase, open at the top, hugged the sides of the Keep, leading up to the Chapel and the Great Hall and, high above on the tower, the Earl of Warwick's standard, with his distinctive emblem, caught the occasional breeze, streaming out in a flash of red and white against the grey cloud-laden sky.

Eleanor waited, taking in the sounds and smells coming from the kitchens, hens strutting and scratching in the dirt, servants coming and going with goods, jugs and pails, children playing noisily in the yard, wagons of stores being unloaded, the clink of metal as the guards polished their sallets and honed their weapons, stopping briefly to stare at the fetching young lass lingering by the gateway. A short time later a dark-haired girl in her late teens, dressed in a dove grey silk gown, beckoned to Eleanor, leading her round through the heat and noise of the cookhouse and up a spiral stone staircase.

"I'm Marguerite," she introduced herself. Eleanor detected a trace of a French accent in the girl's intonation, her umber hued eyes and olive skin tone, redolent of continental extraction, although she had doubtless been absent from her homeland some years, as her English was fluent.

"I am the Countess's personal maid. Wait here Eleanor, my Lady will see you shortly."

Eleanor stood quietly in the cool passageway near the chapel, her eye drawn to the elevated view from a narrow window, overlooking the stables. She could see the grooms washing their sleek thoroughbred steeds, purchased no doubt from the celebrated breeding farm at nearby Jervaulx Abbey and her thoughts turned to that afternoon on the moor. She wondered where the striking youth with the arresting eyes and serious expression could be – perhaps sparring with the young men clattering and clashing in the outer bailey under the watchful eye of the stewards? An abrupt voice startled her and brought her swiftly back to the present as Marguerite beckoned from a heavily-curtained doorway.

"Eleanor, come, this way."

They entered a large, high-ceilinged chamber, where an enormous log fire crackled in the hearth and daylight streamed in through the lofty arched windows, relieving the chill. Several ladies in silk dresses sat sewing and reading, while a handsomely dignified woman in her early forties, wearing a dark red damask gown richly adorned with pearls, her hair pulled back, hidden under a tall veiled hennin, sat at a large desk amongst numerous missives and exquisite leather-bound volumes. Lady Anne Beauchamp, Countess of Warwick, looked up and beckoned the newcomer over. Eleanor approached and bent her knee politely.

"So, you are Eleanor Wildman. Welcome to Middleham castle. Your father was a loyal retainer for the Earl and now your brothers follow in his footsteps. We are delighted you can join us." The Countess's smile was not only an outward show of friendship towards the young girl but an inward recognition that Eleanor's youthful figure and bonny face were doubtless attributes not having gone unnoticed by her husband. *Always easy game for a pretty face,* she adjudged perceptively.

"Thank you, my Lady."

"Can you read, my dear?"

"Aye, a little my lady," Eleanor replied modestly, silently thanking her aunt for her education.

"Good. My daughter Anne has need of another personal maid to relieve Marguerite until she finds a husband and leaves us. Your brothers are progressing well and will soon be completing their arms training. Your family have served us well and we welcome you into our household Eleanor."

"Thank you, my lady," Eleanor curtsied again.

As she lowered her gaze, Eleanor's eye was drawn to a striking diamond-shaped golden locket worn by the Countess, suspended on a gold chain, delicately engraved with religious imagery, edged in pearls, a large deep blue sapphire mounted at the top, glinting in the firelight. Eleanor had never seen such an ornament, the worth of which she could not imagine. Temporarily mesmerised by the shimmering jewel, it was a moment before she realised the Countess was speaking again.

"Marguerite will show you your duties and your living quarters. We will provide your keep and a wage. We hope you will be happy here."

"Thank you, my lady I am most grateful." Eleanor bent her knee once more and followed Marguerite obediently, conscious that the ladies were surveying her silently as she turned away. She hoped they would be kind.

"Hmm... I'll wager it won't be long before our young men will be vying for *her* attentions!" the Countess chuckled aside to her companions, as soon as Eleanor was out of earshot.

Marguerite led Eleanor back down the stairs and across the bailey, through the Eastern gate into the Outer Courtyard, the accommodation part of the castle that she had seen from the lobby. As they passed the tilt yard, Eleanor caught sight of her brothers practising sword thrusts with several other young men. Alarmed by the clash of metal and afeared for their safety, she thought about these youths, only just emerged from boyhood, going into battle to face terrible scenes of death and horrendous injury. Eleanor was astounded by their bravery and awed by their skill. This was a real and deadly serious discipline, a fine line of technique designed to make the difference between life and death, a world away from the carefree boys she remembered sparring happily with wooden swords crafted lovingly for them by their father. They smiled as they saw her, prompting one of the older lads to quip that their sister was a sight better looking than her brothers. Casting her gaze around hopefully for the quiet young huntsman, she realised with a pang of disappointment that he was not there. She wondered when she would see him again and if he would remember the humble maiden who had caught his eye on the moor.

The girls approached a timbered building and ascended a narrow stairway up to a small, sparsely-furnished attic room with two low beds on opposite sides, pushed against each wall.

"You may sleep here with Agnes from the kitchen for now, but when I leave you can have my bed in the lower chamber with Philippa and Isabella," Marguerite offered.

Eleanor had seen Agnes in the kitchen when she walked through – a brassy haired buxom girl with a sullen expression and loud voice. The cook had reprimanded the girl and Agnes had silently mouthed a vulgar expletive behind the woman's back, sneering as she caught Eleanor's eye. *That did not bode well*, thought Eleanor. She had met girls like that in the town, they were usually resentful and unkind, aware of their lowly standing, begrudging anyone who had bettered themselves. Eleanor sighed and resigned herself to keeping out of Agnes's way for now.

Marguerite led Eleanor on a brief tour back through the Inner Bailey, pointing out the guest accommodation and that of the Constable, Marshall, Chamberlain and Stewards, the guards' quarters, the beautiful three-storey chapel and on the South side, accessed by a high enclosed walkway, the private chambers of the Earl and Countess and their young daughters Isobel and Anne. Leaving Eleanor to familiarise herself with the rest of the castle, Marguerite returned to attend the Countess.

It was late afternoon and the kitchen staff were clearing the evening repast. Mixed smells of roast meat and fish wafted up through the stairwells as Eleanor climbed up, passing the Great Hall, now empty save for a couple of servant girls scraping out ashes from the grate below the gaping fireplace, a boy sweeping the soiled rushes on the floor into a pile and a page snuffing out all but a few essential candles. The whitewashed walls were hung with richly illustrated tapestries, depicting scenes of mythical heroes, hunting and bible stories, delicately crafted in threads of intense blues, deep greens and vivid reds, shot through with gold and silver, glistening in the candlelight. Eleanor marvelled at these incredible works of art, so beautifully drawn, flawlessly stitched with expert workmanship and skill.

At the far end of the Hall there was a raised dais where the Lord and Lady would sit and, overhead, a Minstrels' gallery. Another flight of stone steps led upwards to the Solar, where the Earl and Countess and their daughters could relax, read, write and study, the last rays of the setting sun streaming in through the huge arched windows when the rest of the castle was in shadow. Eleanor could not resist ascending higher, on yet another ever narrowing set of steps, but as she neared the top a child's voice echoed down the stairwell. She hesitated, attempting to turn on the steep steps to go down but as she did so, she heard the Countess below calling "Isobel, Anne, come down, its time for chapel."

Eleanor froze, unsure of her presence on the stairway. She could not go down for fear of meeting the Countess again, so chose the less onerous option to go on, in the hope that as the Earl's daughters were only young, they would not admonish her for her trespass. However, as Eleanor reached the top of the turret, emerging into the fresh air, she saw with a start that *he* was there – her quiet young huntsman. He was holding the younger girl Anne up against the parapet, pointing out the route of the hunt.

"Will you take me with you next time Dickon?" Anne was asking him.

"Nay Anne," he laughed. "You're too young at the moment, tis dangerous. Mayhap in a few years..." his voice trailed off as he turned to see Eleanor at the top of the stairs. They stared at each other in surprised silence. Those soulful storm-tinted eyes boring into her once again, Eleanor's cheeks reddened and she and looked away. She started to stammer an apology.

"Oh for... for... forgive my intrusion sir, I seem to have mistook my way."

Richard quickly regained his composure and smiled, setting Anne down, allowing the girls to squeeze past them down the steps to their mother. Anne smiled politely as she hurried by but Isobel, the older girl, shot Eleanor a look of disdain as she passed, her elegant silk gown brushing the maid's plain woollen skirt as Eleanor backed respectfully against the wall. However, to her relief, Richard seemed to welcome the diversion.

"Pray come closer, tis Eleanor is it not?" he beckoned affably. His voice was soft and well spoken, his tonality hovering somewhere on the verge between boyhood to manhood, a slight Yorkshire enunciation softening his vowels.

"Aye sir." Eleanor moved forward. *He remembered!* she marvelled.

"My name is Richard. I've been showing the girls where we hunt."

Now at close quarters with this enigmatic young man, Eleanor could see he was still quite young, probably not much older than herself, but self-assured and well mannered. Undeniably a young man of breeding, he was dressed in a rich, royal blue embroidered doublet and hose with a white silk undershirt, a jewelled dagger sheathed at his waist and a gilded brooch at his shoulder. He stood beside her as she looked out over the battlements, surveying the wide expanse of Wensleydale and up to the elevated ridge above. Eleanor caught her breath at the view spread out before her as her eyes took in the panorama. She had never ventured so high on a castle before and hesitated to approach the parapet, fearing to look down. The Earl's standard flapped gently just above them in the breeze, while Richard pointed out the ruins of the old Norman castle on the hillock to the South, the road to Coverham Abbey, the high moorland tracks, the woods where they hunted the boar and, far to the West, where the lightening sky held the promise of a fair evening, the turrets of Bolton Castle, the ancestral seat of the Scrope family, standing out in sharp relief against the shadowed hills.

"I've loved this place since I was a child," he commented, looking across the fields. Eleanor stood quietly, unsure whether or not to speak.

"I take it you are in service with the Countess now Eleanor," he continued, turning to face her.

"Aye sir, I only arrived today, so I start tomorrow."

"You will be well treated here. The Earl is my cousin on my mother's side."

Eleanor's heart sank at the realisation of their difference in class. A cultured young nobleman like this, she knew, could surely never be hers except in one of her wild fantasies and yet here she was conversing with him like an equal.

"Your brothers were down in the tilt yard earlier, I expect you will have seen them. They started their training just before I did."

Before Eleanor could reply, the church bell of St. Mary and St. Alkelda's rang out, announcing vespers, piercing the stillness, resounding across the town and making Eleanor start. Up here on the roof, the church bells seemed closer, the sound reaching them unimpeded by the thick stone walls that lower down deflected and muffled their tone.

"I have to go to chapel, I'm late," Richard told her, as he moved towards the stairs. As he politely took her hand to help her back down the steps, Eleanor felt a spark of electricity race through her body at his touch.

Can you find your way down now?" he asked, as they reached the passageway, her hand still held firmly in his.

"Aye sir, Thank you sir."

His gaze held hers for a few seconds as his fingers reluctantly released their grip, then he was gone. Eleanor was in a daze. *Dare she imagine a spark of attraction between them?* Instantly dismissing the thought as wishful fancy, she hurried back down to the kitchens where the servants sat at a long trestle table eating broth, bread and meat, washed down with watery ale. She sat down and ate quickly, aware of the stares coming her way and the certainty she would be the topic of conversation once her back was turned. Agnes was already sizing her up as competition for the attentions of the young squires who she and the other servant girls lusted after. She satisfied herself that Eleanor's slim frame was no match for her rather too generous curves and the maid's pretty face no guarantee of submissiveness, judging Eleanor the sort of girl whose virtue would be only prudently surrendered. *No competition*, she decided disdainfully.

It was a relief to Eleanor when she finished her meal and escaped across the outer yard to her quarters. A page had brought up her few belongings from the farm, which she quickly unpacked before falling wearily onto the coarse straw mattress, thoughts racing and pulse pounding as she relived the encounter with Richard, heard again his soft voice, felt the warm touch of his slender fingers around hers and lost herself in those unfathomable eyes which seemed somehow imbued with a sadness she could not read. She realised with a shock that she could not wait to see him again, even a brief encounter would suffice, for she now conceded that would surely be all it could ever be. He had noble blood and she was just a steward's daughter.

Chapter Three

VER THE NEXT COUPLE OF months, Eleanor settled into life at the castle. The Countess found her a couple of silk gowns to wear instead of her old woollen kirtle and Marguerite helped her to brush and tie back the crown of her hair in a neat plait interwoven with ribbon, the ragged ends neatly bound. She was shown how to sew a straight garment seam, execute various embroidery stitches, how to dress the Countess and her daughters, to brush and braid their long hair, smoothing it back neatly under their elaborate hennins. She would play dice and chess with Anne, tried her hand at writing on parchment, admiring the Countess's beautifully illustrated manuscripts, while she learnt about music and history and picked up some basic French vocabulary from Marguerite, whose mother, she learned, hailed from Normandy. Marguerite's mother had fallen for an English chevalier posted to defend Calais when the Earl of Warwick had taken up his captaincy and she had returned with her husband and daughter to England at the end of his service.

Philippa and Isabella, at first somewhat coldly superior towards Eleanor, soon thawed when they judged she was someone they could mould and instruct and who would comply meekly with any task demanded of her. Eleanor was content to carry out her tasks in meek acquiescence, as behoved her station. Ambition was not part of her work-driven nature, despite the unattainable fancies that imbued her imagination. She knew her place and remained at ease with it.

Philippa, the daughter of a knight, brown haired and plain looking with an aquiline nose that gave her an air of arrogance, was in her mid-twenties. Her stern features had not yet attracted a suitor, although Eleanor surmised this assertive lady would not be easily won by flattery. Isabella, a few years younger, was fair with a well-rounded figure but inclined to impatience and quick to make cutting observations. She had had several flirtations with the Earl's retainers but none that tempted her to marry. Eleanor was happy to allow her colleagues their superiority, adapting punctiliously to their routines and methods, enabling her to learn quickly and earn their approval.

The two Neville girls, Isobel and Anne, pale skinned and delicate with willowy figures, fair lashes and brows and abundant waist-length fair hair, were beautiful like their mother but frail and given to frequent bouts of sickness. Isobel was quiet and aloof, sensible of her position as heiress to the Earl's huge fortune, while Anne would happily chatter away and play games with anyone who would join in, seemingly unmindful of her status.

Eleanor was diligent and attentive in her work, with the respect and humility her aunt had instilled in her, keeping mostly to herself and attempting to appear as unobtrusive as possible. She would, however, use every opportunity to spy on the young men training in the yard whilst going about her daily routine. She asked her brothers about Richard or 'Dickon', as he was addressed by his peers, but they said he had gone away. She had heard them talk of the studious young man who had arrived at the castle several years ago, quick witted and intelligent, keen to learn and always kind and considerate to his comrades.

Now she had seen him at close quarters and conversed with him, her interest was roused and she tried to remember all they had said about him, tendering a few innocent questions without sounding overly curious. She could not allow them to know she was attracted to Richard and face the inevitable good-humoured badinage that would ensue, or worse, the embarrassment of him knowing. For the time being she admired the youthful Francis from afar and smiled at the thought of Jane's envy, as she watched him in the tilt yard, competing with the other pages. Clearly younger than Richard, his boyish good looks were not quite mature enough yet for Eleanor to find him appealing but he held promise, she admitted.

Eleanor could not help but be in awe of these young men who trained so long and hard. Mastery at arms was essential if one were to avoid the certain path to an early grave. It was not a game or a sport, despite the jousts, which she sensed were surely only dress rehearsals for death. Chivalric ideals were admirable but would not alter the inevitable outcome, flesh and blood presenting no match for hardened steel. War was brutal and unforgiving for the nobility, punishment severe and absolute. The rank and file were not expected to pay the price of defeat unless caught up in a rout where no quarter was given but it was certain death for a nobleman on the losing side. If victory was yours it was glorious and the rewards great but if you lost, you lost everything, including your head – worse if you were a traitor.

Eleanor tried not to think about it.

Stacked against the wall was a vicious assortment of weaponry; poleaxes, billhooks, halberds, axes and mace; ugly weapons from hell, devised for slashing, stabbing, slicing, impaling, chopping and bludgeoning. Eleanor thought of her father and wondered what hideous death he had met, his broken bones lying somewhere in a mass grave on Towton field. *Pray God it were quick!* She shuddered as a wave of nausea arose from her stomach at the thought of these ghastly weapons encountering soft flesh. *What these men must see and endure on the battlefield must be hell on earth!* she cringed inwardly. Eleanor had nothing but admiration for them. Fortunes were won and lost, husbands killed, wives widowed and remarried, lands redistributed amongst the victors, children disinherited, property destroyed, castles besieged, towns ransacked. Nothing was guaranteed it seemed. No amount of wealth could save you from destruction or premature death.

Now she was in service for this titled family, Eleanor realised that, as a member of their household, she would share in their triumphs and defeats; everything that touched them would touch her also. Her destiny was in their hands.

When Richard returned some weeks later, he could be seen frequently at weapons practise with the other young men or riding out with the hunting party. Eleanor discovered he was a consummate horseman, swordsman and scholar, dividing his time between the hunt, the tilt yard or poring over books, conversing in French or reading in Latin. 'Dickon', she learned from her brothers, had been destined for the priesthood but preferred to build himself up with unrelenting weapons practise, honing his skills for the battlefield, in admiration of his older brother, adhering faithfully to the chivalric ideals he strove to emulate. Eleanor seized every opportunity to catch a glimpse of him, hoping to be rewarded with a smile or even a glance in her direction.

Richard, young Robert Percy and Francis Lovell, were all wards of the Earl and had developed a close friendship. It was the custom amongst the nobility to send their sons away at a young age to be wards to other noble families, to learn their knightly and social skills, which would ensure the future of their dynasty. Discipline and deference were lessons better assimilated distanced from family affections and over-protectiveness. Francis's parents had both died by the time he was ten and Richard, being older by a few years, took the younger boy under his wing. The boys enjoyed each other's company and had a friendly rivalry but the techniques they learned were deadly serious and would one day be used in battle. Their sword play with blunted weapons was fast and furious, leaving them breathless, their shirts soaked with sweat. They would cheer at success or curse in defeat, often uttering a French profanity when English would not suffice.

Their slim youthful physiques benefited from the constant effort, muscle rapidly building up on neck, shoulders and biceps, which ultimately would provide the strength needed to wield the heavy weaponry in mortal combat. Richard, Eleanor learned, had an impairment affecting his spine, causing him to tire easily but determination and dexterity rendered him a competent and fierce opponent, despite his small frame. Once he looked up and spied her watching, flashed her a disarming smile and bowed in mock chivalry, as a knight would bow to his lady. She nodded in acknowledgement and smiled back. Her heart leapt, *if only I could be his...* she fantasised wishfully.

⚜ ⚜ ⚜

SUMMER WAS NO more. The nights had begun to draw in and there was a refreshing cool nip in the air. Changing colours in the vale heralded the approach of autumn, the bright blossomed bell heather now dulled, the furrowed fields a rich reddish brown, the freshly turned ridges revealing a bounty of juicy worms for the gulls flocking behind the plough in noisy droves. The wind soughed in the trees, showers of falling leaves dancing around frenetically, once so uniformly green, now absorbing the rays of the weakening sun turning them every hue of gold, copper and bronze. Along the byways the scarlet hips of the wild dog rose swelled enticingly, their rich sweetness an autumn treat for the blackbirds and thrushes sheltering in the thickets. Eleanor often liked to walk up to the ruins of the old Norman fortress on the hill after she had completed her duties. She would sit by the moss-covered stones looking back at Middleham Castle, alone with her thoughts, watching the torches being lit and gazing at the flocks of starlings flying in ever changing patterns across the darkening sky before settling down to roost on the ramparts.

This evening Eleanor sat on the grassy slope, her arms hugging her knees, taking in the tranquil scene, warming her back in the late afternoon sun and reflecting on her new life. She wondered how Jane was faring at the farm and if John was already turning his lustful thoughts in the direction of the younger girl. *Jane will give as good as she gets!* she smiled to herself at the image of her diminutive friend rendering John's hulk immobile with a well-aimed knee. She thought about her ageing aunt and hoped the old lady would make it safely through the winter's chill. Last winter had been protracted and harsh and Aunt Mabel had been weakened by a particularly virulent fever. Eleanor had nursed her through the worst and thankfully by Spring she had recovered, despite a persistent cough.

Suddenly Eleanor started at the sound of a horse snorting behind her, interrupting her reverie. She looked around and saw the rider pull on the reins and guide his mount over to where she sat. Springing to her feet, her heartbeat resounding in her ears as she recognised him, she smiled timorously.

"My favourite spot too" Richard commented as he dismounted, casting the reins over the branches of a nearby hawthorn bush.

"Pray sit with me awhile Eleanor," he ventured as he sat down.

"Are you enjoying your life here?"

"Oh, aye sir, very much." Eleanor sat down beside him.

"I will miss it when I leave," he sighed. Eleanor's heart sank.

"You're leaving sir?"

"Not immediately but aye, I have to go back to London to join..." he hesitated "...my brothers."

"Tell me about them sir" Eleanor asked politely, trying not to show her disappointment at his forthcoming departure.

"Pray call me Richard, Eleanor, there's little need for formality out here."

He sat back, casually leaning on his elbows, welcoming the chance to talk informally and at the same time admire his pretty companion. Not wishing to awe Eleanor with class and standing, he omitted any reference to title and position. He had no desire to pull rank or intimidate a lowly maiden, trusting she would value him as an equal participant in *affairs de coeur*. He told her about his elder brothers Edward, Edmund and George, his eyes misting over as he described Edmund who had been killed at Wakefield at just 17, along with his father but Eleanor noticed how he became more animated when he spoke of his eldest brother Edward. He was visibly in awe of a man who was the embodiment of all he aspired to be, athletic, charismatic, brave and a great soldier.

He chuckled as he described George, who was closest to him in age but volatile and unpredictable, frequently intoxicated and injudicious but sometimes comically entertaining. George, he told her, had been their mother's favourite and unlike his older siblings had not been sent away as ward of another family, which probably contributed to his somewhat spoiled and arrogant behaviour, oftentimes directed towards his younger sister and brother, Meg and Dickon.

Eleanor listened, studying her companion's profile while he talked. He had a straight nose, a strong chin, well defined brows, long eyelashes and his mouth turned up slightly at the edges. His tawny shoulder length hair fell over his face and he pushed it back from his wide forehead, turning to face her, observing her closely with those soul-searching smoke blue eyes. He asked her about her family and she described her life on the farm, conscious that it was mundane and ordinary in comparison with his. They sat for a while, gazing out over the valley, watching the sun as it sank behind the clouds, turning them pink and gold at the edges. Eleanor realised

Richard was somehow closer to her now and she trembled as he leaned towards her with an admiring smile, taking her hand in his, his gaze steady and penetrating.

"You are a pretty girl Eleanor; will you grant me a kiss? I am in sore need of some feminine attention tonight." He had not been attracted to many girls at the castle but this natural sage-eyed English rose with her inviting lips, svelte figure and cascading hair, the colour of deep burnished copper, now stirred his loins with lustful yearning.

Could this be real? Eleanor thought, *does he really want to kiss me? Oh, how I have longed for this. Does he really like me or is he teasing me?* She thought of John from the farm and how he had teased her about her virtue. Now she hungered for this engaging young man's kiss but fear and embarrassment gripped her and she stood up flustered, attempting to delay the moment and not to appear too eager, or too easy a conquest.

"Sir... pray do not jest with me."

Richard stood up, reaching for her hand and pulling her gently to him, folding his arm around her tiny waist.

"'Tis no jest Eleanor," he replied seriously, his mouth edging closer to her lips as she raised her face to his. She felt her natural reserve ebb away as their eyes met and her pulse stirred at his touch. This was more than temptation Eleanor realised, this was inevitability. He was going to kiss her and she was going to accept.

He brushed her cheek with his and she felt his warm breath on her neck as she relaxed into his embrace, her heart pounding as his mouth found hers. He tightened his grip and pressed her against his chest, the vigour of his kiss both firm and tender. She closed her eyes as electricity shot through her, every nerve ending tingling. Her stomach turned over, her body trembled with latent desire, enticing her to yield to that which she had so long denied herself but now sprung into life.

His kiss left her breathless and he paused to stroke her hair, now falling loosely down her back, the ribbon sliding off and floating to the ground. His breathing quickened and he kissed her again. She could feel his thighs pressing against her, his rising desire evident. Her legs went weak and she thought she might faint.

Without warning, the church bells chimed for vespers, sounding out across the town; Richard looked up.

"Damnation! I have to go. Forgive me. Meet me here tomorrow evening Eleanor, at sundown," he called over his shoulder, as jumping on his waiting stallion, he galloped down the hill.

Eleanor was stunned, in a daze. *Had that just happened?* She ached for him to return and kiss her again. She had not been kissed like that by any man and the sensation thrilled her in a way she had not expected. Their lips seemed to meld together in perfect harmony, as if made for each other and she knew she would give herself to him totally, body and soul if he asked her. She picked up her ribbon, tied her hair back hastily and walked slowly down the incline. Returning to her room later that night, lying bathed in the comforting mantle of darkness, she relived his embrace, his trembling touch, his fervent kisses, his soft voice echoing in her brain with every breath. When Agnes came in, replete with ale, stumbling about and cursing, Eleanor feigned sleep, not wishing to break the spell of *HIM*. Soon her companion's snores ensured she was left to her thoughts, staring into the blackness again until weariness soothed her passion, surrendering her consciousness to merciful oblivion.

How she got through the next day she hardly knew but by sundown Eleanor found herself hurrying back up the hill to the old ruins. Dressed in her favourite sea-green silk dress, a cast-off from one of the Countess's ladies, the ties pulled tight around her lissome figure, she brushed her hair, tied it back loosely and pinched her cheeks to make the colour rise. The air was fresh and she shivered despite the woollen cloak slung over her shoulders. She ran eagerly up the gradient, stopping several times to catch her breath. Beyond the distant Cumberland hills away to the west, the sun was sinking, the sky a confusion of pink, orange then red as the torches in the castle behind her flickered into life.

Would he come? Would he regret the moment of reckless abandon they had shared? *Aye probably,* she told herself, not daring to hope, lest fate dictated otherwise. Her stomach turned somersaults at the prospect of what might be about to happen but the craving he had awakened in her would not be denied. The minutes passed, the sun disappeared behind the distant fells and the first evening star appeared. Eleanor waited, pulling her cloak around her, trembling with anticipation or shivering in the cool air, she knew not which, mayhap a bit of both. *Would he come?* Just as she had resigned herself to returning alone, the rhythmic thudding of a galloping horse approaching at speed set her pulse racing.

As Richard reached the crest of the hill, he jumped down and strode purposefully towards her, grabbing her waist and, without speaking, hungrily pressed his mouth down on hers. Eleanor responded eagerly to his passion, as he threw his mantle down on the grass and gently pulled her down beside him on the soft fur lining. Time seemed to stand still for Eleanor, conscious of nothing else but his lips devouring hers and the intensity of their shared fervour. She felt every nerve in her body come alive. *How she wanted him!* She had hardly allowed herself to believe that this compelling young man she had admired from afar, was himself eager to return her affections. Yet here he was, real and vital, her fantasies made flesh.

"I thought you would not come!" Eleanor whispered, as she took a breath between kisses. Richard smiled with a youthful grin.

"What man would not?" he responded lustfully, drawing her closer to him, his tremulous touch awakening senses she did not know she had, as his hands stroked her body worshipfully.

"Eleanor, will you give yourself to me? I need you. I want you," he murmured urgently, his lips next to her ear, his face buried in her hair.

"Oh Richard, I am yours, I am yours," she sighed eagerly, scarcely believing this was real and not one of the innocent fantasies that had permeated her every waking hour. Now her physical thirst overcame her natural timidity and all thoughts of chastity were banished in the heat of the moment. In her imagination she had resolved to remain unsullied for as long as possible but the lure of total submission for this seductive young nobleman was too strong. This was no daydream, he was flesh and blood, warm and inviting and he wanted *her*. Wild horses could not hold back the surge of yearning that arose in her breast. She *had* to have him.

He fumbled tremulously with his clothes and she laughed as he cursed loudly, his ornate silver belt buckle snapping off in his urgency to undress. He laughed too, the moment relieving the tension between them.

"I needed a new one anyway!" he quipped, as he pulled her towards him, his lips impatiently curtailing her nervous laughter in a furore of exuberant passion.

His breathing quickened and he trembled with growing vigour, kissing her neck down to her breast, sliding his hands up her thighs before gently penetrating her. She gasped involuntarily and let out a moan of ecstasy, rising up to him and pulling him down against her body, revelling in the touch of his skin against hers, allowing his muscular arms to hold her tightly while her fingers caressed his lithe but taut frame. His mouth was warm and tender and her head spun in dizzy euphoria as his body moved as one with hers, his kisses seeming to reach into her very soul.

"Richard, Richard my love," Eleanor whispered ecstatically, as he murmured her name with soaring fervour, then, all too soon for his liking, his craving spent, he lay back on the damp grass before turning to kiss her softly. He smiled at her fondly, as their breathing slowed and the heat of their ardour cooled in the evening air. She smiled back shyly, her face flushed, now acutely self-conscious at the physicality they had shared.

"*Je te remercie, ma belle enchantresse,*" he said, kissing her again. Eleanor determined to ask Marguerite later what he had said, although she would be mindful not to reveal his identity.

Richard helped her up; the young lovers chuckling together bashfully at their state of disarray, picking strands of grass and clover out of their hair, while he attempted to tie the ends of his broken belt together and she adjusted her dress to preserve her modesty. The light was fading fast and they would need to return before darkness fell. The compline bell would soon be ringing out, the household retiring and the guards bolting the castle gateways.

"*Tu es belle ma Cherie,*" he said softly, stroking her hair from her brow, cupping her face in his hands and touching her lips fleetingly before refastening his cloak and leaping back on his horse.

"Come, it's late," he reached down for her hand, pulling her up on the saddle in front of him, gripping one arm around her tightly. As they rode down the slope, the lingering twilight affording just enough light to illuminate the path, Eleanor basked in the warmth of his embrace, his chest pressed firmly against her back, his thighs brushing her hips rhythmically as the horse moved under them. Her senses high on new-found love and desire, she wanted the eroticism of this moment to endure indefinitely, to preserve this giddy bliss, savouring their shared experience of heightened sensuality, as this vital youth walked his mount slowly back to the castle walls, before gently setting her down in the shadow of the gatehouse.

"You go in first. You should not be seen with me," he whispered, "for *your* sake Eleanor, not mine," he added quietly.

She wished she could see his face more clearly in the flickering glow of the torches, just for one more gaze into those eyes, but he eased his mount back into the shadows.

Eleanor rushed to her room, fearing her flushed countenance and ruffled demeanour would give her away, but thankfully the yard was quiet. Shielded in the refuge of her bed, cloaked in the opacity of the night, Eleanor revelled in the memory of his touch, bathing in the intoxication of a newly kindled passion stirring in her, the growing appetite of approaching womanhood. She had tasted the pleasures of the flesh, the forbidden fruit of humankind she had been taught to suppress – and she wanted more. She had surrendered her virtue to this intriguing nobleman and, although she did not yet know it, her heart too.

The festive season was soon upon them and the castle reverberated with fevered activity in preparation for house guests and the bountiful Yuletide fare they had come to expect from the Earl. The public rooms were hung with garlands of winter greenery and huge iron candelabras lit the dark corners with a comforting glow. Eleanor was kept busy helping the Countess and her daughters look their best in extravagant gowns of damask and velvet, plunging necklines and fitted sleeves enhancing their figures, their hair neatly arrayed under matching jewelled headdresses supporting trailing diaphanous veils.

At the Christmas feast in the Great Hall, she had seen Richard seated at the top end of the long trestle table, next to the girls. Isobel appeared coolly detached but young Anne seemed in awe of him and he politely got up to dance with her and other ladies of rank. He wore expensive jewels and clothes of the latest fashion, drank fine wines and ate well but sparingly, occasionally tossing scraps to the hounds that waited patiently at his feet. Eleanor watched enviously, peeping out from behind the heavy arras draped at the back of the Minstrels' gallery and longed to be part of his life.

A few days after the twelfth night revelries, Richard and a number of the young men were preparing to leave again for London. The Earl had already been absent for some days and Richard had been too busy with preparations to speak to Eleanor, despite the occasional heartening smile he sent in her direction. Eleanor felt physically ill at the thought of him leaving. She had thought of nothing else but their love making since that night on the hill and her glowing countenance and distant expression was not lost on Marguerite.

On the eve of the young men's departure, as she sat sewing by the fire, absently staring into the flames, Marguerite interrupted her thoughts.

"Are you in love, Eleanor?"

The directness of the question startled Eleanor and she blushed.

"W...what do you mean?" she stammered, turning her face away and studying her threads intently, stabbing determinedly at the cloth, the needle pricking her finger as her hand shook involuntarily.

"Something is amiss, I can tell. You've scarcely eaten this past week and tis usually a sign. Who is he?" Marguerite teased. "I've seen you eyeing the young men in the yard. Is it Francis? Half the scullery maids are in love with him, although you know he's already married to the Earl's cousin, Anne Fitzhugh.

"Nay, of course not!" Eleanor regained her composure, sucking a droplet of blood from her finger.

"I'm just not hungry, that's all, and anyway even if there was someone, they are all leaving tomorrow so there's an end to it."

"Ha! I knew it. You *are* in love, aren't you? Which one Eleanor? Robert? Ralph? Thomas? You can tell *me*. I can keep a secret," her companion whispered encouragingly.

Eleanor studied her sewing again, but could not prevent a tear welling up and falling onto her hand. A sympathetic ear was all that was needed to open the floodgate of emotion that was bursting to emerge.

"Oh Marguerite, what do I do? I love him so much I cannot bear it! I feel like I'm being torn in two."

"Oh Eleanor, you poor thing. Does he know?"

"Nay, well... maybe, aye, I think he might... but we cannot..."

"He's not married, is he?"

"Nay, but he cannot marry *me*.. I'm lowborn." Eleanor's voice faded to a whisper. Marguerite stopped stitching momentarily and looked up sharply,

"Sacre bleu! Eleanor, is it Dickon? Richard, I mean?"

Eleanor's silence did not contradict her.

"It *is*, isn't it?" Eleanor nodded into her handkerchief.

Marguerite let the revelation sink in for a moment.

"You know he's the king's brother? He's the Duke of Gloucester! Surely you knew?"

Eleanor stared in horror, shaking her head, unable to speak. Her hopes crushed, her newly found inamorato immediately and irrevocably out of her reach, unattainable, forbidden to her by class and status. The Earl's cousin was disparity enough, but *brother to the king?!* She wondered why her brothers had not told her, but then she reasoned they would have assumed she knew. She thought of how she had spoken to Richard like an equal, naïve and innocent, and how she had asked him about his family.

"Why did he not tell me? Oh, I am such a fool!"

Marguerite read her thoughts.

"Huh, Well, he wouldn't say, would he? If he wanted you to submit to him!" She scoffed, then paused, guessing the truth.

"Eleanor... did you...?" she trailed off as Eleanor's sobs became louder, confirming her suspicions. Marguerite smiled to herself. *So, this inscrutable young nobleman is as malleable as the rest of them when it comes to the fairer sex!* Until now she had not noticed Richard showing any singular attachment to any of the young ladies at Middleham and had assumed his impassivity was due to his strict upbringing and social standing.

"Well, isn't *he* the quiet one! Now he's had his fun with an innocent maid he can scurry off and hone his skills on the ladies of court!" she smirked.

"Nay, Marguerite... it wasn't like that!" Eleanor sprang to his defence. She wondered if there was a hint of envy in her companion's cynicism.

"Don't be so naïve Eleanor. I'll wager he's had his eye on you from the start, as a possible conquest. He knows he *must* marry into nobility for political advantage and to keep the bloodline. He is not going to marry a commoner, is he? But he won't be short of maids willing to lie with him. They would like nothing more than to have a peer of his stature succumb to them."

"I'll wager you're his first, though," she added gently, perceiving Eleanor's shocked face. She was unsure of the validity of her statement, knowing how many maidens were enthralled by this self-contained and scholarly young lord, but it cost nothing to allow the maid some consolation.

Eleanor studied her lap, her cheeks burning with embarrassment.

"He is a gentleman and he forced me not. He's not like those who take advantage, I know it. I wanted him. I was willing," she added weakly. "Now I will probably never see him again." A fresh deluge of tears ensued. Marguerite's contempt for certain elements of the nobility who used their position unscrupulously, came to the fore.

"Well, Eleanor you're not the first maid to be deflowered by a nobleman who should know better! They have their way and off they go, nay guilt, nay shame – nothing a few 'Ave Marias' won't absolve when they go to chapel."

"Marguerite!"

"And who's left with the consequences? A ruined maid with a bastard! Your next monthly occurrence had better appear, or you'll be in trouble!"

That night Eleanor climbed the stairs to bed, utterly miserable. Marguerite had made it sound so carnal and crude. *Richard isn't like that – he loves me, I know he does*, she told herself. *What if I'm with child?*

I will lose my position here. What will the Countess say? What will my brothers think of me? What will my aunt say? Where will I go? Oh, I am such a fool. Why couldn't I fall in love with a simple country boy who could marry me and take care of me?

The next day the castle erupted in a flurry of activity as carts were loaded, horses harnessed, their breath steaming in the frosty air; soldiers armed and ready, stamping their feet to allay the cold, the clink of harness and the chatter of excited young men echoing in the stillness as they bade their farewells. Snow had settled overnight, covering Wensleydale in a silent carpet of white, the leafless trees standing out in stark black outline, the weak rays of the winter sun barely warming the huddles of sheep in the fields, their sodden fleeces appearing grey and grubby against the bright pearly snow.

As Richard was preparing to depart with his entourage, Eleanor joined those in the inner bailey who had gathered to see them off. She saw him speaking to the Countess, who embraced him warmly. He was dressed in a heavy fur-lined mantle draped over a doublet and hose of indigo velvet, fastened at the waist with a shining new intricately patterned silver belt buckle, a jewelled sword and dagger at his hip, looking every inch the handsome young knight, he was. *The king's brother no less!* Eleanor marvelled as she watched him, awed by his status but at the same time thrilled that he had been hers for that brief blissful, intimate moment; a moment that had already replayed in her mind again and again.

Swept up in Richard's arms, Anne Neville hugged her adored cousin like a big brother. He kissed the girls affectionately on the cheek and turned to mount his courser. Eleanor, who had been standing behind the Countess with the other ladies in waiting, ran forward as they went inside. Richard had the reins in his hand and his riding boot on the stirrup but stepped down as he saw her. He smiled cordially as she approached, handing him a freshly baked gingerbread cake, still warm from the oven, wrapped in a muslin cloth.

"For your journey, my Lord."

"Sweet Eleanor, thank you," he smiled, taking the cake and placing it in his saddlebag.

"When will I see you again?" she asked hopefully, her face full of expectation, searching his face for some affirmation.

A troubled frown creased his brow and he looked away in discomfort. "It may be some time Eleanor... I can't promise..." he hesitated, trying to find the right words. He felt bad that he had used her and deceived her about his rank. He wanted to hold her and comfort her but he knew his future lay elsewhere and his duty as the brother of the King and a Knight of the Realm would mean he could not commit to this young maid of Middleham, no matter how fair and tempting.

Unbidden tears of hurt and anger welled up in Eleanor and she wanted to lash out at him. Had she meant nothing to him? Was she just easy prey for the rising needs of a lustful young nobleman eager to prove his virility? Humiliated, and with Marguerite's words freshly ringing in her ears, she blurted out, "So, you are content to ravish me and leave me?" before the lump in her throat choked her. The words were out of her mouth before she could check herself.

Richard stepped back, his eyes narrowed, a furrow creased his brow and a surprised look of hurt and disappointment crossed his face.

"I don't recall you rejecting my advances Eleanor," he said coolly. "I'm not accustomed to coercing unwilling young women. You only had to deny me and I would have left you alone."

Mortified at her stupidity, chastened by his anger and desperately wishing to retract her hasty words, Eleanor pleaded meekly.

"Oh, pray forgive me Richard, er, my Lord, be not wrathful I pray you. I meant it not... I just don't want you to go," she added dejectedly, staring at the ground.

"I *have* to go Eleanor," he said, taking her hands in his, like a parent comforting a child, his eyes kinder now, his voice subdued and gentle.

"I am not free to stay here. My duty lies with my brother. I ask your forgiveness if you feel I have dishonoured you, that was not my intention – my feelings were genuine. I hope to see you again, sweet lass, but if not, I won't forget you. Au revoir ma Cherie. God be with you." He longed to scoop her into his arms in a vigorous caress and show her just how much he wanted her; instead with the eyes of his retinue upon him, he had no choice but to leave her dispirited and dashed. His face looked pained and his eyes sad as he mounted, leaned down from the saddle, kissed her tenderly on the cheek and was gone.

Eleanor was desolate. She stood rooted to the spot as this princely youth clattered through the gate, across the drawbridge and out of her life. He waved before he disappeared from view but her eyes were too full of tears and her heart too heavy to respond.

Richard, my one true love, don't leave me here alone, how can I exist without you?

As Richard drew away from the castle, he swore under his breath for his thoughtlessness. He would have loved nothing more than to settle down with an innocent Yorkshire beauty to live a life of quiet contentment, but his path in life was already set. There was no knowing when, or even if, he would return. He was a Prince of the Realm, a Knight of the Garter, that prestigious accolade instigated by Edward III, which had been bestowed on Richard at nine years old and with it the expectation of knightly prowess, upon whom duty to king and country meant no affair of the heart could be permitted to determine his purpose or shape his destiny.

That evening as the sun went down, Eleanor trudged up the slope to the spot where he had loved her, fell on the frozen ground and sobbed and sobbed until she had no more tears to cry, the wet snow soaking into her dress unheeded.

He was gone. Eleanor was bereft.

He was Royalty! He could never be mine. How could a lowly maidservant from a distant corner of Yorkshire ever mean anything to him? she reproached herself bitterly.

Chapter Four

LEANOR IMMERSED HERSELF IN HER work, pushing any thoughts of Richard to the back of her mind but when night fell, alone in the sanctuary of her bed, there he was, his eyes searching her face, his eager lips crushing hers, his quiet voice whispering in her ear. As the weeks went by and her monthly courses showed no signs of appearing, she confided in Marguerite.

"You will have to tell the Countess, Eleanor," Marguerite admonished. "If you can get a young man to marry you before you show, it will save your honour. Many infants fail to reach full term, so if the birth appears to be earlier than it should, nobody will question the timing and your husband need never know. Whatever you do, do not tell her its Dickon's. That must always be a secret Eleanor, or else she will assume you mean to benefit from it or to besmirch his reputation. She will respect your wishes if you want to keep that knowledge to yourself. She knows the ways of men. We've had many visiting nobles and their retinues at the castle over Yuletide, so she won't question it. You're not the first maid to be caught out, believe me."

Eleanor shivered, as much from nerves as from the cold passageway which led into the solar where the Countess sat alone, immersed in her papers and books. She looked up wearily as Eleanor hesitantly approached the desk.

"Marguerite tells me you wish to speak to me privately Eleanor," she said, closing her book and clasping her hands together.

"Aye, my lady." Eleanor bobbed a curtsey and averted her eyes, studying the floor meekly. "I think I might be in trouble, my lady."

"What manner of trouble, Eleanor?"

Eleanor struggled to speak, twisting her fingers uneasily as tears welled in her eyes. "I... er... my..." She could not bring herself to utter the words.

"A man, I take it?" The Countess interrupted.

"Aye, my lady."

"I see. Did he force himself on you?"

"Oh nay, my lady," Eleanor looked up shocked at the suggestion.

"But you were caught up in the moment?"

"Aye, my lady, I'm so ashamed."

"How long since?"

"Nearly two months, my lady."

"Good, that gives you some time. Do I understand then, that the man in question is not free to marry you?"

"Nay, my lady."

The Countess took a deep breath and sighed, echoing Marguerite's words. "Well, you're not the first, my dear, and you won't be the last. Strange as it may seem to you, I was young once and I understand. Go to confession Eleanor and I will pray for your immortal soul."

"Of course my lady, thank you my lady."

"Now..." Anne paused. "We need to find you a husband. Is there anyone here in the castle you have your eye on?"

Eleanor looked up quickly, alarmed that somehow the Countess was able to read her thoughts, but Anne's blank expression reassured her that her secret was safe.

"Nay, my lady."

"Leave it to me then. I presume you don't have a dowry?"

"I know not of one my Lady, but my father may have left provision in his will."

"Very well, I will write to your aunt, but if not, we shall see to it that you have an appropriate sum. That should help. Your father gave his life for our cause at Towton and we should make provision for his daughter. We shall be sorry to lose you, my dear, after such a short time, but needs must. Although" she thought for a moment, "If we find you one of the Earl's retainers, you may be able to remain here in the castle with him and continue your duties."

"I am most grateful. Thank you, my lady." Eleanor hesitated as a concern struck her. "My lady, may I request that my aunt is not apprised of the... er... circumstances?"

"I know how to be discreet Eleanor," the Countess replied tersely.

"Of course, forgive me my lady. Thank you, my lady." Eleanor, abashed at her own crassness, curtsied and left the chamber, her face flushed with shame and humiliation but with her burden of guilt considerably lessened by her employer's kindness. The Countess sighed and walked over to the window. Her prediction had been proved correct and she wondered who had caught her young maid's eye, tempting her into carnal sin. She remembered her own teenage years and the rash cravings of youth, so urgent and all-consuming before marriage and motherhood cooled the fires and calmed the waters.

A month later Eleanor found herself standing at the altar in front of a priest, beside her, a tall dark haired, swarthy young man, a close-cropped beard delineating his jawline, well-built and heavier than Richard but not unpleasant to look at, she conceded. He was the son of one of the Earl's retainers, who was hoping to perfect his combat skills and advance in the ranks. He had agreed to accepting a modest dowry and the promise of promotion, persuading himself that a young wife in the service of the Earl and Countess could only be advantageous for him.

Ralph, at 18, arrogant and full of his own self-importance and martial prowess, thought the maid a little beneath him but he had to acknowledge she was well-favoured, well-mannered and would no doubt make him a dutiful and presentable wife. If it ingratiated him to the Earl and Countess, all the better, he satisfied himself, and if she were reluctant in the marriage bed, he knew of more than one kitchen maid who would be happy to accommodate him.

"I, Eleanor, take thee Ralph Arthur to be my wedded husband to have and to hold... for better for worse... to love, cherish and obey, till death us do part," she recited barely audibly. Aunt Mabel watching from the pew, suspiciously scanned her niece's solemn face, noting her subdued manner but said nothing. Eleanor's heartfelt embrace as she clung to the old lady after the ceremony, told her former guardian all she needed to know.

Eleanor had cried herself to sleep the night before. This was not how it was meant to be! She had always imagined marrying her true love, being swept off her feet to settle down contentedly in wedded bliss. Bitterness and disappointment welled in her. Damn you Richard, Tis so unfair! Why do you get to walk away and enjoy your freedom, bed as many women as you wish, when I have to marry a stranger, a man I do not love and bear a child into the bargain? Instantly regretting her embittered thoughts, she prayed to God to forgive her, kissed her rosary beads and vowed to resign herself to her new life as wife and mother.

The couple lodged in the accommodation annexe to the castle, as Eleanor would continue her duties until she neared her confinement. She was thankful to be away from the tiny garret she had shared with Agnes but now she was a wife she felt a pronounced loss of personal freedom and a sense of duty towards her husband. This was not the life she had envisaged for herself.

Her wedding night she tried to shut out of her mind. Ralph had consumed many tankards of ale at the post nuptial meal and drunkenly pawed over her in bed. His touch was rough and dispassionate, his stubble scouring her skin, leaving red blotches on her cheeks and neck. His preoccupation with self-gratification showed he was undeniably no novice when it came to having his way with a woman. The act of love was uncomfortable for Eleanor and she felt nothing in return, her tense reluctance enough to satisfy Ralph that she had not surrendered her virginity to another man. She was relieved when her husband rolled his weighty bulk off her and slept, his snores frustrating her sleep.

She wept silently, tears dampening the pillow, longing for Richard and the way he had made her feel, imagining him with another maid, kissing her neck, holding her close, running his slim fingers through her hair and fixing her with those fathomless eyes. She hated herself for the way they had parted, longing to retract those words, repeatedly playing in her head. *How could I speak to him like that? What will he think of me? I've made it easier for him to forget me now*, she concluded wretchedly.

Life continued at the castle but quieter and less busy with the Earl away. Eleanor went about her daily tasks and soon felt the fluttering of new life inside her, although it was months before it showed on her small frame.

Chapter Five

OLITICAL EVENTS HAD RARELY FEATURED in Eleanor's thoughts during her childhood on the farm, as the yearly cycle of seasons and animal welfare had shaped and regulated her life, but now, living at the seat of nobility, their struggles for power impacted on the household directly. Now part of the Neville family, she realised she would share in their victories and defeats. Everything that impacted on their lives would determine hers, be it good or bad, famine or fortune.

Cocooned in her insulated world at the farm, Eleanor had been unaware of the countrywide conflicts and divisions between the upper classes, although news of her father's death at the huge battle at Towton in March 1461 had filtered through to them, when Edward Earl of March had won the day for York, despite 28,000 dead. This was Richard's eldest brother, of whom he was so proud and who was crowned king Edward IV soon after.

In conversations with her brothers Eleanor now listened intently as they expounded upon how the country had been split in two, with loyalties torn between the bloodline of the feeble-minded Lancastrian king Henry VI, who was controlled by his French queen Marguerite of Anjou's adherents and the Yorkist line of Edward IV, the son of Richard Duke of York, whose claim to the throne of England was in the view of many, the rightful and more direct claim. York's maternal lineage from Lionel, the second son of Edward III, together with his paternal descent from Edmund, the fourth son, transcended that of Henry VI, who was descended from the third son of Edward III, John of Gaunt. Henry's grandfather, Henry IV, had usurped the throne from his cousin Richard II but his son Henry V's military glory for England at Agincourt had ensured the Lancastrian dynasty's recognition and acceptance. Nonetheless, Yorkist ambition to restore the rightful line of succession continued to linger in the minds of sons and grandsons determined to claim their birth right. The quarrels amongst the ruling classes however, barely influenced the general populace in their daily struggle for existence and whoever occupied the throne was of little consequence to the peasants in the fields, so long as their livelihood was unaffected, Eleanor herself amongst those who had taken scant heed thus far of those at the seat of power.

In 1460, Richard Duke of York and his heirs were confirmed as Henry VI's successors to the throne of England. However, the Duke and his second son Edmund were killed at Wakefield and their severed heads placed on Micklegate Bar in York by the vengeful Queen Marguerite of Anjou, determined that her son would not be passed over as heir.

Following her husband's death at Sandal, Cecily Duchess of York's nephew, The Earl of Warwick, joined his cousin Edward Earl of March, the Duke of York's eldest son, against the Lancastrians. Together they fought and won the battles of Northampton, St. Albans and later Towton, after which the victorious Edward then claimed the crown for the Yorkists by right of victory and his father's ancestry; his youth, charisma and military prowess the embodiment of everything a monarch should be. The befuddled Henry remained confined in the Tower to ensure his heir could not claim the throne while he lived.

The mighty Earl of Warwick, the man labelled 'The kingmaker' was acknowledged to be the driving force behind the meteoric rise of his cousin, now Edward IV and the Earl fully expected the king to heed his advice and counsel.

However, in his Northern powerbase at Middleham castle, the Earl's household had gradually become aware of a widening rift between Warwick and the king; dissent simmering under the surface since the summer of 1464, when Edward had inopportunely announced his marriage to Elizabeth Grey, the widow of a Lancastrian knight and daughter of Richard Woodville, 1st Earl Rivers, which had taken place in secret, months before it became known. It was rumoured that the attractive widow was already with child by Edward before their betrothal, hence the delayed disclosure, and had either miscarried or lodged the infant with another family before publicly assuming her role as queen. Edward, ever the slave to his loins, remained bound by his promise to reward her with the crown. Either way, the news was met with astonishment, surprise and rumblings of disapproval. Nevertheless, Edward was king and none could or would gainsay him.

The Earl of Warwick had been busy on a diplomatic mission in France negotiating with king Louis XI for a bride on Edward's behalf, thus ensuring a lasting alliance between England and its old Gallic enemy. However, upon his return, Edward's marriage announcement at Parliament left Warwick chagrined and sidelined, all his efforts with Louis amounting to naught and there was nothing he could do but accept it. A king was expected to marry well, preferably into the European nobility, in order to strengthen his country's position through a trading and military alliance, but Edward's ill-considered marriage to a young English widow brought no advantage and undermined Warwick's credibility with the French king, leaving the Earl red-faced and humiliated.

Queen Elizabeth, Edward's self-seeking new bride, having employed her beguiling beauty to snare her prize, then ensured through her marriage that her two sons from her previous union and numerous siblings now benefited from newly bestowed titles and favourable marriages. As a result, this recently elevated family enjoying the king's favour had alienated much of the nobility, not least of whom was the Earl of Warwick, who was among those convinced that allegations of necromancy and witchcraft aimed at Elizabeth's mother Jacquetta, the widowed Duchess of Bedford with regard to her bringing about Edward's union with her daughter had some truth in them, and that she was even now plotting Warwick's downfall.

The Earl's resentment festered in the background through the next few years until, on returning to England from a further diplomatic mission in June 1467, he was again shocked to find that Edward had replaced his brother George Neville as Lord Chancellor with Robert Stillington, Bishop of Bath and Wells, a man who, it would later come to light, held a secret that could nullify Edward's impromptu marriage to Elizabeth. The Neville's long held position of influence with the king was gradually being eroded and their counsel ignored.

The Earl had nevertheless continued negotiating with king Louis for an alliance with England, whilst Edward had been brokering entente with Burgundy *against* the French king. While Warwick was away, Edward had mounted a lavish tournament in which his new brother-in-law, Anthony Woodville, Lord Scales, would joust against the Burgundian champion, Antoine. In March 1468 Edward had sealed his alliance with Burgundy, arranging for his sister Margaret to marry Duke Charles, leaving Warwick furious as, yet again, his negotiations with the French king on Edward's behalf had been discounted, his advice scorned, and his carefully orchestrated mediation with Louis XI ignored, leaving him embarrassed and belittled.

The queen had given birth to two daughters since her marriage to Edward but the fertile Elizabeth, having already had two sons by her first husband, knew it would not be long before a new son of York would supplant the king's brother George, Duke of Clarence, currently heir apparent. George, resentful of the Lancastrian biased Woodville family's influence over Edward, now saw his position under threat and turned to his cousin the Earl of Warwick, their old Yorkist ally, for support. The two noblemen began to scheme against Edward and agreed it would be mutually beneficial for George to marry Isobel, the Earl's eldest daughter; the Duke of Clarence therefore, acceding to the huge Neville patrimony and the Earl happy to welcome the king's brother as son-in-law.

Young Richard, Duke of Gloucester, the youngest of the York brothers, found his loyalties torn between his cousin Warwick, under whose wardship he had been educated and disciplined at Middleham, and his close family bond, which demanded unswerving devotion to his brother the king. He had accompanied Edward and his sister Margaret to Canterbury on her way to marry Duke Charles of Burgundy in June 1468. It was during this summer that Eleanor had encountered the young Duke of Gloucester at Middleham and she now understood why he had had to leave Yorkshire and return to London to take up his many Ducal obligations. Conscientious and dutiful, awed by the achievements of his elder brother, Richard did everything that was asked of him by the king and was shortly to be showered with positions of great responsibility, despite his youth and inexperience.

The king's favouritism for his earnest youngest brother had further alienated his ebullient brother George, whose siding with Warwick, had added to Richard's confusion, as he loved them both. He had grown up with George, sharing their exile to Flanders together as children, sent away for their safety, along with their sister Margaret, after the sacking of Ludlow in October 1459. However, when forced to make a choice, he chose to be loyal to Edward, the statesman and soldier he had always admired and longed to emulate, rather than the volatile and headstrong George who, although a charismatic and gifted orator blessed with the family's classic good looks, was rarely sober and inclined to indiscretion and unpredictability.

Richard's years of hard training had built up his slender physique and perfected his skills in preparation for battle, despite the pain in his back persisting and gradually impacting on his stamina. He was, nevertheless, determined to be the chivalrous knight and loyal brother Edward deserved to have by his side. Despite his slight frame and reserved demeanour, this studious fourth son of the Duke of York was determined not to be outshone by his older siblings. His first big test on the field of battle was to come sooner than expected and, to his dismay, against one who had once been his guardian and mentor.

Chapter Six

PRING 1469 MARKED A CHANGE of pace at Middleham
Castle and soon the vulnerability of their position was
brought home to Eleanor as the events of the year
unfolded. Eleanor had heard raised voices and was
aware of tensions within the household. The Countess appeared
strained and distracted. The Earl had briefly returned to raise troops
and arrange for his family to leave for Warwick Castle. Eleanor
heard him raging furiously to the Countess,

"That upstart parvenu, that bitch!" he railed, red-faced. "Since
Edward married that avaricious harlot, she and her insignificant
family have turned the king's head and bewitched him into doing
their will, aided, I'll wager, by that witch of a mother! She drips
poison into his ear until he is so besotted, he betrays his own family
in favour of hers."

"Richard, my dear..." began the Countess, shocked at her husband's
outburst.

"Nay, Anne, this has gone on too long. All my negotiations with
the French king have come to naught, with Edward signing an
alliance with Burgundy against France! My requests to marry Isobel
to the Duke of Clarence and Anne to Gloucester have been refused,
yet suitable marriages have been negotiated for *all* the queen's
insignificant siblings! Doubtless she has been bending the king's
ear to curb my influence. Well, I've had enough! Clarence is with
me and if I can persuade Gloucester to join us, Edward and his new
Woodville clan's pretensions will be curtailed. Isobel *will* marry
Clarence, despite the king, and we will soon see who holds the reins
of power! George is one of us now and Richard owes his allegiance
to me, after all I have done for him."

"Richard is loyal to his brother and I doubt you will divert him,
my Lord."

"Our cousin is young and has been brought up in our midst. I don't see him as being a problem to us... not yet anyway." The Countess thought it better not to contradict her husband for fear of a further outburst, but could not help but feel anxious as to the outcome of his resolve. Any conflict with the king of England was unlikely to end well, no matter how high and mighty a subject may consider himself to be and if the Earl failed, it was not only his future he jeopardised but that of his whole family.

Eleanor tried to make sense of what she had heard. Richard, she worried, would be caught in the middle of this dispute and his loyalties would be tested to the limit, with the Earl and his brother George in conflict with his brother Edward, the king. Soon Richard would soon have to stand by his fealty to one or the other. If he chose to be loyal to the king, which Eleanor felt certain he would, she might not see him again at Middleham and as part of the Neville household, she would be seen as being in opposition to her former lover's family.

Richard was not the only one with divided loyalties. Francis Lovell, also Warwick's ward, to whom he owed loyalty, now left Middleham for his father-in-law Henry Fitzhugh's seat at Ravensworth. The Fitzhughs were long-time adherents of the Nevilles but Francis had formed a lasting friendship with Richard and felt bound by his affinity to the Yorkist cause, in support of his friend, to whom he would remain faithful for life.

Following Richard's departure to join the king at court, Eleanor was forced to resign herself to her duties, blocking out all thoughts of him and throwing herself into her life as Ralph's wife. However, now Ralph and the other retainers, including Eleanor's brothers, were called upon to join the Earl. Middleham again became a hive of activity; messengers came and went at all hours; armed retainers gathered from miles around, weapons and armour crafted and repaired, horses purchased and supplies stockpiled. A few days before the soldiers' departure, as they prepared to retire, Eleanor sat on Ralph's bed reflecting upon the wisdom of the Earl's actions.

"What will happen Ralph? Will there be war?" she asked her husband anxiously.

"I hope so!" he replied hungrily, with a virgin soldier's thirst for action. "The Earl is going to challenge the king. Even his brother the Duke of Clarence is with us. The king is being manipulated by unwise counsel from the queen's Woodville family, they must be curtailed."

"I thought it was treason to fight the king?"

"Aye, so it is but the Earl is confident he can persuade the king to heed his advice. He is more opposed to the ill-advised elevation of the queen's kin than to the king himself. After all, it was through the Earl's support that he got where he is."

"What about the Duke of Gloucester? He is loyal to the king but also to the Earl!" Eleanor did her best to sound casual and not show inordinate interest in Richard.

"Dickon will keep out of it I should imagine but if it comes to a fight he will side with the king. A brother trumps a cousin when it comes to family loyalty."

As her husband climbed into bed Eleanor clutched her stomach protectively, thankful that the thoughts and anxieties whirling in her head for the father of the quickening life inside her, were voiceless. While Ralph's breathing almost immediately slowed into noisy slumber, Eleanor lay wakeful and unsettled. What sort of world would her child be born into? Would it be fatherless and would its mother even survive the perils of birth?

Ralph, as always swaggeringly self-confident, was excited to be serving at last, eager to use his martial skills for real and not just in mock combat in the tilt yard. Cutting a dash in the Earl's scarlet and white livery which Eleanor had to admit suited him, he readied himself proudly, honing and polishing his weapons meticulously. On the troops' day of departure Eleanor bid her husband farewell as he kissed her roughly on the cheek, patting her swelling belly possessively.

"Make sure he's a boy!" he quipped jovially, but Eleanor knew his jest was not as light-hearted as it appeared. He was hoping for a son to mould into his own image and fully expected his wife's body to acquiesce, convinced that the more he believed it the more it would come to pass. He was a man and he would beget men, he reasoned egoistically, for fortunately for Eleanor he remained in carefree ignorance of her unborn child's true paternity.

Eleanor's tearful farewells to Edward and James, displayed a mixture of pride and fear for her brothers who could hardly contain their excitement as they donned their surcoats adorned with the Earl's emblem and selected their weapons. They hugged their little sister warmly and promised to return with gifts for her child and herself. She tried to stay positive but the knot in her gut persisted. *Will I ever see them again?* she wondered. She knew that fighting against the king was treason, their futures doubtful and their loyalty open to question if they were on the losing side.

"God keep you both," she said softly, through a mist of tears.

The Countess and her daughters were excited at the prospect of leaving for Warwick castle, the splendid seat of the Earls of Warwick on the banks of the River Avon It had taken a week of preparation, packing of coffers, loading of carts, food supplies, weapons, armour and harnessing of horses before the company left Middleham. The usual hubbub of the castle was at once hushed with only a small number of kitchen staff, maids and nursery staff left to look after the children, although there was still a detachment of guards to keep the castle defended and the young pages instructed, not yet ready to become fully disciplined soldiers. Alone in Ralph's chamber Eleanor enjoyed having the entirety of the bed to herself, instead of being elbowed to the edge and for once, unbroken sleep without her husband's constant snoring and heavy breathing beside her.

Marguerite was now betrothed to a young man, whom Eleanor had seen riding out with the hunt, skilfully managing the hawks and an excellent shot with the crossbow. He was part of the Earl of Northumberland's household and the couple had left for Warkworth castle, the impressive ancestral Percy seat, lost to the family after the 3rd Earl fought and died at Towton but now owned by John Neville, situated in its commanding position on the East Coast. Eleanor envied Marguerite's happiness and felt abandoned and alone. *How did I end up like this?* she reproached herself, coupled to a man she could not love, carrying the child of another with whom she could never hope to share a future. Her only consolation was that she would advance in her position as personal maid for the

Countess when she returned, although she felt duly obliged for her kindness towards her.

Richard had been away for many months fulfilling his duties as the king's loyal servant and brother. He was nearly 17 and ready to take on whatever was asked of him by Edward. He had long dreamed of righting the wrongs done to his father Richard Duke of York, killed by the Lancastrians at Sandal castle in 1460 along with Richard's older brother Edmund, Earl of Rutland who at the same age, had been caught fleeing to Wakefield after the battle only to be slain pitilessly by Sir John Clifford in revenge for the death of his father. Clifford had shown no mercy to the adolescent youth who had pleaded for his life, as the vengeful knight raised his sword, retorting bitterly "Thy father slew mine and so will I do thee."

Richard Duke of York's legitimate claim to the throne had been ratified, naming him and his heirs the rightful successors after the death of king Henry VI but queen Marguerite's forces had seen to it that this would never happen. She was not content to sit back in meek compliance while her son was disinherited. The Duke's eldest son Edward, Earl of March had now restored the House of York to the throne but young Richard of Gloucester would not relinquish his aim of one day avenging his father and brother's death.

In June, a Lancastrian rebel uprising led by one 'Robin of Redesdale' against king Edward, had started in the North and spread southwards. The rebel leader was rumoured to be Sir John Conyers, a retainer of the Earl of Warwick, who by association was implicated, if not the instigator. Warwick had successfully enticed George, Duke of Clarence to join him in opposing his brother Edward, the Duke having been equally enraged by the unworthy queen's rapid family advancement and influence. Encouraged by Louis XI and the promise of a lucrative alliance between France and England, the Earl had hatched a plan to restore the simpleminded Henry VI back on the throne in place of Edward, as despite the young king's popularity there were still many disaffected nobles who wished to re-instate the Lancastrian king, now languishing in the Tower and recognise the young Prince Eduard of Lancaster as his heir.

Many were surprised that the mentally challenged king Henry had been able to father a child in his catatonic state and rumours persisted that the Prince was the son of the Duke of Somerset, a firm favourite of Queen Marguerite, who had fled North after the battle of Towton and then to France with her son. At first the confused king, deeply religious and devout, appalled at the idea of carnality, had exclaimed that the babe must be the product of the Holy Ghost but later acknowledged the child as his heir. Marguerite was now waiting in the wings ready to seize her chance to regain her lost power in England and saw the disaffected Warwick as the perfect means to enable this, despite their former enmity.

Richard, together with Edward and his queen, meanwhile, were on a pilgrimage to the shrine of St. Edmund and Our Lady of Walsingham in Norfolk, thereafter spending a week at Richard's birthplace, Fotheringhay Castle, which had belonged to their father. Richard had only vague childhood memories of the old Northamptonshire castle, standing tall on an elevated mound beside the placid water meadows of the River Nene, where he had played happily with his older siblings Margaret and George – a time of peace, a carefree idyll before the threat of war obliged the family to retreat to Ludlow Castle, the Mortimer family stronghold on the Welsh border, owned by Richard's paternal grandmother, Anne Mortimer. This was the last time seven-year-old Richard had seen his father, who had marched off to face the Lancastrians, leaving Duchess Cecily alone with her three youngest children – Margaret, George and Richard – at the mercy of the approaching forces.

While the Duke of York was forced to flee to a temporary safe haven in Ireland, due to the defection of his commander, Andrew Trollope, to the enemy, Ludlow was sacked and his family taken into the custody of Cecily's sister, the Duchess of Buckingham. Their terrifying ordeal had left a lasting impression on Richard of the perils of war and as he matured would fuel his resolve for redress.

Now ten years later and returned to their family seat at Fotheringhay, the York brothers learned that a force of rebels a was advancing south, outnumbering their own and that Warwick and Clarence were behind the uprising. Edward sent word to the Earl of Pembroke, Devon and Lord Hastings to join them at haste as he himself made for Nottingham Castle with his small retinue.

Some days earlier, the Earl of Warwick, his brother-in-law the Earl of Oxford and the Archbishop of York had sailed from Sandwich to Calais, along with Warwick's two daughters and the Duke of Clarence. Demonstrating her approval for the match, Cecily Neville, the Duchess of York, once known for her beauty as the 'Rose of Raby' but more recently as 'Proud Cis', had waved off her son George and his fiancée Isobel on their journey to France, with gifts and best wishes. The Duchess may not have been quite so approving had she known the Earl's full intentions and her son's involvement in his traitorous schemes against his brother, but for now she was happy for him to wed her beauteous great niece, heir to the Neville fortune. The couple were married at Calais Castle on 12th July. The Earl then publicly issued a manifesto listing all his grievances against the king and his adherents. There was no turning back now, Warwick had shown his hand. Leaving his daughters in France, he and the Duke of Clarence, now his new son-in-law, returned to England a few days later and began the march North towards Edward.

Warwick's army intercepted the Earl of Pembroke's Royal forces at Edgecoat on 26th July and battle ensued. Pembroke and the Earl of Devon were killed and soon afterwards the queen's father, Earl Rivers, and one of his sons, Sir John Woodville, were captured by Warwick and beheaded without trial. Warwick's intense hatred of the Woodvilles had culminated in an explosion of violence against the family he saw expropriating his counsel. The rebellious Earl then took the unprecedented step of capturing king Edward, who was at Olney, having been outnumbered and subsequently deserted by his followers. Unable to oppose Warwick without an army, Edward allowed himself to be taken into custody by the Earl's brother, George Neville, the Archbishop of York. From there he was taken first to Warwick Castle, then to York and finally to Middleham, as the Earl's prisoner. He knew, however, that Warwick would not resort to regicide and meekly accepted captivity while awaiting the Earl's next move. He was quietly confident that his status was inviolable and his cousin would soon learn from his mistake.

Richard, who had been with the king, was not perceived as a threat by the Earl and had been allowed to go free.

BACK AT MIDDLEHAM, Eleanor's confinement came in July. After a night of discomfort and intermittent pangs, she awoke to a rush of warmth as her waters broke. The long labour that ensued exhausted and appalled her. Childbirth was the battle all women had to face sooner or later, with no guarantee of the outcome for either mother or child, or both. *How do women endure this time after time?* She wondered in dismay as the pain increased. The midwife mopped her brow offering words of encouragement but the pain was overwhelming. The contractions felt to the young mother like some evil torture in which a belt was increasingly tightened around her extended belly, each successive paroxysm more agonising than the one before, sapping her strength until she felt she could endure no more. She whimpered and moaned, her fingers clinging tightly to the bedpost for what seemed like an eternity, the short-lived relief at the end of each contraction menaced by dread of what was coming next, until eventually, hours later, the child slipped out onto the blood-smeared sheets.

"You have a girl," the midwife told her, but Eleanor could not care, as long as the ordeal was over and the pain would stop. She thought of Ralph and how disappointed he would be that the son he had fully expected was a girl. *My fault, no doubt,* Eleanor reflected dispassionately. She was relieved, however, that his absence forestalled any doubts he might have had about the gestation period of this newborn that was plainly full term.

She named the child Elizabeth, after her mother. She was a small baby, pale and slight, like her father, Eleanor marvelled. She wondered how something so small could hurt so much. As she cradled the infant against her milk-swollen breast, she wondered too if Elizabeth would inherit her father's eyes and chiselled features or her own softer, more rounded face. Soon the memory of the pain she had endured faded as the love for her child overwhelmed her. *She is MINE and HIS, nothing can change that. She is living proof that he loved me once. If only I could tell him!* Eleanor yearned. *He would love her as I do, I am sure! Oh Richard! Richard, where are you?*

After a month's rest Eleanor went back to her duties while the child was nursed with the children of other retainers. She was glad Ralph was not there to resume his marital rights, although Eleanor was sure Agnes had obliged him during the long months of pregnancy. The girl would flirt with him whenever possible and Eleanor had caught them whispering together in dark corners, his chest pressed up against the maid's ample bosom, barely constrained by her tight bodice. Eleanor cared not, she did not love him, although sleeping in a big bed accompanied by Ralph's snores had been almost preferable to the cramped stuffy attic room, she had shared with the sullen kitchen maid. Eleanor was struck by the unfairness between the sexes. While a husband's philandering and sensual pleasures outside marriage were tolerated, a wife was expected to stay chaste. With a fertile woman in an almost constant state of pregnancy and with the ever-present risks of childbirth looming, a husband could almost be forgiven and usually was, for seeking relief elsewhere for his prurience. Now Eleanor had Elizabeth, her focus changed with the state of motherhood and with Ralph away, she felt she could endure almost anything, so long as her child was safe.

In the Earl's household, rumours were rife. Isobel's marriage to the Duke of Clarence had come as no surprise to Eleanor, since she had heard the Earl and Countess discussing it. She thought of the pale sylphlike girl, poised and beautiful but who was prone to bouts of sickness becoming the wife of the contentious and headstrong George, whose winning looks gave the lie to the conflict within. Eleanor had seen the Duke dining in the Great Hall, regaling the guests with amusing anecdotes, his loud voice and raucous laughter becoming ever more pronounced as he eagerly drained each successive goblet of its intoxicating contents. Fairer in colouring than Richard, his good looks certainly appealed to Isobel, who regarded him with rapt adoration but Eleanor wondered how she would cope with his volatile character, so diametrically opposed to that of his quiet and contemplative younger brother. Richard would listen in silence to his brother's stories, smiling politely until he himself became the butt of the joke, bringing an unwanted flush of colour to his cheeks.

"I hear the king has a new lapdog. He gazes up at his master with doe eyes and his tongue hanging out – he obeys his every command!" quipped George loudly on one occasion, casting his eye around the hall for acknowledgement.

"Oh, how sweet! What's his name?" Anne had exclaimed innocently.

"He's called Dickon!" George had replied facetiously, grinning over the lip of his goblet, gleefully watching his young brother squirm with embarrassment while the Hall erupted with muffled guffaws and stifled titters. Isobel happily fell in with the laughter generated by her idol but Anne's smile swiftly evaporated when she saw she had unwittingly contributed to a joke on her revered cousin. All eyes turned to Richard who glared at his sibling testily, muttering a profanity under his breath.

Typical older brother! Poor Richard! Eleanor had empathised, as she watched from a discreet distance. Now she smiled at the memory, pondering why George had chosen to break the family bond, betray their trust and side with Warwick? No doubt greed and ambition had played their part in the mind of the covetous Duke! She knew Richard would have been pained and dismayed by his disloyalty. He would prefer, she fancied, to suffer George's brotherly taunts than to have to face each other on opposing sides of a battlefield.

The household was shocked and uneasy when they learned the king had been taken prisoner by the Earl. This meant that they would all be considered rebels and the future of the castle and indeed the Neville's themselves, would hang in the balance.

An air of uneasy expectation pervaded the castle, while the household waited for news and some days later, Eleanor was woken in the dead of night by the sounds of riders entering the inner bailey. She peeped out of the casement to see the yard full of soldiers and men carrying flaming torches.

In the flickering light she saw the Earl and another very tall man wrapped in a thick hooded cloak dismounting and hurrying into the Earl's private apartments, accompanied by several guards. Nobody spoke and before long silence descended upon the bailey again. In the morning, the pages and ladies in waiting were summoned to the Great Chamber.

The Earl stood in front of the fire, his face drawn and weary.

"We have an important guest with us," he informed them. "He is under guard and will stay within the confines of the castle, however you must make him as comfortable as possible and see to his every need. Do not disturb him this morning but you may attend him later."

So the rumours were true! Eleanor had heard stories that the king had been captured without a fight. *The king of England here in Middleham! Richard's eldest brother!* She was shocked but at the same time curious to see this man she had heard so much about, not the least from Richard.

Later that day, when a page came to ask for clean bed linen and wine to be brought to the king, she took her opportunity. She was shown to the guarded chamber and entered quietly.

A tall, flaxen-haired man, his flowing locks falling in undulant waves over wide shoulders, dressed in the finest clothes, stood with his back to her, gazing into the fire, initially unaware of her presence.

Eleanor hesitated, unsure whether it was her place to speak.

"Your Grace..." she ventured timidly, as he turned his face towards her. She caught her breath, dropping her knee in a deep curtsey.

He must be the handsomest man I have ever seen in my life! she thought to herself as she took in his intense blue eyes, tanned face and perfectly chiselled features, *like a golden God of Greek mythology* she imagined, the absolute embodiment of the sunne in splendour emblem he wore. She perceived a slight similarity to Richard in the strong jaw and arresting eyes but he was about ten years older, of heavier build and a good six inches taller.

She paused, not quite knowing whether to continue with her task or wait for a command. He was her king but was being kept under guard, simply as a high-ranking nobleman, whose authority had been curtailed.

"Come here my dear," he said kindly, settling himself down on a chair next to the hearth, *looking every inch a monarch on his throne,* Eleanor opined. She understood immediately why Richard was awed by him – she was in awe of him herself.

Timidly, she approached and placed the wine jug on the table and the sheets on the bed.

"I see Yorkshire lasses are just as fair as the maids of London, if not more so!" he remarked, surveying her face and figure with an approving stare.

Eleanor's cheeks reddened and she looked down demurely. Edward leaned forward, grabbed her hand and kissed it slowly, smiling up at her appreciatively, fixing her with his sapphire eyes. She had heard of his reputation with the ladies at Court, and indeed anywhere he travelled, be they of noble birth or otherwise, and could quite see how they would be captivated by this charismatic Adonis.

"*Comment vous appellez vous, mademoiselle?*" he asked.

Eleanor had by now picked up enough French to understand this short question.

"Eleanor, your Grace." She thought she detected a shadow cross his face but then he smiled.

"A pretty name for a pretty girl! Pour me some wine, Eleanor."

He released her hand and sat back into the chair, watching her intently, taking in her slim shoulders and rounded breasts still swelled from recent child-bearing, spilling invitingly over her neckline as, reaching down, she filled the goblet with the rich red liquid and handed it to him. He took it from her slowly in his heavily-ringed hand, his fingers lingering on hers, all the time disconcertingly scrutinising her face and cleavage. Eleanor blushed, quickly turned away and began to spread the linen over the bed, but as she did so she heard him get up and stand behind her. Suddenly she felt his hand on her waist and his breath warming her neck as he leant down and kissed her bare shoulder. Startled, she turned to face him, trembling at the closeness of this alluring man, his mouth inches from hers, her senses struggling to resist the overwhelming urge to accept his kiss. Flustered and embarrassed, she tried to pull away from his embrace.

"Forgive me your Grace but... I am married!" she protested, her hand resting on his richly embroidered doublet. He stepped back, releasing his grip, laughing.

"So am I, my dear, but that doesn't make me any less of a man, I can assure you!"

Eleanor was confused. Here was her king, whom she could not easily refuse, but she wanted him to know that she took her honour and her marriage vows seriously and, despite her husband's lack of faithfulness, she was determined not to debase herself. She backed away, busying herself by hurriedly smoothing the bedsheets and drawing up the coverlet.

Irritated, but admiring her resolve, Edward turned back to the table, took another generous draught of wine and sat down again. Resting his head against the carved, high-backed chair and closing his eyes, he dismissed her with a casual wave.

"Off you go then Eleanor, tempt me no longer," he exhaled, with a long breath of indifferent resignation. He heard the rustle of her dress as she curtsied and left the chamber, smiling to himself at the maid's discomfiture as the heady combination of arousal, fatigue and sweet intoxicant consumed him. If this maid was unwilling, he would have no difficulty finding another more amenable. As king he knew he could have had his way regardless, but he respected women and was not unchivalrous, nor unmindful of their virtue, unlike many of his courtiers, who would use their positions to ensure compliance.

Eleanor was abashed and confused. *Should I have refused him? He is my king. I am his subject! What should I have done? Have I disobeyed my king?* she agonised. On her return to the solar, Philippa looked up eagerly.

"Well, is he as handsome as they say, Eleanor?"

"Aye, he's like a Greek God!" Eleanor replied absentmindedly, as Philippa noticed her concerned expression.

"What's the matter Eleanor?"

Eleanor bit her lip. "I think he propositioned me... but I refused him! Oh Philippa, I spurned the king!"

"King or not Eleanor, that does not give him the right to have you!" Philippa scoffed with indignation, reminding Eleanor that Marguerite would have surely concurred with the judgement.

"Never fear Eleanor, plenty of willing maids at Middleham will have no scruples about becoming the king's whore! He will admire you for your refusal. They say the queen refused him unless he pledged her the marriage bed."

"I've heard she's very fair."

"Aye, and she uses it to her advantage. They say her mother's a sorceress and that she and her daughter beguiled the king with necromancy!"

"Huh! I would not have thought it necessary given his immoderation when it comes to women!" Eleanor countered drolly, smiling at her most recent introduction with her hot-blooded sovereign.

"Nay, probably not, but she was determined to be queen, nothing less would suffice!"

Eleanor thought about the queen, who she was quite sure knew all about her husband's romantic dalliances, but she knew many aristocratic marriages were based on nothing more than gainfulness and the benefit each could bring to the union. This made it even more surprising that the king, the most sought-after suitor in the land, had been persuaded to marry one so disadvantaged. For some love developed over time but for many, wedlock remained simply expedient. Eleanor's parents had married for love, as most commoners did, and she had determined to do likewise before her moment of recklessness with Richard had forced her into a marriage of convenience with Ralph.

The talk in the castle was all about the king and why he was being held captive by the Earl. They heard there had been a battle at Edgecoat, where Warwick had killed the Earls of Pembroke and Devon, along with the queen's father and his younger son, Sir John Woodville. Edward, who had hitherto never lost a battle, had been surrounded and outnumbered and wisely allowed himself to be taken prisoner. The Duke of Gloucester had apparently been with the king, but they heard he had been allowed to go. Eleanor wondered where he was and what he would do. Now, with Edward under the Earl's control, would Richard stand by his brother or his guardian? In her heart Eleanor knew it would be the former and, come what may, Richard's loyalty would not be shaken. He would stand by his brother, despite the affection and indebtedness he felt for his cousin. Warwick had misjudged his young ward and unwittingly made an enemy of his former charge.

Over the next few weeks, despite Edward being kept under guard, he was allowed relative freedom, even joining a hunting party and attending mass at St. Mary and St. Alkelda's, a short walk from the castle. The townsfolk came out to catch a glimpse of their charismatic young statesman, whose reputation as a warrior and tactician was the stuff of legend. George Neville, the Archbishop of Canterbury, joined him at the castle while the Earl was kept busy attempting to quell unrest along the Scottish borders. However, to Warwick's dismay, he underestimated the widespread allegiance to a king who had not actually been defeated in battle and whose subjects still looked to his authority to bear arms. Without the king's command, the Earl could not raise enough troops. London was in turmoil, Parliament was cancelled and with the Scots threat looming, the only avenue left to him was to allow his Royal prisoner to travel to York to sanction the mobilisation of troops.

Eleanor had kept herself busy and just far enough from Edward to prevent any further advances. It was not that she did not find him appealing, quite the opposite, in fact. She could not trust herself not to fall under the spell of his animal magnetism, but becoming a king's concubine was not something she could justly contemplate. She thought of Richard and what he would think of her had she been intimate with Edward. The king's pious younger brother, although no puritan, deplored the loose morals so prevalent at Court and if he had held any regard for her integrity it would surely have been lost had she been tempted. She thought about her brothers Edward and James and their disapproval had their sister become the king's doxy. *Nay,* she told herself *I am better than that,* although upon witnessing some of the other ladies' maids showing no such scruples, openly flirting with their honoured guest, she had to admit to a pang of envy – God-like good looks, an outstanding warrior *and* a king of England – an intoxicating fusion of power and physical perfection that was hard to resist! A fact borne out by Edward's many admirers, courtesans and sycophants, charmed by his charisma, bonhomie and arresting masculine presence.

Eleanor had heard no word of her brothers since they had left with the Earl's retinue. She feared for their safety but she contented herself that they were well, having heard nothing to the contrary.

She also thought about Ralph and wondered how he was faring and whether he thought of her at all.

Probably not, she mused cynically. *Too busy drinking and wenching, I'll wager!*

Edward soon left the castle, either of his own volition or by the consent of his captor, Eleanor was unsure which. He made his way South and was joined at Pontefract by the Duke of Gloucester, Lord Hastings and the Earl of Northumberland, who had not so far supported his brother Warwick. Together they entered London to a rapturous welcome. The Earl had been outwitted, Edward was no longer a prisoner and the House of York had triumphed again. Unfortunately, it was not to last.

Edward's immediate concern was what to do about his cousin, the Earl of Warwick, and his own troublesome brother, the Duke of Clarence. They were now traitors, having plotted his demise, but Edward was initially reluctant to attaint them. Warwick was a strong Northern nobleman who possessed vast swathes of the land and had the allegiance of many devoted followers. There would be a power struggle in the North without him. The House of York was weaker without their cousin's backing, and the king hoped to win back his brother's allegiance by reconciling him to their cause.

Richard, Eleanor discovered from the talk in the castle, had been sent to Wales, not only to raise troops and put down rebellion by Welsh rebels but also to recover the castles of Carmarthen and Cardigan, a task he carried out successfully. Edward had rewarded his youngest brother's loyalty with the office of High Constable of England, which had previously been held by the late Earl Rivers, whom Warwick had so summarily beheaded. He was also granted the lordship of Sudeley Castle and the offices of Chief Justice in North Wales, Chief Steward of the Duchy of Lancaster and the Earldom of March. He was still only seventeen.

Chapter Seven

Y MARCH 1470, RICHARD WAS at Hornby Castle in Lancashire, assisting the local Harrington family over a dispute with Lord Thomas Stanley, who claimed the castle by right of Stanley marriages to the Harrington heirs. Stanley, middle-aged, a straggly beard sprouting from his pointed chin, his shifty eyes exemplifying his habit of changing his allegiances according to their usefulness, controlled much of Lancashire and Cheshire. He, along with his brother-in-law, the Earl of Warwick, held the North-West in his sway and was resentful of Richard's interference. The Harringtons ultimately lost the dispute but became Richard's staunch defenders for life. He could not know it, but Richard's opposition to the Stanleys in support of this family, would later have a profound impact on his destiny.

Edward then recalled Richard to him, after a new skirmish with rebels in Lincolnshire, where papers were found incriminating Warwick and Clarence in a bid to depose Edward and place Clarence on the throne. Edward could no longer procrastinate and ignore their treason. George's ambition had gone too far now. He and his dissident cousin were now proclaimed traitors and a price put on their heads. The king also took the Earldom of Northumberland from John Neville, Warwick's brother and restored the family seat to Henry Percy, Neville being placated instead with the Marquisate of Montagu, an action which was later to have unforeseen repercussions for Edward.

The Earl of Warwick and the Duke of Clarence had no choice now but to escape. They took, the Countess and her daughters out of Warwick Castle and boarded ship to Honfleur. Isobel, who was heavily pregnant, gave birth to her first child on board ship during bad weather but sadly the child did not survive and was buried at sea. In France Louis XI welcomed them and after a meeting with Henry VI's exiled queen Marguerite, who kept the Earl on his knees in deferential supplication for fifteen minutes, it was agreed that his younger daughter Anne, aged 14, would be formally betrothed to Marguerite's 16-year-old son, Eduard of Lancaster. This was to take place in early December, although it was agreed that the marriage should not be consummated until Henry VI had been restored to the throne, which Warwick was now poised to facilitate with Louis XI's backing. As Marguerite's former adversary Warwick's volte face was just the fortunate happenstance she needed to regain her status and ensure her son's succession, but despite forcing the chastened Earl to grovel at her feet, she was cautious not to be fooled by false promises and empty words.

The talk at Middleham now centred on the Earl's daughters, heedlessly swept up in their father's ambitious plans. *Poor frail Isobel* thought Eleanor, who must have had a difficult and terrifying ordeal giving birth on a storm-tossed vessel, only to lose the child shortly afterwards. And young delicate Anne, barely out of childhood, betrothed to the Lancastrian Prince Eduard, who by all accounts, although well visaged, exhibited a spoiled and haughty nature with a bloodlust for brutality, inherited no doubt from his vindictive mother. Being the two most wealthy heiresses in the country, these delicate Neville girls were pawns in their father's dangerous game with no choice in their destinies and no regard given to their frailties or desires. As simply valuable commodities to be haggled over and passed to the most high-ranking bidder, they were jockeyed to offer the most advantageous alliance. Eleanor thanked her fortunes that she was left to her quiet life in the castle with her daughter whose illegitimacy would protect her from such exploitation.

By August Richard had been appointed Warden of the West Marches bordering Scotland, a post previously held by the Earl of Warwick but Edward now sent word for him to ride South as they had received information from sources in France that Warwick and Clarence were soon to return with the aid of the French king to restore the House of Lancaster to the throne. The tables were about to turn again and this time in Warwick's favour.

The king also summoned Marquis Montagu to join him at Doncaster but Edward had failed to grasp John Neville's reaction to the loss of his Northumberland Earldom. John had previously been a loyal supporter of the Yorkist cause but the loss of his Earldom was an insult he could not ignore. The disgruntled Marquis promptly switched his allegiance back to his brother the Earl of Warwick, who had landed at Dartmouth, along with the Earl of Oxford. To swell their numbers, Jasper Tudor was approaching from the South West gathering Lancastrian support along the way. Edward learned of John Neville's defection and again found himself heavily outnumbered, caught between the two Neville's.

This time the king had no choice but to flee the country, given Warwick's 30,000 strong army and reputation for ruthlessness towards his enemies. Edward, accompanied by his loyal youngest brother, made his way to the East coast where they sailed for Holland. Meanwhile the queen who was expecting Edward's third child, sought sanctuary at Westminster with her mother and daughters. It was 2nd October 1470, Richard's 18th birthday.

In their haste to escape, the York brothers left with nothing to their name, once across the Channel, having to rely on Charles of Burgundy's governor Louis de Gruuthuse to avail them of money and clothes until they could reach safety and seek harbourage with their sister Margaret, the Duchess of Burgundy. Duke Charles had initially been reluctant to support the fugitive king openly but now Louis XI of France declared war on the Duchy enabling Charles to show his support for his brother-in-law, king Edward.

Back in England the Bishop of Winchester released the bemused and bewildered king Henry VI from the Tower where he had been kept and paraded him through the streets of London in disarray. George Neville, the Archbishop of York installed himself in the Tower apartments and the next day Warwick rode into the capital accompanied by the Duke of Clarence, the Earl of Shrewsbury and Lord Stanley. Warwick called a Parliament returning his brother George to the Chancellorship, creating John Neville Lord Montagu, reversing the attainders of Lancastrian nobles and agreeing peace with France. queen Marguerite was expected but did not arrive. She was cautiously biding her time in France with her son and his betrothed Anne, the Countess of Warwick and Isobel until she could be assured of Warwick's success.

In early November, Edward's queen still in sanctuary at Westminster, gave birth to a son. There was now a new male heir to the Yorkist throne, whose arrival supplanted George Duke of Clarence, the former heir. However now Henry VI had been declared the true king of England and by December Prince Eduard of Lancaster had been officially married to Anne Neville. The succession was determined that only if Anne failed to produce a male heir, then any sons of Clarence would become heirs. Edward IV was declared a usurper and along with Richard Duke of Gloucester, was attainted.

Across the water, the York brothers' forced exile was not to last long. Edward had all this time been planning to regain his kingdom with the aid of Duke Charles who had supplied him with ships, money and men, in expectation of the king's support for Burgundy against France. Edward was not going to relinquish his throne, so hard won at Towton, especially after ten years of relative stability, discounting the skirmishes at Hedgeley Moor and Hexham in 1464, which quashed remaining Lancastrian resistance. By early March 1471 he was fully equipped and ready to set sail again for England, finally landing after a storm-tossed voyage, at Ravenspur on the Yorkshire coast, eventually re-joining his brother Richard and Earl Rivers, the queen's brother, having succeeded to his father's title, who had sailed on another vessel.

Together with around 1500 men they made their way warily Northwards to York. At first, they met with some resistance under the new Lancastrian authority and were only permitted to enter the city under the guise of claiming Edward's Dukedom. Surprisingly neither Henry Percy the new Earl of Northumberland, nor John Neville, Lord Montagu, did anything to intercept Edward after he left York. Possibly Percy was loath to jeopardise his recently restored Earldom, granted to him by Edward and similarly Montagu, torn by divided loyalties, needed the backing of his brother's army before committing himself. As a result, the fugitive king's numbers were soon swelled by the arrival of Lord Hastings who brought an extra 3000 men to the Yorkist cause and together they moved Southwards, gathering support as they went.

The Earl of Warwick, still awaiting the arrival of queen Marguerite, moved up to Coventry to await support from Clarence, Oxford and Montagu but did not count on the untimely defection of the Duke of Clarence, who had been gradually persuaded by means of letters and messages from his mother, brothers and sister to reunite with his family. As a son of York, he had long been viewed with distain and suspicion by the Lancastrian regime and had become increasingly disillusioned since the readeption of Henry VI. Realising that his position was gradually being undermined by the Neville's and with the marriage of Anne to the Lancastrian Prince of Wales, his succession was becoming more and more unlikely. Feeling aggrieved and marginalized, accordingly, on 3rd April when Clarence's army met up with Edward's forces near Banbury, George, Edward and Richard, the three York brothers, instead of opposing each other across a battlefield, embraced and were reconciled in friendship and forgiveness – blood ties that could not be severed by their brother's short-lived and somewhat imprudent estrangement, despite the divergent aspirations of their errant sibling.

Edward, once more in a position of strength, attempted to negotiate a surrender with Warwick, who now holed up at Coventry refused to leave, so in the absence of a solution Edward resumed his progress to the capital, where the Archbishop had paraded the unfortunate king Henry through the streets, in a futile effort to gain favour. The plan backfired when the pathetic figure of the unworldly, addlepated monarch, grinning imbecilically, with his unkempt hair and grubby clothes, simply emphasised the contrast between this puppet king Henry of Lancaster and the larger than life warrior and admired statesman Edward IV of York. The choice was obvious, if not predetermined. As a result, on April 11th Edward entered London to reclaim his throne with no opposition. He rushed immediately to Westminster to greet his queen and infant Edward, his new son and heir. The Yorkists were back in power and with Warwick's cause weakening, the Earl's life was forfeit.

Chapter Eight

T MIDDLEHAM CASTLE NEWS REPORTS of the changing tide of events had caused confusion, fear, uncertainty, sorrow, joy and agitation all in equal measure as the Earl's fortunes fluctuated. Since the capture and release of king Edward, the mighty Earl of Warwick's influence had been shown to be losing potency but rose again with his alliance with the French king and readeption of king Henry. Now with the return of king Edward, the Earl, having inspired treason and dissent, was in danger of losing everything including his life. Eleanor was cheered to learn however, that Richard had returned to England with his brother, her fear of never seeing him again now allayed by renewed hope.

What would become of the Earl? What would become of his family? Eleanor worried. She feared for the Countess who had been so kind to her and the girls Isobel and Anne, now both married, the elder to the perfidious Duke of Clarence and her sister to the Lancastrian Prince of Wales. Either way, one of them was bound to be on the losing side and what of the Countess? *What would happen to her? What would happen to Middleham?*

Despite her fears for the family she lived with, Eleanor also feared for the father of her child. She shuddered to think of him on the losing side facing the executioner's block because of his unswerving loyalty to his brother and his determination to avenge his father. *Where was he? Did he ever think of her? What perils had he encountered in his flight to Burgundy? What dangers had he faced when confronting rebels? Had he found a new love? When would he have to face his first test in battle?* As the household prepared for the Easter festivities, Eleanor would not have long to wait for an answer to at least one of her questions.

Down in London, the three York brothers Edward, George and Richard now at the head of the Royal army, moved out of the city to confront Warwick, who had been joined by the Earl of Oxford, Exeter and Warwick's brother Lord Montagu. Edward shrewdly brought king Henry to the field to prevent the possibility of Marguerite of Anjou's forces taking the capital behind him. The two armies met at Barnet and camped within a mile of each other, Warwick unaware quite how close the Royal army was stationed. Edward wisely instructed his troops to keep silent and refrain from lighting fires so as not to give away their positions.

During the night Warwick pounded the enemy lines with cannon fire, which unbeknown to him overshot Edward's men, causing little damage. By morning, a thick mist had enveloped both armies, whose commanders failed to see they had lined up unevenly, each right wing overlapping the enemy's left. Richard at 18, had been given the honour of leading the vanguard on the right, facing Exeter, Edward in the centre facing Montague, with George and his reserves behind him and Hastings on the left facing Oxford. Warwick was at the rear of his army with his reserves. It was Easter Sunday, 14th April 1471.

This was Richard's first major battle, the event he had trained long and hard for during his years at Middleham but ironically against the very person in whose household he had been nurtured. This slightly built young man, coping with the early signs of scoliosis, bravely took his chance to show his loyalty and devotion to his brother, revenge his father and implement his chivalric ambitions in the pursuit of glory for the House of York.

He was eager to put into practise everything he had learned and striven for in his long years of discipline and mastery at arms and was ready to demonstrate to Edward that his faith in his young brother was not misplaced.

Despite it being the teenager's first taste of mortal combat, Edward confidently placed Richard in charge of the forward attack force, knowing from his own experience that the bravado of youth would fuel his brother's prowess before the brutal reality of warfare had time to strike home.

Inspired by the glorious exploits of his illustrious ancestors, Edward III and his son the Black Prince, at Crecy and Poitiers and more recently his own victory at Towton, Edward resolved his unseasoned brother would earn his spurs. A baptism of blood was the initiation every young knight had to face – victorious or slain, glory would be his, on earth or in heaven, in defence of God's anointed.

In the early dawn, shrouded in the opacity of the dense disorientating cloud vapour, the battle began. Richard charged his vanguard into Exeter's flank pushing them back towards Montagu and Warwick. As they slashed and crashed their way in heavy hand to hand fighting, on the other side of the field Oxford routed Hastings' men and chased them back into the town, looting as they went. Some of Hastings' men escaped to London with premature news the battle was lost but unbeknown to them Edward still held the centre, a fearsome figure standing tall, wielding a heavy sword, mowing down all who surrounded him. Along with Richard's, his troops were still holding their ground against Montagu when Oxford's men returned to re-join the affray.

In the confounding mist and swirling fog of battle, however, Oxford's banner and livery, the De Vere silver star, was mistaken by his men for Edward's insignia of the sunne in splendour and as a result they unwittingly set about attacking their own forces. Frantic cries of 'Treason' went up, at assumed treachery within the ranks. Montagu was killed and in the confusion Oxford's men fled, along with their commander and the Earl of Warwick. Edward had given the order for Warwick to be captured alive but by this time it was too late; the Earl was chased and cut down mercilessly by over-zealous Yorkist troops suffused with bloodlust and the heady hysteria of victory.

Richard Neville, the mighty Earl of Warwick, the 'kingmaker' lay dead, stripped of his armour, his ambition and his cause. Edward was saddened that his cousin who had up until now been a loyal supporter of the Yorkist crusade, had met his death so ignobly without a chance to account for his actions or declare his motives for his defiance. To Edward's further shock and sadness, as the battlefield was cleared, John Neville's corpse was found to be wearing Yorkist colours beneath his armour. Montagu had not been able to reconcile the conflict within; blood or bond was the cruel choice his conscience could not make.

Edward's resolute belief in his youngest brother had been justified. The battle won, the brothers greeted each other warmly in the elation of victory, smiles of joy and relief lighting up their faces, their exhausted bodies soaked in perspiration, their heavy armour battered and muddied, dripping with the blood of the vanquished. Richard had acquitted himself admirably in this his first battle, with only a modest flesh wound as a badge of honour; a deep gash from wrist to elbow, inflicted on his forearm as he parried a blow aimed at Lord Hastings fighting beside him. Watching his young sibling walk off to have his wound attended to, Edward could not have been more proud.

As Richard removed his gauntlet, sticky with blood, the adrenaline rush of mortal combat subsided and the burning pain of his injury kicked in. Richard winced, muttering an oath, followed by a grateful prayer for his survival but he could not suppress a smile of relief at winning his brother's approval. Later, having his lesion dressed in the medic's tent, he looked up as George staggered in, cursing blasphemously, wiping away blood streaming from a deep cut on his temple, half blinding him. Despite his unsightly, throbbing injury, having slaked his thirst with a long draught of ale, George sank down wearily beside his brother, grinning as he offered his rare, if grudging, approbation.

"Well done Dickon! Bloodied at last! Who'd have thought the little shrimp had it in him! I see I shall have to watch my back!" he guffawed, ruffling his brother's hair in an effort to disguise his renewed respect. Richard beamed. It was not often George bestowed praise, which rendered it all the more valuable, especially in his own discomfort.

Meanwhile, on the South Coast, queen Marguerite with her son Prince Eduard and his new wife Anne had at last landed at Weymouth and were joined by the Earls of Somerset and Devon. The Countess of Warwick, having herself landed at Portsmouth, immediately fled into sanctuary at Beaulieu Abbey upon hearing her husband had been killed. Marguerite, whose initial thought was to return to France, was persuaded by the Duke of Somerset and a growing army of support from the West Country to head North, join with Jasper Tudor in Wales, and engage with Edward's forces, which they judged would be exhausted and depleted after their victory at Barnet.

When Edward's spies learned of her plan, the king immediately marched in pursuit, his knights and troops still euphoric, buoyed up by their recent success. Invigorated, re-energised and renewed by the buzz of victory, the Royal army marched Westwards with blistering speed, despite the heat. Marguerite's army, after resting in Bristol, pressed Northwards but was refused entry to Gloucester, having no option but to trudge on in the unseasonably hot weather, chased relentlessly by Edward.

The two armies gradually converged at Tewkesbury, with Richard again leading the vanguard for Edward, aided by cannon and fresh troops. The Yorkists smashed into the Lancastrians, who initially held their ground but after fierce fighting finally broke ranks after a renewed flank attack from Edward's mounted spearmen waiting in the woods to their left. Somerset's troops turned and fled towards the River Avon, where many of them were killed or drowned in their heavy armour, unable to get across. Marguerite's son Eduard was cornered by Clarence's troops and killed, despite the youth's pleas to his brother-in-law. A few Lancastrians, including Somerset, fled to sanctuary in Tewkesbury abbey, where Edward's men surrounded them, later evicting them to face trial and execution.

Surveying the blood-soaked, body-strewn aftermath, Edward, George and Richard, grim-faced and depleted, reflected upon the grievous toll this bitter feud between York and Lancaster had exacted. The clash and parry of combat had re-opened Richard's wound and he had struggled to keep his advantage. His mood, as with his brothers, was one of relief at survival, rather than the jubilation of conquest.

Surely now England could be at peace? How many more of their countrymen would have to die needlessly before amity prevailed? How many more times would they have to cheat death? For now they could relax but they knew, as sure as night follows day, their time would come. Richard quickly dismissed the cold shiver running down his spine, wilfully blocking out the embryo of an unwelcome image materialising in his mind, before uttering a silent prayer and spurring his horse away from that spectacle of carnage. He could never quite shake off a conviction that he would not make old bones and having survived two ferocious battles which, save for good fortune could have gone either way, his deep-seated foreboding seemed ever more indisputable.

Marguerite, her spirit and resolve crushed and broken by her son's death, submitted meekly to captivity, along with Anne and the other ladies who had been sheltering in a nearby religious house from whence they were taken to London as prisoners, while Edward returned triumphant and victorious. Henry VI, who was back in the Tower incapacitated by his delirious state of mental withdrawal, lost control of his reason upon hearing the outcome of the battle of Tewkesbury and the loss of an heir to the Lancastrian throne, knocking himself senseless in a fall and dying as a result.

Many rumours arose as to the manner of his death with Edward being implicated as facilitator and even Richard's name was intimated. Eleanor knew that with his strong faith, fear of damnation, sense of honour and belief in the code of chivalry, Richard would never have raised his hand against an anointed king, let alone one who could not defend himself.

With the main focus of the Lancastrian cause no longer extant, the country settled down to Yorkist rule but the underlying resentment and hunger for revenge that lay dormant in the minds of sons who had lost fathers and brothers would smoulder under the surface, waiting for that spark of opportunity to ignite.

For now, the future looked bright for the Yorkists, but the ambitions of a scheming mother for her only son and the machinations of a power-hungry bishop, would one day culminate in a Lancastrian resurgence that would change the course of history.

Chapter Nine

N MID SPRINGTIME 1471 WENSLEYDALE basked in the warm protection of the lofty moorland peaks; the blackthorn twigs now erupting into showers of snow-white blossom, Lenten lilies quavering along the grassy banks, their golden trumpets heralding the return of the sun, everywhere fresh green buds, swelling and unfolding to clothe the bare branches. Young lambs kicked their heels playfully beside the River Ure, as it lazily followed its untroubled course down to the vale of York and somewhere in the woods a cuckoo's familiar call echoed over the tranquil scene. Daily life in this far-flung corner of England seemed a world away from the power struggles taking place 250 miles to the South.

Gradually word filtered through to the castle that there had been a great battle at Barnet and the Earl, their Lord and master, together with his brother, was dead, his grand plan to restore Henry VI to the throne thwarted. Panic ensued in the household, the uncertainty of their position hitting home when they learned the Countess was in sanctuary and Anne a prisoner in London, after a second bloody battle at Tewkesbury. Many were in tears for the Earl who had been their protector and benefactor but who had rebelled against his king and paid the ultimate price for his perfidy.

Eleanor had heard nothing of her brothers for months but from talk she heard from returning soldiers she soon learned that they had been seen amongst those who had escaped Northwards after the battle of Barnet and were probably hiding out somewhere until they felt they could return in safety. Despite her worry for them and her sadness for the Earl and Countess, Eleanor eagerly listened out for any news of Richard. She heard that he had fought his first major battles with the utmost courage and valour, emerging victorious to share in the acclaim and rewards no doubt his grateful brother would bestow on him. She pictured him in the heat of combat, wielding a heavy battle axe as she had seen him do in the tilt yard, unrelenting, unflinching, unshakeable in his resolve, to emerge gore spattered and dripping with sweat under his weighty armour, his spine aching with every twist and turn. She had nothing but admiration for this young man whose bravery at just 18 years old amazed her and whose loyalty was unshakeable.

She longed for the day when she could safely enlighten Elizabeth about her valiant father.

There was news too of Ralph. He had been killed at Barnet and Eleanor was now a widow. She felt a pang of remorse for the swaggering youth who had marched off so confidently to fight for the Earl. Despite his arrogant indifference to her, she felt sorry that a young man in his prime had to die, probably an agonising death, surrounded by carnage and the screams of the dying. No man should have to end his life in that way simply to resolve the dynastic feuds of the nobility. It seemed a waste of youth and ability in one so full of self-assurance and soldierly potential. She was, however, grateful to him for marrying her and saving her the shame of bearing a child out of wedlock. She also felt the relief of once again being free to remarry if she pleased, although this time she vowed it would be for love.

Eleanor was still a youthful 17, pretty and wholesome and although she did not realise it, the object of desire of many a young soldier at the castle, who eyed up this young widow lustfully. She had often sensed them watching her as she walked through the yard, the odd ribald comment prompting boorish amusement and muffled guffaws as she hurried past, feigning ignorance.

Eleanor was not wholly unmoved by their attentions. Lying alone in her bed, she craved that intimacy and heightened sensory thrill that came from flesh against flesh, shared body heat, the urgency of mouths feverishly pressed together, the electricity that shot through her when a virile young man ran his hands over her trembling body, holding her with his powerful arms, asserting his masculinity, worshipping her body with his. Often, she ached with frustration, hankering for the love of a man she could call her own, someone she could love with abandon, basking in a shared passion from one to whom she could relinquish her soul, her whole being.

Richard, she knew, could never be totally hers, despite a fondness that she was sure he had once felt for her. She had to be content that he had singled her out to be his first lover and now could never deny her those moments of intimate ecstasy they had once shared. Many a long night she had spent lying awake, imagining his return and with it the vague hope he might renew his passionate relationship with her.

By May king Edward had been busy redistributing the Earl of Warwick's lands. His brother George Duke of Clarence was the new Earl of Warwick, through his marriage to Isobel, the Neville heiress. Now based at Warwick Castle, he was given the bulk of the Beauchamp and Despenser lands belonging to his mother-in-law who was still in sanctuary.

Richard, already Constable and Admiral of England, Warden of the West Marches and Great Chamberlain, was made the chief steward of the Duchy of Lancaster in place of Stanley and was granted the Lordships of Middleham, Sheriff Hutton and Penrith. Richard resigned his offices in Wales to the Earl of Pembroke, to concentrate his jurisdiction in the North.

Edward needed to fill the power vacuum left by the Earl's death and his youngest brother, having so admirably acquitted himself on the battlefield, presented the obvious choice. Richard was poised to come home to the place he had grown to love and the people who had nurtured him.

Before he could do that however, he had to resolve his dispute with his brother George, who was protective of his Earldom and his wife's vast inheritance. Isobel's sister Anne was now a widow and free to marry again. Richard had long felt a connection and a protective fondness to his cousin Anne with whom he had grown up at Middleham and she had held him in great affection, oftentimes imagining their future together.

Richard knew the late Earl had for many years considered him as a match for his younger daughter and addressed his feelings about Anne to Edward. However, George was vehemently opposed to Richard's proposed union with the heiress and tried everything to prevent the marriage. Despite Edward's mediation, Richard and George soon reached an impasse, neither willing to acquiesce.

Anne went missing for some months, concealed, it was assumed, by George, who was determined his brother would not gain from her inheritance but Richard's persistence in his search for her paid off and it was rumoured, he found her disguised as a scullery maid in a London hostelry, from whence he took her to sanctuary. Following this he and George, after much argument in the presence of the king, were made to agree to Richard marrying Anne Neville but resigning his office of Great Chamberlain to George. The Duke of Clarence would also keep the Earldom of Warwick and Salisbury, in return for which Richard would keep Middleham and many of the deceased Earl's other estates in Yorkshire.

In due course, by the next Springtime of 1473, following the necessary papal dispensation for the betrothal of cousins and despite George's rancour, Richard and Anne were married at St. Stephen's Chapel, Westminster. Richard had always been protective of his young cousin during his years at Middleham and he knew the Earl had once considered him as a match for Anne. There was no doubting Anne's long held devotion for Richard, which had not diminished during his absence and now he and Anne were returning home as man and wife.

It was not long before news of the young Duke's impending marriage reached the household, forcing Eleanor to banish any thoughts of assuming relations with her former lover and bow to the inevitable outcome she had anticipated. Eleanor's subdued and thoughtful demeanor did not go unnoticed and some put it down to the news of her recent widowhood.

"I am sorry you are widowed Eleanor," Isabella commiserated one afternoon as the ladies sat sewing.

"Thank you, Isabella. Poor Ralph. I hope he didn't suffer." Eleanor stood up, laying down her embroidery frame on the coffer and walking over to the window.

"I hope my brothers are safe," she mused, speaking her thoughts out loud. "What will happen to us all?" she turned anxiously to her compeers. "Are we tainted by the Earl's treason? What will happen to the Countess and her daughters?"

"Nothing will happen to us Eleanor," Philippa reassured her. "We were not party to the Earl's actions. The Countess will be safe in sanctuary at Beaulieu, although she will forfeit her lands and property. Isobel resides at Warwick with her husband and Anne will be the Duke of Gloucester's Duchess when they marry. He will be our new Lord."

"Aye, it will be good to see them again," Eleanor stared back out of the window.

"I'm glad they are to be married," Isabella commented. "Anne was always smitten with Richard and making her his Duchess means he will keep Middleham Castle in the family."

"As long as he minds not Lancaster's cast-off!" Philippa replied cynically, as Eleanor shot the older girl a disparaging glance.

"Poor Anne. Richard would know it was not her wish that her father married her to Prince Eduard. By all accounts he was cruel and vindictive," she countered.

Isabella stared askance at Eleanor, suspecting she might have a more than passing interest in the Duke and Duchess.

"I hear Duke Richard fought valiantly. The king gave him the vanguard – an honour for one so young," she said pointedly, studying Eleanor's face for the slightest hint of a reaction but Philippa interjected.

"The king was a similar age when he fought at Towton."

"Aye, but Richard is of much slighter build and his back is not straight. I've seen it when he changes his shirt," Isabella couldn't resist the goad. Eleanor turned sharply and sprang to his defence.

"He's a skilled fighter despite it! He tires more easily, that's all."

Isabella glanced at Philippa, smirking satisfactorily to herself. *I knew it!*

"Someone's carrying a torch!" she whispered, as a knowing look passed between them and Eleanor, out of earshot, continued to gaze vacantly out of the window.

"They are so brave, these young men. What they must face..." her voice trailed off as she envisaged the bloody initiation awaiting every young soldier on the battleground, not the least of whom was her former lover.

THE EXCITEMENT WAS palpable as the household of Middleham Castle prepared for their new Duke and Duchess, the valiant young man of 19, the Earl's former page, who had proved himself outstanding on the battlefield, loyal and dependable, his beautiful young bride of 16 who had already gone through so much, having been married, widowed, kept prisoner, disguised, concealed, discovered and finally married again. There was no animosity towards Richard or Anne as new master and mistress of Middleham; they were part of the Neville family and were welcomed home as the rightful and beloved recipients of this Northern stronghold.

Eleanor was eager yet nervous to see Richard again. So much had happened since their last parting words. She knew, of course, that he was now lost to her, wedded to Anne and would inherit his wife's share of the Beauchamp and Neville fortunes, and she had to concede that the pretty young ladies' maid who had once caught his eye could no longer feature in his life. Richard was the second highest ranking knight in the country and had already proved himself on the field of battle. The serious, shy boy who had entered his cousin's house as page would return as their Lord and master, owner of Middleham, Sheriff Hutton, Penrith, Carlisle and many other estates across the North.

How can I speak to him now? How should I address him? Should I act as though nothing ever occurred between us? Will he even remember me? Eleanor wondered. It had been over four years since their moment of bliss on the hill. Four long years in which the quiet teenager to whom she had lost her heart had become a man, been bloodied on the battlefield and no doubt loved other women, maybe even fathered children. She wanted so much to show him Elizabeth but now that he was married to Anne, Eleanor deemed it neither apt nor timely. Any feelings she had once held for the king's youngest brother could not be acknowledged and would have to be locked away in the innermost recesses of her heart.

The Duke and Duchess's party arrived late in the evening. They dismounted and went straight to their apartments, tired and dusty from their long ride. Eleanor was called upon with two other ladies to help Anne undress and unpack for the night. Anne greeted them warmly and delighted to be back in Middleham, her childhood home, she immediately secured the services of her mother's personal maid, with whom she had shared laughter, tears, hopes and dreams. The Duchess had matured into a graceful young woman, still pale and delicate, her youthful exuberance now curtailed and refined into a poised and sophisticated peeress like her mother. In her short life she had undergone so much, been married to a prince, widowed, lost her father, seen her mother lose her inheritance, been a fugitive and a prisoner, yet now at last wed to the Duke of Gloucester, her childhood companion, the man she loved – the man Eleanor loved.

Eleanor ached with envy at the thought of Anne and Richard together in the intimacy of their recent matrimonial union but she was happy that Anne would hereafter find a kind and caring husband in her childhood friend. Eleanor had always liked the Earl's good-natured youngest daughter and was glad to be of service to her. She helped to bathe the Duchess, dress her and brush out her fine fair hair, falling to her waist, Eleanor thought, like a champagne-coloured field of ripe bearded barley. Eleanor tried, unsuccessfully, to erase the image in her mind of Richard burying his face in his wife's silken tresses, holding her close, worshipping her body with his, as he had done with her that evening so long ago.

Eleanor caught her first glimpse of Richard later as he passed by the chapel. Her pulse missed a beat and she darted back into a dark doorway before he noticed her. She was not ready to face him yet and her careful rehearsal of a measured calm and polite greeting, was dispelled by a sudden discomfited shyness. She perceived he looked older, his lost boyhood now subjugated by maturing masculinity, still handsome and slender but his features more defined, his complexion darkened, lines around his eyes conspicuous where he had squinted in the sun. *What he must have seen and endured since they last met! How proud of him she was!* He had proved himself a fearless warrior in two huge battles, sharing in his brother's glory and being showered with the spoils.

If only he were mine! she craved. He was the knight of Eleanor's dreams; her wild imaginings incarnate but he belonged to another and was as far from her as ever he could be.

Chapter Ten

ONTHS WENT BY AND LIFE at the castle settled into routine once more. New retainers joined the Duke's retinue and the tilt yard was busy as usual with young men learning their craft. As an experienced military commander Richard was keen to make sure he was ready to answer the call to arms should it be needed – and it frequently would be.

Eleanor had seldom seen Richard since their arrival but he had smiled at her once or twice and she had caught him glancing at her discreetly as she went about her duties. She was envious of his closeness with Anne but also relieved that two people she had loved and who had grown up together were reunited after so much uncertainty. Anne was a sweet gentle lady, still retaining some of that childhood naivete, graceful and frail with an alabaster complexion, but never terribly well, often prone to bouts of sickness and coughing. Eleanor worried about the ordeal Anne would have to endure should she fall pregnant and if her narrow hips, weak constitution and small frame could bear the rigours of childbirth.

It wasn't long before the Duchess confided in Eleanor that she was with child. It would be her firstborn, Richard's child but not his first; Eleanor kept that knowledge to herself, although the thought arbitrarily struck her that any issue of Anne's would be Elizabeth's half sibling and yet, despite sharing a parent, they would always be a world apart in position and wealth.

Eleanor had also found out from overhearing a casual remark by Anne that Richard had fathered both a son John and a daughter Katherine while he was at Court. Jealousy welled up in her at the thought of him sharing his bed with other women but she had to acknowledge he was a young man, vital and virile, on the threshold of manhood, a knight of the highest order, yet not unmoved by the temptations of a fair maiden, not yet skilled in seduction but learning the art of intimacy through the urgent, lustful demands of youth. Richard was attractive and available and four years was a long time; he was hardly likely to have been celibate. Suppressing her secret torment, Eleanor forced herself to accept that it was inevitable, nature taking its natural course, awakening in this young man the purpose of mans' existence to procreate and survive.

It was high summer; above the town the sun blazed down on the heath where moths and butterflies danced around fragile harebells bobbing their wafer thin lilac heads soundlessly in the breeze as it softly wafted the resonant notes of a curlew's trilling call across the upland summits and away over to Swaledale. Far below, verdant pastures bloomed in clouds of colour; yellow buttercups, blue meadow cranesbill, bright pink rose bay willowherb, wild orchids and white ox-eye daisies jostled for position, overhung by a tangle of hedgerows, where trails of white-petalled dog roses, the emblem of Yorkshire, sprinkled the thickets like star clusters in a sky of green. Birdsong filled the air, swifts and swallows wheeled and darted to and fro in their constant search for flying insects, their scythe-like wings slicing through the haze; below them peasants bent double, labouring in the fields, sweating under the hot sun, gathering another harvest.

Released from her duties for the afternoon, Eleanor wandered down through the cobbled streets of her home town, past the rows of close-packed thatched cottages and stone-faced townhouses, towards the river Ure, with Elizabeth, now just turned four. Several townsfolk who knew Aunt Mabel, hailed them with a friendly greeting and a comment about the agreeable day, watching the pair approvingly as they walked by. Mabel's ward had done well for herself, they weighed. Eleanor politely echoed their sentiments and prompted her daughter to wave back in acknowledgement. The little girl with amber coloured curls tumbling down her back, skipped along happily beside her mother and before long set to muddying her dress along the water's edge, crouching down to watch the frogs hopping across the mud, landing with a plop into the water. Little Bess laughed then squealed in fear as a dragonfly buzzed around her head. She ran to hide behind her mother, who laughed mockingly.

"It won't hurt you Bess. Look how beautiful it is with its shiny blue body and delicate fairy wings." Bess was not convinced.

A light breeze whispered through the willows bending low over yellow flag irises crowding the banks, their long-tapered leaves stroking the surface where tiny water boatmen skimmed across the tension and below them in the clear water, minnows darted erratically above the dappled stones of the riverbed. The air was warm, the sky an intense blue as cotton-wool clouds billowed high into the atmosphere in ever-changing shape, occasionally blocking the sun, while soaring skylarks sang in full voice, filling the air with rippling waves of joyful high-pitched warbling. Picking daisies together, the young mother showed Bess how to make them into a chain, slitting the stalks with her fingernail and threading the flower head through one by one, joining the last onto the first to form a floral necklace. Carefully placing it around her daughter's neck, she pulled her long hair through gently, so as not to break the fragile stems.

"There you are, fit for a princess!" Bess beamed with pleasure and skipped on.

"Shall we see what time of day it is Bess?" said Eleanor, reaching down for a dandelion seedhead.

"Blow as hard as you can and count the times you need to blow the seeds away, that will tell you what hour past midday it is."

Elizabeth blew as forcefully as she could and by the third breath all the seeds had gone from their naked stalk.

"Three!" she chortled gleefully, then stopped abruptly as a lone rider approached from the direction of Coverham Abbey. The child grabbed her mother's hand, pressing against her skirt shyly as the nimble chestnut stallion was reined in and slowed to a walk, while they stepped aside to let the rider pass. Eleanor shielded her eyes from the sun and saw with a shock that it was Richard. He halted beside them, patting his horse's neck to quieten him.

"A fine day for a walk madam," he initiated, his voice deeper than she remembered, the teenage boy now full-fledged to adulthood.

Eleanor bobbed a curtsey, still holding Elizabeth's hand tightly. "Aye, it is, my Lord."

"How are you, Eleanor?" he asked, fixing her with a mesmeric stare. Her heart missed a beat. *He had not forgotten her!*

"I am quite well, thank you my Lord," Eleanor blushed at the memory of their past encounter, steeling herself to appear calm.

"I am glad to hear it Eleanor," he replied, before jumping down from the saddle and leading his mount beside him. As they walked on slowly, Elizabeth pulled her hand away from her mother's overly tight grip and ran ahead. Eleanor was silent while the man she yearned for walked beside her, waiting for him to speak, sneaking a glance at his profile as he watched his pretty daughter chasing butterflies along the path. *How I long to tell him* Eleanor thought wistfully. She wondered if he would see himself in her child, although she knew he could never acknowledge her publicly as his.

She studied his face, which had matured and darkened with the sun, a shadow of stubble growth now noticeable on his jawline, no longer the fresh-faced youth she had first met. He looked strained and his perceptive discerning eyes even more joyless, if that were possible. She thought about the battles he had fought, the supreme courage he had shown and the terrible things he must have seen. The four years he had been away had been turbulent in the extreme, his life in danger almost constantly. Surrounded by death, treachery and deceit, he had been one minute a fugitive, the next, elevated to great heights as the wheel of fortune turned. He had grown into manhood, ruggedly appealing, the embodiment of chivalric prowess, a knight who had won his spurs, victorious in battle and unrelentingly loyal. Eleanor wondered how many young maids had fallen under his spell since the day she watched that raw unseasoned youth of sixteen, charging off to offer his fealty, his life, his destiny, to his brother the king.

As if following her line of thought, he asked, "How old is your daughter Eleanor?"

"This is her fourth year, my Lord."

He walked on silently, watching Bess intently.

Eleanor's thoughts raced, the awkward silence between them thankfully broken first by Richard.

"What is her given name?"

"Elizabeth, my Lord."

He paused, frowning slightly, the name perhaps reminding him of his brother's choice of bride.

"I am sorry to hear you are widowed, Eleanor. I hope you are able to provide for Elizabeth."

"Aye my Lord, I can manage. I am happy to continue serving the Duchess as long as she needs me."

They walked on in pregnant silence, thoughts wrestling, each waiting for the other to speak, the Duke acutely conscious that this attractive widow had relinquished her virtue to him and Eleanor unable to voice the love and longing she still held for him. Time and position occupied an ever-widening abyss between the former lovers, which polite conversation could not bridge. As a passing cloud briefly cast them into its shade, Eleanor shivered, earnestly searching for appropriate words of pleasantry to impart to this man she idolised. She peeped sideways at Richard, averting her eyes quickly as he returned her stare, unspoken words vacillating between them. As the sun broke through bathing them in warmth once more, they were both relieved at the diversion when Bess came running back to them.

"Look, a lady beetle!" she held out her hand, unfurling her fingers carefully as the red spotted insect crawled over her palm, then spread its tiny wings and flew off. Richard looked down into the child's face and smiled.

"You will have good fortune now Elizabeth," he told her. He stopped leading his horse and turned to face Eleanor.

"She will turn heads one day," he said quietly, watching the girl as she trotted off down to the water's edge. He was tempted to add 'like her mother' but he knew such a remark was inappropriate now he was a married man. Lasciviousness and perfidiousness, so ubiquitous in his brothers, were not part of Richard's character and despite his wish to atone for his youthful indiscretion with Eleanor, he knew Anne did not deserve her husband's disloyalty in expressing admiration for another woman, especially now she was with child. The romantic dalliances of youth were an assumed part of growing up but with maturity should come moderation, self-discipline and honour.

Richard was now looking intently at Eleanor. She gazed back longingly as his eyes searched hers and she had to look away for fear of blurting out her secret. She trembled and her heart raced at the proximity of his lean figure, which she noticed, he held a little awkwardly as if in some discomfort. Standing so close to him once more, Eleanor felt that surge of feeling she had withheld for so long; she ached to embrace him and feel his lips on hers one more time but she knew the gulf between them could never now be narrowed – he was wed to another, the Lord of Middleham, her master, her protector but never again her lover. She understood that even if he still held feelings for her, he would not show it out of respect for Anne, his wedding vows and his ingrained moral integrity, so at variance with his brother's libertinism.

"If you need anything Eleanor, you only have to ask," he said gently. Eleanor sensed he wanted to say more, when just then Bess called to her mother from the riverbank, eager to show her something and the moment passed. It was to Eleanor as if for that brief moment of immobilising eye-contact they had been locked in a soundless bubble, devoid of everything around them save for their shared experience, until the child's cry shattered the illusion and reality burst in.

"Thank you, my Lord", Eleanor replied meekly, though in her heart she was crying out *Richard, I want for nothing save you, the father of my child, stay with me and be mine'*. Instead, she stood immobile, watching him turn away, re-mount and trot the stallion down the path, waving to Bess as he passed her. Bess waved back, happy in her innocence, clasping a fistful of marsh marigolds, unaware this noble stranger's blood ran in her veins.

Eleanor's eyes filled with tears, partly for her daughter, bereft of a father and partly for herself, robbed of the love she craved. *I will tell you one day my sweet girl, I promise,* she vowed silently.

Not long afterwards, one evening after Anne had withdrawn to her chamber, Richard sent for some bread and wine before retiring. His page was engaged in feeding the dogs, so Eleanor took the plate and flagon of wine up to him, hoping for another chance to converse with him. As she entered the solar, he was sat at the desk, engrossed in papers and books. He did not look up as she placed the jug and platter on a chest by the hearth and turned to go. Hearing the rustling of her dress he raised his head wearily, his face relaxing into a smile when he saw who it was.

"Eleanor! Thank you... I sent for Thomas..."

"He is busy with the dogs, my Lord," Eleanor interrupted. "I was passing and offered to help."

"I am glad to see you Eleanor..." Richard hesitated and put down his quill.

"I wanted to ask you something... Pray sit down Eleanor, pour me a drink and yourself too." He passed her his goblet to fill and she took the spare goblet she had brought and filled them from the jug.

"Thank you, my Lord," she replied, sitting down on a low bench beside the hearth.

"Pray call me Richard, we are alone Eleanor."

He took a draught of the sweet liquor and let it warm his throat, closing his eyes momentarily, as he rested his head against the high-backed carved oak chair. Eleanor waited politely, his classic facial features and long lashes reminding her of his brother Edward, when he had sat before her. She sipped at the full-bodied wine sparingly, fearful that the rich intoxicant she rarely tasted undiluted would soon dull her senses, perhaps encouraging her to be unguarded. When Richard opened his eyes a moment later, he regarded her fixedly with a direct stare.

"Is she mine, Eleanor?" The intensity of his gaze and the abruptness of his question threw her off guard and made her jump. There was no doubting to whom he referred.

Eleanor nodded, looking at the floor.

"Aye, Richard she is," she whispered, relief flooding over her and tears welling in her eyes as the burden of her secret lifted. She heard him take a deep breath, perceiving a look of hurt in his eyes as she looked up. As he scrutinised her face, his expression caused a stabbing pain of remorse and self-reproach to pierce Eleanor's breast. The last thing she wanted was to wound the man she adored.

"Why did you not tell me, Eleanor?" He frowned, visibly annoyed, but whether at himself or her, she was unsure.

"Forgive me Richard. You left and..." Her voice trailed off. She hadn't meant to castigate him.

"I *had* to leave Eleanor. You could have got a message to me. I could have provided for you. Clearly you do not have a very high opinion of me!" He studied her face keenly.

She was stung by the unfairness of this remark from the man she had worshipped for so long, held in such high regard, loved to distraction.

"Oh, nay my Lord, I respect and admire you. I did not wish to burden you, my Lord. You had your duties and I was ashamed of my... situation."

"So you married Ralph and passed Elizabeth off as his," he said flatly.

Eleanor blushed. He made it sound so base.

"Aye, but the Countess..." She stopped, realising she had broken a confidence.

"The Countess?" Richard exclaimed, glancing up surprised. "*She* knew of this?"

"Aye, she arranged for my marriage and dowry."

"Oh, I see..." he hesitated, frowning. "Did she know the child was mine?"

"Nay Richard, of course not. I would never have given that away. But if the Countess returns she may see the likeness, as you have done Richard. Bess... has your eyes and your colouring."

"I know," he sighed, with a pained expression, swallowing another mouthful of the heady red liquid.

"I suspect Anne will perceive it before too long," he spoke as if to himself, twirling the goblet in his pliant fingers. Noticing the purple slash of fresh scar tissue branding his hand and forearm, Eleanor involuntarily drew in a swift intake of breath.

"You are injured?" she stared in alarm.

"T'is only a scratch Eleanor, nothing of consequence," he replied, brushing aside her concern and pulling his sleeve down further; a reminder of Barnet he would prefer to forget.

Eleanor realised how little she knew of his life and the events that had transformed him from boy to man. She wished so much she could be part of his life, share his pain, his joy, keep his secrets but the gulf between them was as wide as it could be. Anne was now his confidante, his partner in life, his companion, his lover. Eleanor was his past, not his future.

They sat in absorbed silence for a while. In the candelabra the melted stubs of wax were threatening to extinguish themselves, casting flickering shadows across the wall hangings as Eleanor sat twisting her fingers uncomfortably. Distracted, Richard drained his goblet and reached for the flagon again.

"I will provide for Elizabeth Eleanor; you will not be left wanting on my account." He heaved a sigh, refilling his cup and offering the jug to Eleanor, who shook her head politely. The wine was already benumbing her senses – any more and she might recklessly profess her love. He put the jug down and took another long draught of liquor.

"I cannot acknowledge her as my own, as she has been brought up as Ralph's, but thank you for raising my daughter and keeping her safe. She is a lovely child, a credit to you." He commended her with a measured stare.

"...and to you Richard," Eleanor responded, wanting him to know how much she appreciated him as her child's father.

"Nay, I have done nothing," he remarked ruefully, looking away, guiltily aware that he had taken advantage of a virtuous maiden knowing he could never be bound to her.

"You are part of her Richard, that is enough," she said truthfully, hoping he would accept her flattery as genuine.

"Thank you, Eleanor." For a fleeting moment as their eyes met, she was back there on the hill drowning under his spell but he shifted in his chair, discernibly discomforted.

"I never meant to cause you any pain Eleanor. I... I was young... and you captivated me, forgive me."

"There is nothing to forgive Richard..." Eleanor longed to continue '*I loved you*' but instead she said "...I have Elizabeth."

He smiled again, appraising her appreciatively, noticing her once girlish figure had filled out and blossomed into womanly curves, her freckles faded, her lips full and sensuous, still as desirable, if not more so, as the innocent young teenager who had first caught his attention.

"You cannot be short of admirers Eleanor," he complimented her candidly.

"You should find a husband to take care of you."

Eleanor ached to reply *I already have and you are here! Now you would give me away?* She could not let him see that his remark hurt her in its heedlessness and disregard for her private heartache, despite the tribute, however she recognised he would be unaware of the depth of her feelings towards him. *If only I could declare my love* she wished silently.

Before she could think of a suitable response there was a commotion at the door and two large wolfhounds bounded into the room, followed by the Duke's page, Thomas. Richard, taking advantage of the interruption to gather his thoughts, turned to stroke the dogs, fondling their ears playfully. Eleanor, seizing her chance to avoid further awkwardness, stood up, bobbed a quick curtsey, "My Lord..." and was gone before he could speak.

She stopped in the passageway, leaning against the wall, closing her eyes and steadying herself, fighting those long-suppressed feelings which had risen to the fore. She could hear her heart thumping loudly in her ears from the fusion of wine, the flush of exhilaration from their meeting and the relief of unburdening her secret. *At last, he knows Elizabeth is his!* Composing herself outwardly at the sound of approaching footsteps, Eleanor ran to her chamber and threw herself onto the bed. In her heart Richard had been and always would be her husband, the only man she wanted and yet the one man she knew she could never have.

The following day a page brought her a purse of coins, attached to it was a parchment note. *'For Elizabeth'*, signed *'R. Gloucester'*. Eleanor conveyed her thanks to the page and put it away safely, not intending to use it unless absolutely necessary. Money was not what she wanted from Richard, she only wanted *him*.

Chapter Eleven

ARLY IN 1473 RICHARD HAD had to confiscate the lands of the elderly Countess of Oxford, whose son John de Vere, Earl of Oxford, an attainted Lancastrian since his escape from Barnet, had been making trouble in the Channel. Richard could not risk the Countess assisting her son in financing a rebellion. He offered to accommodate her at Middleham but she was afraid of the North country and saw this as a threat, which it was not intended to be. Many enemies of the House of York would use this and every other excuse to find fault with Richard's motives, as would become clear with the passing of time and Oxford would not relinquish his cause to bring down Yorkist rule and reassert Lancastrian supremacy. Destiny would ensure their paths would someday cross again on a battlefield in Leicestershire that would settle the score one way or the other.

At the end of April king Edward had arrested the Archbishop of York, George Neville, for a conspiracy between him and the attainted Earl Oxford. Edward sent the Archbishop to Hammes Castle outside Calais. George, Duke of Clarence was somehow implicated in Oxford's plan. His simmering resentment of Edward's preference for Richard would not go away and he had not forgotten that a Lancastrian parliament had recognised his position as heir before Edward's queen had produced a son.

At Middleham Anne had given birth to a boy. Eleanor did what she could to try to alleviate the Duchess's pain and discomfort as the midwife fussed around her. It was a long difficult labour. Richard was away, for which Eleanor was grateful. She did not want him to witness Anne's ordeal or hear her tortured cries. The midwife was afeared for both mother and child, as Anne bled profusely, draining her of the little strength she had. The child, when it emerged, was undersized and weak but survived, as did his mother, to everyone's great relief.

The babe was baptised Edward, which was no surprise to Eleanor, given Richard's adoration of his elder brother. Edward of Middleham was now Richard Duke of Gloucester's legitimate heir, in fact his only *legitimate* child. Anne took months to recover from the birth and on the Duke's return his delight at his new son was tempered by concern for the health of both his wife and child. Eleanor tended the Duchess and gradually young Edward rallied, thanks to the ministrations of his wet nurse, while his mother slowly regained her strength as the warmer weather took hold.

Now that Eleanor had confided in Richard about Bess, she felt a sense of relief, although she still could not bring herself to confess to Anne. With Anne having had her own child by Richard, it did not seem well judged to enlighten her and in any case, it was not her place. Richard could do so himself if he deemed it appropriate. Young Elizabeth played happily with the other children but more often by herself. Sometimes, Eleanor noticed, Richard found time to come and talk with his natural daughter, taking her down to the stables to see the horses, lifting her up on their sleek backs and leading her round. She had an instinctive aptitude for riding, *no doubt from him*, Eleanor pondered.

Her heart filled with pride and joy to think he was fond of the child they had made together. She smiled inwardly as the thought struck her that he could surely not forget who Elizabeth's mother was! She could not deny, however, that every time she looked at her daughter, Richard's eyes would be staring back at her, reminding her of those precious moments they had once shared. Chiding herself for her jealousy of his love for Anne, after all he was the king's brother and could not have married anyone of lower status than the Earl's daughter, she bound herself to be satisfied with her circumstance.

There were comments in the kitchen that he had only married Anne for her inheritance but although part of this may have served to enhance his standing as Duke of Gloucester and the new Lord of Middleham, Eleanor knew they loved each other. Richard was unlike his brother George who was grasping and desirous, a man who would stop at nothing to advance his wealth and position.

In May Richard attended a Royal Court in Nottingham, where he and the reinstated Earl of Northumberland, Henry Percy, had pledged that Richard would be of good lordship to the Earl in return for Percy's faithful service. There had been tensions between them due to their overlapping responsibilities for the North. The Earl resented Richard's superiority over him since the death of Warwick, from which Percy had hoped to benefit. The Percy's had long held control over the North before king Edward had seen to promote his younger brother in Warwick's stead. However, for the time being they agreed, albeit unenthusiastically, to coexist and share control in a mutually advantageous collaboration. Richard was aware that despite outward appearances of co-operation, only time would tell if the previously Lancastrian magnate would prove to be loyal to the House of York.

All this time, the Countess of Warwick had been in sanctuary at Beaulieu Abbey. Anne had been worried about her situation and had spoken with Richard about it. Eleanor had overheard Anne asking Richard if he would help her mother. Richard had replied that as she had been the wife of a traitor, there was not much he could do for her, despite his sympathy for her position. His brother George had been granted her Beauchamp estates which she had inherited from her father and king Edward had ensured she would no longer benefit from her huge wealth. Anne persisted, persuading Richard to speak to the king, assuring him that the dowager Countess posed no threat and that Anne would welcome the companionship of her mother during Richard's frequent absences.

In due course, to Anne's delight, the king allowed Richard to assume responsibility for his mother-in-law. She was summoned to join them at Middleham, travelling up from her cloistered sanctum under the protection of Sir James Tyrrell, Richard's faithful councillor, who had fought by his side at Tewkesbury. George, far from happy when he heard the Countess was joining Richard's family, sensed he could be about to lose his share of her property, which did nothing to lessen his simmering resentment of Edward's obvious preference for their younger brother.

The Countess arrived home to a tearful reunion with her daughter, eager to introduce her mother to her new grandson, Edward of

Middleham. Anne and the Countess were able to share their private grief for the loss of the Earl of Warwick, their husband and father, who had dared rebel against his king and had paid the ultimate price for his treachery. Anne Beauchamp had come home to this quiet corner of England where she could live out the rest of her life in peace and seclusion under the protection of her one-time ward, Richard Duke of Gloucester.

Eleanor was warmly greeted by her former mistress, who commiserated with her on her widowhood and enquired after her daughter. Eleanor was shocked at her appearance. The Countess looked ashen faced and haggard, lines of worry etched on her brow, her cheeks sunken, streaks of grey starkly visible in her hair, her only ornament a large silver crucifix resting on her plain and unadorned widow's gown, the sombre black emphasising her years. Her eyes sad and distant, her fortitude crushed, her husband dead, her wealth redistributed, she was but a shadow of her former dignified self but she was home and she was safe. Eleanor helped her unpack her few possessions, her richly illustrated manuscripts and some precious items of jewellery amongst which Eleanor was heartened to see the beautiful golden pendant with the sapphire stone she had so much admired on their first meeting, which now seemed far removed from the Countess's present harsh reality. The pearls had been removed, possibly as a gift to the Countess's benefactors, and Eleanor marvelled at how quickly and decisively fortune could change a life from that of privilege to one of privation.

Soon after her arrival, the Countess guessed Eleanor's secret when a sudden realisation of the child's paternity struck her while she watched Elizabeth playing. The child's fine bone structure and pale countenance reflected her father's genes; her similar colouring, her eyes the same soft blue grey, her strong chin, her slim fingers, her serious and somewhat distant expression as she clasped her fabric doll, quietly amusing herself. The likeness to Richard was unmistakable.

"Your secret is safe with me Eleanor," the Countess had whispered, smiling knowingly.

Chapter Twelve

INCE ACQUIRING THE LORDSHIP OF Barnard Castle, strategically placed between Richmond and Penrith, Richard was busy recruiting retainers, consolidating his authority and cultivating acceptance in the area as the new Lord of the North and was seldom at home. New soldiers, archers, grooms, pages and scribes joined the growing household at Middleham.

Eleanor was lonely. She acknowledged she could not spend her life yearning for someone she could never have and there were plenty of eligible men at the castle to arouse a young widow's interest. A few had made tentative advances but none held more than a mild attraction for her... that is until a new contingent of bowmen arrived.

One, the captain, stood out from the rest. He was tall, broad shouldered and immensely strong, a masterpiece of male physical beauty, hard for a companionless young widow to ignore. Eleanor would find an excuse to walk past the training field whenever she could, just to catch a glimpse of him. She watched as he stretched the six-foot longbow to breaking point, his sculpted muscles tanned and taught, releasing the arrow straight, fast and exactly on target. Eleanor cringed at the thought of the unfortunate recipient of that formidable force. She admired the archer's powerful physique, his rugged Nordic descent apparent in his features, his long blond locks, tied back with a leather thong, looking in every way like a mythic hero, fresh from the pages of some fantastic Viking saga. She watched discreetly as he cast off his shirt, wet with perspiration before dousing his naked torso with a bucketful of water and a frisson of excitement awoke her senses. Sensing her scrutiny, he cast her a beaming smile of encouragement as she walked by.

One day as archery practice finished, Eleanor took the captain a tumbler of ale. He was sat on a bench at the side of the tilt yard undoing the laces on his leather bracer but looked up with a friendly grin as she approached.

"I thought you might like a drink," she said, offering the tumbler to him. He took it gratefully, as she studied his intense blue eyes and generous mouth, his smouldering masculinity awakening in her a desire for bodily contact that had lain dormant for too long.

"Thank you, madam." He spoke with a deep-toned, pronounced Northern accent.

"I'm Eleanor, the Duchess's maid," she replied.

"Aye, I know," he said, bluntly, with the refreshing honesty of his class, studying her pretty face before running his eye over her womanly figure. She realised he must have enquired about her.

"And I am Phillipe." He took her hand and kissed it politely. "My mother was French," he added in explanation.

"Where do you come from?" Eleanor asked courteously.

"Barnard Castle, madam. The Duke has called upon us to join him for training."

"Oh aye, of course." Eleanor could think of nothing else to say that would not show her ignorance but she had heard of the imposing castle, perched on its escarpment, high above the River Tees about a day's journey to the Northeast of the Pennines, which was now under Richard's jurisdiction. Richard had recently ordered structural improvements to the accommodation including a new oriel window, affording a far-reaching view along the river towards the north-west and the waterfall known as High Force.

Phillipe took a gulp of ale, studying Eleanor keenly as he drank. She watched him shyly, trying not to appear unduly interested but as their eyes met she could not disguise the attraction she felt and looked away embarrassed. Thankfully, he spoke first.

"Was that your daughter I saw you with?"

"Oh aye, Elizabeth, she's five now," said Eleanor proudly.

"Is your husband..."

Eleanor interrupted before he could finish.

"My husband was killed at Barnet," she said quickly, needing him to know she was not bound to anyone, thereby appearing wanton.

"My condolences madam," he offered, studying her impassive face as he took another long draught of ale, observing her all the while, correctly surmising she was by no means consumed with inconsolable grief at the loss of her husband. Eleanor blushed, reading his knowing expression and was relieved when a bowman approached to speak with the captain, diverting his attention.

"I must be about my duties, the Duchess will be expecting me," Eleanor turned to go, suddenly self-conscious that she had been so familiar with a stranger.

"Fare thee well Eleanor, thank you for the ale," he smirked, with some satisfaction at her abashment, aware that the offer of ale had just been a convenient pretext for contact.

He watched her walk back to the gate. The bowman who had come to speak to him made a vulgar remark and they both laughed. Eleanor, out of earshot, looked back but Phillipe was busy stacking his weapons. She failed to notice him look up at her again when she looked away. In the sanctuary of her bedroom that night, she lay awake thinking of him, imagining his taut body close to hers and his muscle-bound arms gripping her tightly. She wondered wishfully if fantasy would become reality.

She would not have long to wait.

With Christmas festivities in full swing, the castle was overflowing, the main rooms brightly lit by dozens of extra candles and lamps, dried rosemary and lavender strewn on the floors, the heady aroma mingling with the delicate scent from the bowls of rosewater on the tables; there was feasting and dancing in the Great Hall for lords and ladies from miles around.

Richard and Anne made a striking couple, dressed in finest silks and velvets, pearls and precious jewels dripping from their fingers and adorning their clothes. The Countess, now restored to her former home, appeared relaxed and revived, having reclaimed her elegance and poise and was smiling again, dressed in finery provided for her by her daughter.

It was almost like the old days of the Earl's legendary hospitality and the Duke and Duchess had made sure they were not to be outdone by comparison. With tables groaning under huge quantities of festive food, minstrels played from the gallery and entertainers charmed the guests, while below them the kitchen clamoured with noise and confusion.

Eleanor was feeling faint with the stifling heat from the huge fireplaces and the suffocating atmosphere in the kitchen. Craving some fresh air and having a few moments to herself she crept out and climbed the winding stairs past the Great Hall, leading up to the battlements. A jester was performing his comic antics, which Eleanor always found somewhat ridiculous and oft verging on insolence but which inexplicably to her appeared to be accepted by all without offence. For the present though, she was grateful his tomfoolery gave her the perfect excuse to absent herself momentarily while the guests were distracted.

Climbing the cool stairway, she welcomed the comforting shadows away from the brightly lit hall while the sound of laughter and music drifted upwards, gradually diminished by the thick stone wall spiralling upwards as the width of tread decreased beneath her time worn soles. As Eleanor reached the top and stepped out into the clear cold night air, she gasped in wonderment, awestruck by the vast dome of inky sky outspreading above, ablaze with stars. It seemed to her as though the world was enveloped inside a huge black orb punctured by countless pinpricks, through which shone the dazzling glare of heaven.

Leaning against the parapet, cooling her face, mesmerised by the millions of twinkling points of light, lost in thought, she recalled her first encounter with Richard, when a voice behind her jolted her back to the present.

"Beautiful, aren't they Eleanor?" Phillipe was resting against the wall, a tumbler of ale in his hand. She wondered how long he had been watching her from the shadows. Part of her was excited by the encounter but another part wanted to flee.

"Aye, they are wonderful!" she exclaimed, her face flushed.

He came forward and stood beside her, setting the tumbler down, placing his hand upon her shoulder and pointing upwards to the heavens. *Too late.* Flight would be discourteous now that she had hesitated and fear was replaced by curiosity, although she was glad the darkness hid the colour rising to her cheeks, betraying her abashment. Eleanor pretended not to notice Phillipe's hand, now progressing to her waist, as they stared at the spellbinding sky.

"See that bright star, that's Sirius, the dog star, the brightest star in the sky," he pointed. "Now look up, there's Orion, the hunter, see his belt, the three stars and his sword. Over there is the Plough and if you follow the line of stars straight up," he traced the line with his arm "that's Polaris, it always points to the North.

"You know about the stars?" Eleanor observed, trying her best to sound casual and appear unperturbed by his proximity.

"Aye," he chuckled. "It helps pass the time on the eve of battle, camped out in the field with nothing better to do than stare at the night sky and think of beautiful women," he grinned, looking directly at his comely companion, fixing her with a salacious stare.

Eleanor averted her eyes uncomfortably.

"My father was a seaman," he clarified, but a polite discussion about navigation was not his intention. They both knew they were postponing the inevitable. Phillipe edged closer to Eleanor, unsettlingly so, his vicinity instantly banishing any thoughts she had of continuing the conversation, as her heart pounded in her ear, obliterating everything, save for the immediacy of his presence. Her instinct told her she should move away from him but her propriety was outdone by a need for contact long forgone and she allowed him to close his other arm around her, her flesh tingling and her body quivering at his touch.

"You're cold," he assumed." Here," he took off his jacket and wrapped it around her shoulders.

"Thank you... Now *you* will be cold!" she smiled demurely, before instantly regretting the comment that prompted his reply.

"Not if you warm me with a kiss Eleanor," he ventured, moving ever closer, sensing her battle with temptation. She knew she had fallen for his trap but felt powerless to resist his mesmeric attraction, her whole being aching with repressed longing; a combination of curiosity and carnal need for this virile young man welling up, tempting her into submission. There was something irresistibly hypnotic about latent power that she knew could crush or caress her at will, a fine line separating prurience from purity – something in a woman's psyche that found subjugation a pleasure when initiated by the animal attraction of a compulsive force. Part of her wanted to know she had the power to conquer this exemplar of masculinity with the delights of her sex and render him helpless in her arms. It gave her a feeling of control over him that fuelled womankind's innate desire for pleasures of the flesh – a primal instinct for procreation shared by all forms of life. This man's rugged allure was compelling and Eleanor capitulated.

"Just one then," she lowered her eyes shyly as Phillipe drew her towards him in a crushing embrace. Feeling her relaxed and yielding, he lifted her chin and pressed his lips onto hers so hard it took her breath away. Eleanor couldn't help herself, she kissed him back, every nerve in her body alert, as he impelled her against the parapet wall. His face felt rough and his half-grown stubble scoured her soft skin; his strong fingers, hardened with the constant friction of bowstring and ash, caressed her neck and wound themselves into her hair, as pulling her head back he clamped his mouth down on hers. She could sense the strength in his arms and the power in his thighs pressing against her. Her body ached for his and her pulse raced with pent up craving for the intimacy she missed but she realised at that moment, immured in his embrace, that what she felt was pure lust, pure wanton desire. It was not love. She wanted his manhood, his corporeal being, not his undying affection. *That makes me no less unchaste than Agnes from the kitchen* she chided herself. *If I let him have me, I am no better than a harlot!*

Within her, the conflict between her body aching for physical contact, fighting against her mind focusing on the sin of temptation, was too much for Eleanor. *What am I doing?* She thought of her churchly upbringing, Aunt Mabel, her daughter, of Richard. Ashamed of herself, she drew back, catching her breath and forcing herself to break free from his grip.

"You have had your kiss and... I have to go," she said breathlessly, her hand pushing against his chest and easing herself away from the wall. "Forgive me but I cannot..."

She pulled his jacket off her shoulders, thrusting it at him assertively before hurrying down the steep winding steps, trying not to trip up on her skirts, chiding herself for her moment of weakness.

"Eleanor!" he called after her, cursing profanely in frustration, before draining his tankard and throwing it forcefully over the ramparts into the moat below.

The muffled splash alerted a guard at the gate who scanned the battlements then peered down over the drawbridge and into the darkness. After a few moments of listening, he shrugged and returned to his post. Many an object had ended up in the murky water either by accident or design, to sink irretrievably into the sludge at the bottom of the trench. Out on the moonlit moors, a frost was beginning to form, a barn owl swooping down from the church tower flapped by silently by like a white ghost and a distant screech from some unfortunate prey pierced the quietude of the dale. Music and laughter still emanated from the Great Hall, long after Eleanor's tears of shame, frustration and self-reproach dampened the pillow of her lonely bed.

The next day the Duchess was unwell, keeping to her chamber while the Countess was immersed in her books. Eleanor had little to do. She determined to find Phillipe to apologise for her demurral, feeling bad that she had tempted him. She was not in the habit of enticing young men, permitting them a taste of her feminine charms, then refusing them with a rebuttal and she did not want him thinking ill of her. She was not a coquette and was eager to explain her reluctance and beg pardon for her impropriety. A hoarfrost had formed in the night, coating every branch, berry and twig in delicate fronds of ice, transforming Wensleydale into a shimmering wonderland as Eleanor wrapped herself in a warm mantle and made her way down to the tilt yard, every breath she nervously exhaled steaming in the freezing air.

The myriad of ice shards clinging to every surface, sparkled in the watery sun against a cloudless sky but down in the tilt yard all was quiet and there was no sign of Phillipe, in fact no sign of any of the bowmen, they had left. Eleanor had missed her chance and she surmised he would no doubt be denouncing the fickleness of women to his fellow archers. She hoped he would not give her away; she could not bear the thought of her indiscretion somehow reaching Richard's ears. What would he think of her? Phillipe was hardly likely to admit she had denied him after her initial compliance and titillating gossip would not willingly surrender its appeal to the blandness of truth.

After church she sought out the priest to hear her confession and duly did her penance, the holy father's unperturbed response affirming that she was not alone in her transgression, the familiar theme of which he had heard many times before and, in fact, made up the bulk of his confessionals. *The sins of the flesh are just the substantiation of our human frailty which the Lord will forgive if we are contrite*, he had told her.

Chapter Thirteen

N THE SPRING OF 1474, the Countess's lands were split between Isobel, Anne and their husbands George and Richard. Although the Countess was aggrieved her property had been divided up as though she was already dead, she understood that, as the wife of a traitor, she was entitled to nothing less, despite frequent entreaties to the king. It was to ease her plight that Richard and Anne offered to look after her within the family at Middleham, where she was able to take care of her frail daughter and watch her grandson grow.

Richard was busy establishing his lordship and creating bonds with Northern families, many of whom were formerly in the service of his cousin the Earl of Warwick. By his marriage into the Neville family he was accepted readily as their new Lord, with Anne at his side and the Countess still residing in her late husband's home. Although Richard enjoyed the trappings of wealth and the advantages of nobility, he was mindful of the plight of the lower classes and cognisant of their needs, memories of his flight to the Low Countries with Edward after Warwick's rebellion ever reminding him of the precariousness of their position and the generosity of good people.

While Richard had been kept fully occupied on the border, strengthening the fortifications at Carlisle Castle and dealing with frequent skirmishes by Scottish raiders ignoring the peace treaty, life at the castle continued routinely, the time of day marked by the bells of Middleham church and the monastic communities nearby which rang eight times a day at Lauds (dawn) Prime (Sunrise), Terce (mid-morning), Sext (midday), None (mid-afternoon), Vespers (sunset), Compline (retiring) and Matins (about 2am). For the sons of the well-bred, a daily timetable of early mass, breakfast, learning, penmanship and conduct, dinner around noon, riding, hunting and hawking, knightly training, supper, chapel, evening relaxation and then bedtime, kept them fully occupied and in a state of readiness for their Lord's call to arms.

One afternoon in late summer a page came to find Eleanor.

"Two gentlemen are asking to see you outside the North gate madam."

Curious, Eleanor walked down to the guardhouse, wondering why on earth she would be at two strangers' bidding. The guard showed her through the arched entrance and out into the sunshine. Two men were sitting on the grass with their backs to her, they looked dishevelled and dusty, their long matted hair of a strangely familiar auburn hue, the leather of their shoes split, their garments worn and frayed.

"May I help you sirs?" Eleanor enquired as they turned and leapt to their feet.

"Hello little sister!"

With a cry of delight, Eleanor ran to her brothers' arms, holding them as if she would never let them go. They hugged and kissed her tenderly, as tears of joy ran down her cheeks.

"Oh Edward, James, I thought I would never see you again!" she cried, alternating between smiles and sobs, looking from one to the other, taking in their unkempt beards and their once muscular frames, now thin and malnourished. They hugged her again and stood back to look at their sister, now blossomed into a sensuous and desirable woman with their mother's iridescent eyes gazing back at them.

"Look at you Eleanor!" exclaimed Edward. "Married life must be suiting you!" How is Ralph? How is your child?"

Eleanor studied their faces, bronzed and weatherbeaten from months of travelling, looking older and more mature, more masculine, no longer the excited youths she had waved off five years ago. Edward had a freshly healed scar furrowing his temple and she noticed James was limping slightly.

"Ralph was killed when you fought at Barnet," she told them quickly, accepting their commiserations but not wanting to elaborate. Her face brightened as she told them of their niece.

"My daughter Elizabeth is six now. You must see her! She will love meeting her two brave and manful uncles at last!" She walked with them arm in arm, one on each side of her and took them into the castle grounds. "The Duke of Gloucester is the new Lord of Middleham and Anne Neville is his Duchess," she explained.

"Aye we heard, so we thought we would take a chance and return. We are pleased for Richard and want to offer our services. Do you think he will have us?" queried James.

"Of course he will! Battle veterans are invaluable to him. Many of the Earl's retainers have joined him now. He will be grateful for your loyalty and will know you were only doing your duty for the Earl. Go and see the captain of the guard and introduce yourselves, although…" Eleanor hesitated, wrinkling her nose, "…perhaps a bath would be a good idea before you see the Duke?"

They laughed and Eleanor giggled as they embraced again.

"I can't wait to hear about your adventures. I will come and find you after supper when I have finished my duties. Oh, did you know the Countess is here too?"

"The Countess? We heard she was in sanctuary." Edward was surprised.

"Aye, she was, but the Duchess asked Richard to allow her to return to Middleham to help with little Edward. She lost her lands though, to Isobel and Anne."

"At least she is safe and reunited with her family."

Eleanor rushed to impart her good news to Anne and the Countess.

"My brothers have returned!" she exclaimed excitedly to Anne.

"I'm so glad they are safe Eleanor, Richard will be happy to see them again. I hope they will join him?"

"Oh aye, of course! I know they will be happy to do so my lady."

Later Eleanor found her brothers chatting in the tilt yard to some of the younger pages. They were now clean shaven, dressed in fresh linen shirts and woollen hose, their hair washed and drying in the warm evening air. She had brought them some ale, meat and bread and they sat down together on a bench, as the sun sank low in the western sky.

"Tis so peaceful here. We have missed Wensleydale and you too of course, Ellie."

"Where have you been all this time?" she asked.

"Earning our keep on the land mostly," sighed James. "We were separated at first after the battle and I was convinced Edward was amongst the dead."

"Me too," interrupted Edward, rubbing his scarred forehead. "I blacked out after the battle but when I came to it was near dark and peasants were rummaging through the bodies for spoils. An old hag was crouching over me. She thought the devil himself was after her as I opened my eyes and sat up!" He chuckled recalling the old lady's curse and shriek of fear. "I must have resembled a ghoul from Hell, the state I was in!"

"No change there then!" quipped James, nudging his brother's ribs affectionately with his fist.

"You were none too pretty yourself!" retorted Edward. They laughed together while Eleanor studied their faces, markedly older now, their features more than ever resembling their father.

"We feared to return at first, not knowing the situation so we tried to make a living wherever we were. We had a lot of help from strangers along the way. They gave us farm work to earn enough to continue on our journey North."

"What was it like? The battle, I mean," Eleanor ventured, a morbid curiosity overruling her dread of a truthful reply.

"It was hell on earth, Ellie," James began, and a torrent of words spilled from his memory while his sister listened attentively, aghast at the horrors he portrayed. He spoke of the noise, the agonised screams from both man and beast, the fear, the blood, the exhaustion and dread of frantic hand-to-hand fighting, bodies being trampled into the mud, crushed under foot and hoof in bloody pools of rampant slaughter. James relived the scene as all around them men fell with heart-rending cries hideously wounded, limbs dangling uselessly or reduced to a grisly truncated stump. Eleanor thought of Ralph and hoped his death had been quick. She could almost smell the blood and fear, hear the moans of the injured, her brother's words graphically portraying the silent dead, trampled heedlessly underfoot, their gaping flesh, the horror of violent death etched forever in the glassy depths of their lifeless eyes.

Eleanor's face was ashen. Edward shook his head at James to stem the flow of his outpourings. Their sister need not know what carnage they had witnessed. As James wiped away a silent tear, his brother went on to describe the confusion in the fog, the terror when they thought they had been betrayed by their own side, the desperation and panic when they knew the battle was lost, and their sadness for the Earl, who had been chased and mercilessly cut down by hot-headed Yorkists, in gratuitous savagery. Edward shook with emotion as he spoke and had to put down his tankard. Their father had died for his cause and afterwards the Earl had become a father figure to them. They had always been well treated under his care. He deserved a more honourable death, despite his disloyalty. Even King Edward, they were sure, would not have wished quite such an ignominious end for his rebellious cousin.

As fugitives, the brothers had had to hide out for days in fear of their lives, they told her, discarding their livery and weapons, mingling with the labourers in the fields and sleeping rough in barns and woods. Slowly they made their way Northwards, picking up titbits of information as they went. They heard about the second battle which had taken place at Tewkesbury, apparently even more brutal, when the French queen was captured, her son killed and her forces routed at Bloody Meadow in a deluge of slaughter and butchery, where many had drowned in the River Avon in a frantic attempt to escape the bloodbath. War, they concluded, was a savage, barbaric and unrelenting hell. There was nothing glorious about it for the losers and even the victors deplored the human toll their success exacted.

Eleanor's heart filled with pride and respect for her brave brothers who had now become men, embracing them once more with a hug and a kiss, thankful that they had survived. As she bid them goodnight and climbed the stairs to the Duchess's chamber, her head full of images of death, she thought of Richard, fresh from the trauma of his first battle, having to march immediately to his second, knowing what bloodshed was to come, yet ready and willing to face it once more.

Where do they find the courage? she wondered in astonishment, at the same time recognising the capacity of youth to believe in their own invincibility, a notion that would surely vitalize their daring. Nevertheless, she was thankful that her fairer sex afforded her the benefit of avoiding such terrifying engagements, which only served to increase her admiration for these intrepid young men.

When the Duke returned from the Borders a few days later, he welcomed Edward and James, listening with interest to their story. They pledged their allegiance to him and set about building themselves up in readiness to serve again. They had heard of his prowess in combat, despite his slight physique, were humbled by his bravery and pleased his loyalty had been rewarded by the king. They understood how hard it must have been for him to take up arms against his cousin and benefactor who had welcomed him into the bosom of his family and taught him the skills he had now had to use against his mentor.

THE YEAR PASSED peacefully and as another autumn approached, with the castle stores stocked to overflowing with fine wines and food for the seasonal celebrations and merry-making, Eleanor took her daughter foraging. They went blackberry picking along the hedgerows, now crowded with fruit and swelling red rosehips, gathering nature's bounty to be made into jams and sweet pies for the winter feasts. Elizabeth, her mouth full of succulent ripe blackberries, laughed with her mother at her juice-stained fingers and purple tongue. They selected the best windfall apples, picked the swelling pumpkins from the kitchen garden and watched the swallows gathering along the ramparts before they disappeared southward ahead of the winter storms. As the fallen leaves piled up on the woodland floor, the heavy-laden sweet chestnut trees gradually released their bounty of shiny nuts bursting forth from spiky green cases, to be eagerly gathered by the village children for roasting on the hearth.

Eleanor would be careful not to repeat her actions of the previous Christmas, determined to keep herself chaste, dedicated to her duties and her daughter. If any man showed interest in her she vowed she would not be the one to make the first move. Any thoughts of love and lust she pushed to the back of her mind, the occasional smile from Richard sufficing to appease her longing and strengthen her resolve.

Occasionally she had ridden out with the Duchess to visit friends in the valley and beyond. Riding a gentle dun-coloured mare from the Duke's stables, Eleanor loved these excursions, jogging along the bridleways with the wind in her face and the ever-changing vistas unfolding before her. She was transported back to her childhood when she would ride out with her brothers, relishing the freedom to go where they pleased, covering so many more miles than was possible on foot, enjoying the elevated viewpoint afforded from horseback and the pleasure of keeping boots dry and away from puddles.

On one such outing, as the colours of Wensleydale turned from gold to burnt orange, the party rode westward towards the ancestral seat of the Scropes at Bolton Castle further up the dale, an impressively situated square fortress with a commanding view across the valley and over Wensleydale forest to the steep slopes of Penhill, rising skyward to the south. More modest in size than Middleham, with a central quadrangle enclosed on all sides and with bright south-facing rooms overlooking extensive gardens, the castle was nonetheless a luxurious residence as well as a stronghold. Eleanor had caught the eye of one of Lord Scrope's young retainers. He introduced himself as William Metcalfe, a cousin of the Metcalfes of nearby Nappa Hall. He was out hawking with Lord Scrope's huntsmen when they met the Duchess's party trotting along by the river near Aysgarth falls. They stopped to rest in a clearing near the river to let the horses drink while Eleanor and Anne dismounted to watch the cascades of water tumbling down the gorge, spilling relentlessly over step after step of shallow limestone terraces.

While the Duchess conversed with Lord and Lady Scrope, Eleanor sat on a fallen tree trunk, gazing into the falls, mesmerised by the crystal-clear bubbling, gurgling torrent as it swirled between the rocks, wending its way ever downwards. A lightening flash of iridescent blue caught her eye as a kingfisher shot across her field of vision and disappeared into a crevice in the muddy embankment on the far side of the river. As Eleanor watched quietly, a plucky little dipper plunged into the ice-cold water and flew up again, his white throat shining out of the murky shadows, characteristically dipping and hopping on the limestone slabs, his beak stuffed with tasty morsels. The heavy rains had made it hard going for the little bird but he persevered seeking out the slower outflow in sheltered corners.

Interrupting her contemplation, William had come to sit beside her offering her a leather tumblerful of ale. She accepted gracefully, whilst veiledly appraising his lithe physique and rugged masculine features. He reminded her a little of Richard, although his brown hair was cut shorter, his ruddy complexion tanned and weather-beaten. Eleanor took in his full lips and smiling hazel eyes, echoing the dusky depths and brimming pools of the river Ure as it tumbled past boulders in its way and found herself attracted to him.

They chatted cordially, William telling her about his hunting exploits and Eleanor talking of her life and her daughter Elizabeth. He smiled at her appreciatively, his eagerness appearing undeterred by the fact she was a widow and mother. Eleanor found him engaging, friendly and well mannered, his soft Yorkshire accent akin to her own. He told her about his goshawk, Maia, a beautiful grey bird with a delicately striped breast, sitting patiently nearby, her fierce talons gripping her perch tightly, her hooded head inclined to one side intently recording and analysing the sounds of the river. William had trained the keen-eyed raptor as a fledgling and she had learnt to respond instantly to her master's call. On the ride home with the Duchess, Eleanor found herself lost in thought about this likeable young man and his affinity with the natural world.

She saw Will on several occasions more before the winter weather took hold and each time, they enjoyed each other's company, talking seriously of war or laughing hysterically as the master of hounds slipped into the freezing water attempting to retrieve his wind-snatched hat from an overhanging branch. Upon their departure Will would kiss her hand politely as she mounted her horse and the last time they parted he had kissed her cheek affectionately. During a pause in conversation, he had impulsively turned to her with a question he had been mulling over for some time but until now had held back for fear of rejection.

"Eleanor, would you consent to be my wife?"

Eleanor hesitated, taken by surprise.

"I... I'm not sure Will. I am very fond of you.... but marriage?"

"I make a good living and would take care of you and Elizabeth," he pleaded, grasping her hands earnestly.

"Oh Will, may I have a little time think about it?"

Eleanor needed to digest his proposal and wondered what Anne would say.

"Of course you may Eleanor, but my smitten heart won't stand the suspense for too long!" He clutched his chest in mock agony and they both laughed, relieving the solemnity of the moment. His parting kiss on the cheek was tender and heartfelt and as he watched her go, she looked back, returning his wave, pondering his question and how she would answer him.

Will was among the retainers as the Christmas festivities got underway at Middleham. Eleanor had seen him arrive with Lord Scrope, her suitor dashingly attired in a new doublet of emerald green. She knew it would be impolite to keep him hanging on for an answer. While she untwined the braids in Anne's hair that evening, teasing out the crinkled tresses, Eleanor took her chance to broach the subject of marriage.

"My lady... may I ask your advice?"

"Of course you may, Eleanor."

"You may know I have been friendly with William Metcalfe from Castle Bolton..." she hesitated, embarrassed.

"Aye, I noticed you seem to be getting on very well," smiled Anne knowingly.

"Well, the thing is my lady... he has asked me to marry him."

Anne turned to face her, surprised.

"Oh, I knew he liked you!" she beamed. "Do you love him?"

"I... I know not," Eleanor replied truthfully. "I do like him very much but marriage?"

"You could do worse Eleanor, and he will be a good father for Elizabeth."

If you only knew, Eleanor thought to herself.

"Aye, I suppose so, thank you my lady." Eleanor put down the hairbrush and left the chamber, encouraged by Anne's support and wondering at her own foolish hesitance which she realised was only a consequence of her own insecurity. Her experience with Ralph had taught her that marriage without love was a bastille of resentment and acrimony from which there was no escape. Now she had met a suitor who would make a caring and loving husband and with whom she could find love. What more could she desire?

She found Will the next day as he prepared to join the Duke's hunt, grooming a glistening ebony stallion in the stable courtyard. He beamed as he saw her, putting down his brush, theatrically bending one knee to the ground and kissing her hand.

"Do you have my answer, Eleanor?" he entreated, gazing up at her imploringly.

"Aye Will, my answer is yes, I *will* marry you," she laughed happily as, grinning enthusiastically, he jumped up to embrace her, before cupping her face in his hands and kissing her gently on the mouth.

"My lovely Eleanor, I will make you happy, I promise," he vowed sincerely. She returned his kiss, trembling slightly at the realisation of what she had just agreed. She knew Anne would be telling Richard and she wondered what he would think of her and if he would consider Will a good stepfather for his daughter.

A few days later the Duke summoned Eleanor to him. He was busy scrutinising documents but looked up readily as she entered the room.

"Congratulations on your betrothal Eleanor," he smiled at her and her heart skipped a beat as she searched his face for any sign of disapproval, but there was none.

"Thank you, my Lord." Eleanor wanted him to be envious and was rewarded by his next remark.

"William is a lucky man," he said truthfully. "He will look after you and Elizabeth, I have no doubt. We have provided a small dowry for you, Eleanor. Anne and I hope you will continue here with us."

"Thank you, my Lord. I would not wish to leave you my Lord."

"Good." Richard watched her pensively, searching for an appropriate approbation and as she turned to go he added, "I hope you will be happy Eleanor." He spoke with genuine feeling, his voice gentle and less formal now, directed at her on a more personal level. For a fleeting moment the gulf between them disappeared, as their eyes met and Eleanor was back there on the hillside entwined in his arms. Embarrassed, she studied the floor, wondering if he had read her thoughts.

"Thank you, my Lord," she whispered, looking up at him hesitantly, fearful of her own transparency. He held her gaze for an instant with those absorbing eyes, confirming unspoken what she needed to know.

EASTER 1475 FOUND Eleanor wedded again. She walked up the nave of St. Mary's and St. Alkelda's wearing a gown of deep cobalt blue silk gifted to her by Anne, a garland of Spring blooms woven into her hair, beaming happily as she stood at the altar with Will beside her, looking suave and athletic. This time she said her vows sincerely, silently asking God to forgive her and make her a good wife to Will. He was a good man and he loved her; she could ask for no more. She smiled sadly to herself at the thought of Aunt Mabel, who had passed away the previous winter but who would surely this time have approved of the match. Elizabeth stood obediently behind her mother, holding a posy of early blossom and greenery, excited to be dressed in a pretty dress of cream silk, embroidered with suns and moons – another gift from Anne's childhood wardrobe, the original draped sleeves now tapered to fit Bess's slender arms, in accordance with the current fashion.

Will was kind to Elizabeth, treating her as his own, teaching her about nature and the animals of the forest. She was thrilled when he promised to take her out hunting when she was older. The young girl could see her mother was happier and more content, though she felt a pang of jealousy that Eleanor's love would now be given in part to Will. She would no longer be the sole focus of her mother's attentions, enjoying the exclusivity of her mother's love. Unused to having a father, having a man in the family would change the dynamic for Bess and it would take her time to adjust to the intrusion.

Eleanor's wedding night was in complete contrast to the one she had shared with Ralph. Will worshipped her, kissing her tenderly at first, then with rising passion as she responded willingly, desire surging through her body, the years of longing falling away, his full lips enveloping hers, kissing her soft skin, revelling in her nakedness. She reciprocated with increasing fervour, his sinuous firm body entwining with hers as their flesh became one. Eleanor gave herself to him wholeheartedly and for once did not think of Richard as the pleasure of the moment enveloped her body and mind. She had grown into a desirable woman, motherhood now accentuating her curves and she readily basked in the attentions of her admiring husband. She was happy and the ache in her heart for Richard softened and lay veiled in the corners of her mind, like a precious jewel locked away in a sealed casket, enshrouded and dormant, eclipsed by the light of her new love.

Unfortunately, the honeymoon period was not to last long, before duty and distance separated the blissful newlyweds.

Chapter Fourteen

N February 1475 Richard had been given the position of Sheriff of Cumberland for life and by June had been awarded the lordship of Skipton Castle, which must have seemed poetic justice since it was the ancestral home of the Clifford family, the son of whom was responsible for his brother Edmund's death and had earned the nickname 'Butcher' Clifford as a result. Richard was also granted the remaining Neville lands in the North, formerly belonging to Lord Montagu, whose Southern lands were granted to George, Duke of Clarence.

It was not long before talk of war would again infiltrate the peaceful Dales but it was not from Scotland, where a treaty of peace had been ratified, with the promise of king Edward's daughter Cecily to king James's son. Now firmly established as a Northern magnate, Richard was poised to assist the king in any new venture that required his support and so, following the treaty with Scotland, Edward's focus changed.

The king now turned his eye to reclaiming the throne of France, lost so ineptly since the disastrous reign of Henry VI. Edward had not forgiven Louis XI for funding the Earl of Warwick's rebellion and had been negotiating with Charles, Duke of Burgundy, against the constant threat from his aggressive neighbour. Consequently, by July 1474 Edward and Duke Charles had signed a treaty of alliance against France.

The people of England had longed to repeat the glories of their victory at Agincourt under Henry V, which had become the stuff of legend. Edward now hoped to unite the country once again in a renewed offensive against their old enemy, issuing a proclamation in February, summoning all lords and captains of retainers to assemble their armies at Portsdown by late May. He had been raising funds for war from his subjects by means of 'benevolences', which amounted to a gift of money, freely given, not taxation and although this system was unpopular, Edward's charismatic charm and the promise of renewed glory for England, meant he eventually succeeded in funding his new war effort.

The Duke had begun to gather retained men across the Northern strongholds to support the king's venture. A cacophony of sound invaded the castle, from the hundreds of extra recruits gathered under Richard's banner, the forge busy day and night, the kitchens straining under the extra load, the surrounding fields invaded by regimented rows of tents housing foot soldiers, archers and spearmen, called to arms from far flung towns and villages.

Since the fall of Richard Neville, the new Lord of Middleham had succeeded in gaining the allegiance of many Northern families including the Scropes, the FitzHughs, the Greystokes, the Dacres, the Metcalfes and the Conyers to name but a few. His reputation for combative excellence, fairness and good lordship, regardless of rank had ensured Richard a loyal following. Phillipe would no doubt be amongst them, Eleanor surmised, so made sure she kept away from the encampment. She hoped that since her marriage to Will, the archer would keep her brief lapse of decorum to himself.

As Duke of Gloucester, Richard needed to establish his own livery, favouring for his insignia the image of a white boar (*le sanglier blanc*), signifying to Richard the many qualities of character he admired. Will told Eleanor of its significance. Far from being a timid animal, the boar would not flee when confronted, instead was likely to attack, he explained. Small and tenacious, it was a fierce opponent, renowned for protecting it's young. The boar was also the symbol of St. Anthony, he told her, patron saint of religious houses and in his legend only the boar protected the saint from demons, representing spiritual purity, resistance to temptation and defence of the weak. All these chivalric values, Eleanor knew Richard embraced, having spent many hours reading about his illustrious ancestor Edward III, who had encouraged his son Edward, the Black Prince, as he was known, in heroic deeds and excellence on the battlefields of France, emulating the Arthurian knights who inspired them. Another legend concerning the Irish saint St. Brigid, told of a hunted boar finding sanctuary in her monastery, where she cared for it and kept it with her own pigs. Lastly, Will reminded Eleanor, Richard's father was the Duke of York and the Roman name for York, Eboracum, was often shortened to Ebor, an anagram of which was Bore, a spelling often in use for the wild pig. Eleanor could not imagine an emblem more apt to epitomise the Duke's identity as he prepared to march into battle.

For his motto Richard decided upon '*Loyaulte me lie*' – loyalty binds me – signifying his homage to the memory of his father, his fealty and devotion to his brother king Edward, his family, his people, his steadfastness to the code of chivalry he strove to follow and his faithfulness to God. Eleanor thought the maxim suited him perfectly.

New standards, badges and surcoats were ordered, emblazoned with Richard's white boar motif, training was in full swing, new weapons forged and honed, retainers summoned from all over the Duke's dominions and by the end of May 1475 they were leaving Middleham to join the armies of the king and the Duke of Clarence in Kent. The popularity of Richard as Lord of his new Northern stronghold was affirmed in the largest contingent of troops brought to swell Edward's forces.

Eleanor had said a tearful farewell to Will as he prepared to leave to do his duty for the Duke. They had enjoyed no more than two months of each other, during which Eleanor was the happiest she had been since she had fallen in love with Richard. She had given all of herself to Will, body and soul. He had loved her almost every night, except on returning late from the hunt, when he had flung himself exhausted on the bed and slipped into unconsciousness within a few minutes. Eleanor lay close to him as he slept, sharing his body warmth, watching his chest rise and fall and listening to his rhythmic breathing. She felt safe and beloved, happy and comfortable, sharing his life and enjoying his company. She knew she could want for nothing more.

Oftentimes she would go down to the field to watch Will training the hawks, swinging the bait around as they swooped down low, deftly plucking the tasty morsel from the string. He would let her hold the magnificent birds, perched on a thick leather glove, gently stroking their soft feathers. Eleanor loved to hear him talk. He taught her so much about the natural world, the plants and animals of the forest. He was not an indiscriminate hunter, being mindful of their lifestyles and precarious existence alongside mankind, and would only hunt for food, killing only where necessary and allowing nature to thrive in its own environment. Man must exist in harmony with nature, not in conflict, he told her, so as not to upset the fine balance of life and its daily struggle for survival.

The couple often strolled through the woods by the river amidst carpets of wild garlic, the heady redolence mixing with the pungent smell of woodsmoke percolating through the coppice from the charcoal kilns. Will showed Eleanor the red spotted fly agaric toadstools sprouting at the base of the tree trunks and stopped to listen for the green woodpeckers noisily tapping the bark in search of larvae, or the buzzing of the bees crawling into foxglove trumpets, to emerge moments later, pollen laden and gorged on nectar. He pointed out the bushy tailed red squirrels scampering away in the undergrowth as they walked by, before pausing to embrace her tenderly, while Elizabeth capered along behind, collecting poesies of woodland flowers and chatting merrily to herself.

Will shared his many amusing stories with Eleanor, they laughed together like children and at night they held each other close and discussed the day. Eleanor was content. The affection she held for her husband sustained her, mellowing the heartache deep within her for her first love.

When the time came to go Eleanor clung to him and wept, imploring him not to leave her. Will held his blossoming wife tight and promised to bring her back something beautiful from France. He was confident that once again England would be victorious over their old enemy and he was proud to wear the Duke's new livery adorned with the white boar.

The household turned out to see the men depart. Richard kissed Anne and his young son Edward tenderly, before mounting his charger. He set off at the head of his entourage, resplendent in his new scheme of deep mulberry red and rich blue, looking magnificent, majestic and noble, his standards fluttering aloft in a sea of colour. Eleanor's heart swelled with pride for the father of her firstborn and longed to fling her arms around him in a fond embrace, as she had with Will, but watching from above, she knew better than to interrupt his family farewells. Richard was her Lord and master and the devotion she felt for him was no longer fitting, as behove her position now she was married to Will. Instead, she held Elizabeth up at the casement to wave the company off.

Emotional farewells had been said to her brothers but their mood was upbeat, full of excited expectation at the promise of conquest in France. This time they would be fighting for their king and victory would be glorious. They adjudged French peasants would be no match for their well-trained, battle-hardened troops and legendary English archers. England would be great again and the triumph of Agincourt would be eclipsed by the sunne in Splendour and the House of York. They had no doubt of it.

"God speed, my love, return to me soon," whispered Eleanor, watching the entourage disappear from view. As always when men went to war the rousing farewells from the womenfolk were tinged with dread of injury or death; the prospect of a loved one buried in a far distant foreign grave, never to return, an all too distinct possibility.

After the company departed in a glorious procession of colour and noise, the castle descended into silence once more, made all the more marked after the frantic preparations and hubbub they had become used to. Now that all was quiet again, Middleham, and indeed the whole country, waited with eager optimism for news of the glory they fully expected.

King Edward IV, along with his brothers Richard Duke of Gloucester and George Duke of Clarence, left England on 4th July with a huge invading army gathered from all over the land, Richard's contingent being by far the largest, a fact that did not go unnoticed by his appreciative brother. They landed at Calais, where they assembled before marching towards Rheims. However, within a few days the promised support from Burgundy did not arrive. Duke Charles had used most of his resources in a fruitless siege at Neuss and could be of no use to Edward. To compound matters, as the English army advanced they were blocked from entering the Burgundian towns. They camped briefly at Agincourt, which only served to remind them what had been lost since the unfortunate reign of Henry VI, whose calamitous tenure had expunged his father's victories and divided loyalties throughout his realm. Edward's longed-for aim of restoring England's dignity with the splendour of a triumph against their old enemy was rapidly losing momentum.

At Omer, the York brothers were welcomed by their sister Margaret Duchess of Burgundy, in place of her husband, where the brothers were happy to see her and spend some time with her. The army moved on to Peronne to eventually meet up with Duke Charles but the gates of the city were closed, forcing them to camp in the fields. Some of Edward's disgruntled men went South but were killed in a skirmish with the French. The Count of St. Pol of Luxembourg had promised to hand over St. Quentin to the English in return for Champagne, after France was conquered. Duke Charles suggested to Edward to take up this offer before he himself rode away again. However, on approaching the town of St. Quentin with a small detachment of troops, a force rode out to attack the English and guns were fired. Several Englishmen were killed or captured, betrayed by the Count's broken promise. The bedraggled survivors marched back to Edward through heavy rain, re-joining the rest of the demoralised company, who had received no help from Duke Charles.

Faced with the prospect of the coming winter, with food scarce and money running out, Edward had received a tempting offer from Louis XI of France, who was now threatening Burgundy, for a lucrative truce instead of war, which would benefit them both. Edward would receive 75,000 crowns to leave peacefully and for this would be rewarded with a pension of 50,000 gold crowns. Furthermore, it was agreed that Henry Tudor, who had been living in exile in Brittany, would be handed over.

Edward considered the king's offer, which, it was agreed, would last for seven years. Despite the loss of face, his army was still largely intact, he could return with full coffers before the winter set in, benefit from a promise of mutual military support and a lucrative trade agreement and England would, for now, be safe from the threat of French invasion. Discretion, being the better part of valour in Edward's eyes, he accepted Louis' terms.

Louis then opened the town of Amiens to the disgruntled English soldiers, who, having been robbed of their chance to fight, gladly took full advantage of the food, drink and women on offer. To his shame and disgust, after several days Edward had to resort to forcibly removing his drunken men from the town, leaving them to sober up in the fields, much to the amusement of the French, who sneered contemptuously at their age-old enemy, robbed of their dignity and purpose.

With the Treaty agreed as arranged, the two kings met on the bridge at Picquigny where, as a precaution against treachery, a screen had been erected between them. The Duke of Clarence, the Earl of Northumberland, Lord Hastings and other nobles accompanied Edward, who was richly dressed in cloth of gold and adorned with precious jewels, while Louis by contrast, was modestly attired. The two kings spoke together amicably, validating the contract with their signatures, after which Louis showered Edward's nobles with expensive gifts and pensions, relieved for now that his country had been saved from English aggression.

However, Edward's brother-in-law Duke Charles was outraged. He railed at Edward and stormed off in fury, his words falling on deaf ears. Edward's alliance with France would now pose a bigger threat to his Duchy, as he could no longer continue to rely on England's support against the French king, leaving him vulnerable and exposed.

Richard was equally furious with his brother's capitulation to the French king. It went against all his ideals of chivalry and patriotism to accept what was, after all, a bribe. He refused to attend the signing and made his feelings clear that the honour of England had been compromised and the house of York disgraced. He would have to take his men back to England minus the military glory and the promise of the spoils of victory they had expected, along with the ridicule of the French people and the bewilderment of his own.

Louis attempted to win his favour by showering him with expensive plate and horses. The Duke of Buckingham was also left incensed and departed early for England, with Richard and many others, although some stayed on and joined Duke Charles's army.

Shortly after Edward returned to England, he ransomed Marguerite of Anjou for 50,000 crowns. As for Henry Tudor, he somehow managed to avoid capture, having been forewarned and made his escape, the ultimate result of which would, in years to come, change history and bring to an end over 300 years of Plantagenet rule.

Chapter Fifteen

Y September 1475 Richard had arrived back at Middleham with his full complement of faithful retainers but without the glory of conquest they had been assured. Eleanor hugged her brothers before running to Will's waiting embrace. He looked strained and tired, a shaggy beard now concealing his jawline, his stocky frame noticeably thinner after months on the move with ever dwindling supplies. The mood amongst the men was sombre, not the joyful elation of victory but one of frustration at being cheated and duped, their weapons unbloodied, their pride dented, their cause discredited. Eleanor, along with the rest of the womenfolk, was simply relieved to have her man returned to her in one piece. A woman would sooner favour a father, husband, son or lover restored to her alive and full-bodied, despite defeat or dishonour, than for him to die victorious and never come home.

"Forgive me sweetheart, I have not brought you your promised gift," Will admitted sadly to his blossoming wife, noting the fresh rosy bloom in her cheeks.

"Oh Will, it is of no matter. I only want you. I am just content you are home. I have some news Will," she hesitated, embarrassed to say the words. "I am with child."

"Eleanor my love!" He exclaimed joyfully, lifting her up, embracing her tenderly as she laughed shyly.

"Have you told Elizabeth?" he enquired, setting her down more gently than usual.

"Nay, not yet. I will tell her soon."

Quiet and preoccupied, Richard kept to his chamber, seeing no one. The brother he had idolised and followed faithfully had betrayed their father's memory, traded his self-respect and wounded England's pride. Edward had been bought off, reneged on the alliance he had agreed with Duke Charles who, Richard thought, had every right to be angry, despite the Duke's failure to mobilise his army to help Edward. Lack of support was not a good enough excuse to save the face of England's much celebrated invasion force. Edward was forced to crack down on dissent by delivering hard justice to anyone breaking the law, while Richard and the Duke of Northumberland together addressed discontent in York and the Northern borders.

The castle settled back into routine once more, Middleham's Christmas festivities came and went but around the country unrest continued as returning troops vented their frustrations.

Will was sorry to hear from Eleanor that Lord Scrope of Castle Bolton had died, but by January 1476, Elizabeth Scrope, his widow, sent her 16-year-old son Thomas to Middleham to serve under Richard's care and protection. Will was pleased to see young Thomas, who had often accompanied him on the hunt and whose interest in birds of prey matched his own. Richard soon after arranged Thomas's marriage to one of Anne's cousins, thereby securing his near neighbour's loyalty and affection.

Eleanor enjoyed her second pregnancy. She felt wholesome and maternal, loving the fact she was carrying and nurturing this precious burden for Will, his first born. Elizabeth was fascinated by the idea and hoped for a sister to play with. Anne and the Countess offered congratulations and Richard commented how motherhood suited her, her healthy complexion and burgeoning figure not going unnoticed by him.

"I am delighted for you Eleanor, you seem happy," he told her one day. She assured him she was and thanked him, uplifted that he had been mindful of her wellbeing. *He does care*, she thought elatedly.

Richard was away for long periods but when at home would find time to play with little Edward and fuss over him. Anne was still frail and often kept to her chamber while Edward was looked after by his nurse Isabel Burgh and Anne Idley, the mistress of the nursery.

Eleanor's second birthing came in early February. There had been a smattering of snow on the ground and the dark stormy days seemed unending as rain lashed down on the Dale, filling the rivers to bursting point, crashing over the waterfalls in a thundering deluge of mud and debris. The memory of her first confinement haunted Eleanor and she dreaded the ordeal she knew would come. Her labour was a little shorter this time but the pain just as intense. Will waited patiently, praying that his wife and child would be safely delivered. He heard her moans but the midwives kept him away until the cries of the newborn signalled its birth.

When they allowed him into her chamber, Eleanor was lying back on clean sheets, her body sponged and clothed in a fresh gown, her hair smoothly brushed and falling over the pillow, holding her child tightly wrapped against her breast. She beamed joyfully at her husband as he entered.

"You have a son, Will. Look how perfect he is!" Eleanor exclaimed.

Will carefully cradled his infant son and took him to the casement, gazing adoringly at this new-born stranger, marvelling at his tiny fingers, toes and wisps of light brown hair.

"He looks like you," Eleanor observed proudly. "I would like to call him William."

Will could not see how this tiny wrinkled being with its red face, tightly closed eyes and squashed nose resembled anyone at all, but was delighted his wife wished to honour him in naming his firstborn after him.

"Thank you, my sweet, William it is!" He kissed William's head gently and handed the babe back to his mother, kissing her forehead before rushing off to impart the news to everyone he saw.

Elizabeth's initial disappointment at having a new brother soon diminished as she proudly helped her mother care for the baby, who was too young anyway to be a playmate. Instead, she could indulge her innate maternal instincts and acquire a sense of importance in nurturing her little brother.

⚜ ⚜ ⚜

FOLLOWING RICHARD'S DISAPPOINTMENT in France, his attention turned to his father, Richard Duke of York, who had been buried, along with his son, Edmund Earl of Rutland, at Pontefract following their deaths in 1460 at Sandal and Wakefield. In July Edward and Richard exhumed their father's and brother's bodies and transported them back to the family seat at Fotheringhay in Northamptonshire, with great pomp and ceremony, where they were reinterred in new tombs at the magnificent church next to the castle. The procession of coffins draped in black, pulled by black horses, travelled for eight days with Richard acting as chief mourner, riding ahead of the cortege alongside the Earl of Northumberland and Lord Stanley. Edward, his queen and their two daughters joined them at the church for the funeral mass and interment the following day, after which Edward laid on an elaborate feast at the old castle, so peacefully situated by the banks of the meandering River Nene.

As Christmas 1476 approached, Middleham Castle's household was stunned by tragic news from Warwick. Isobel, George of Clarence's Duchess, had died ten days after giving birth to a son, Richard's namesake, who followed her to heaven shortly afterwards. Isobel had been ill for some time and the birth was more than her weakened body could take. Anne and the Countess were grief stricken. The castle plunged into mourning for the elegant and beautiful Duchess, who left her two children, Edward and Margaret, and her husband George, inconsolable with grief. Down at his magnificent Earldom in Warwick, the already highly volatile and unstable George sank into a frenzy of anguish, blaming everyone and everything for his wife's demise. Since Barnet, his head injury had resulted in blinding and debilitating headaches, inflaming his already schizophrenic temper, which, with Isobel's death, descended into frequent psychotic episodes of manic depression and irrational fury.

Two weeks later in Europe, Charles Duke of Burgundy died. Edward, George and Richard's sister Margaret was now widowed and Charles's daughter Mary from his previous marriage, now his heir. Margaret had her eyes on a union between her recently widowed brother George and her stepdaughter Mary, which would make George the new Duke of Burgundy. However, king Edward quashed this idea in favour of his brother-in-law Anthony, Earl Rivers, presumably at the behest of his queen, although this proposal was soon rejected by Mary. The Duke of Clarence however was incensed as, yet again, his ambitions appeared to have been thwarted by Edward. His position as next in line to the throne after the death of Henry VI and Prince Eduard of Lancaster, had been usurped by his brother and now his chance to become Duke of

Burgundy was again frustrated. His anger was soon to erupt in a mania of rage and indignation.

At Warwick Castle, the resentment and anger which had built up in the Duke and festered for many months since Warwick's rebellion, now erupted, bursting forth from George, who in his wrath accused a servant, Ankarette Twynyho, of having poisoned his wife. The unfortunate woman was tried and sentenced to death by the terrified jurors and promptly hanged, along with another servant, John Thursby, who was also blamed for the infant's death.

George was now treading on thin ice, his impulsiveness and unpredictability exacerbated by his bereavement. Edward was furious that his brother had taken the law into own hands, executing two innocent servants. To further complicate matters, the king arrested two men who had supposedly plotted his death by witchcraft, one of them being a retainer of the Duke of Clarence, who was implicated in the charges of necromancy against the king. One of the men, Thomas Burdett, was connected to the household of Eleanor Talbot, whose name would appear later in connection with Edward's marriage to Elizabeth Woodville, and may have had information that threatened the legality of the marriage and therefore that of their offspring. Edward had them executed.

Assumed to be in possession of this new information concerning Eleanor Talbot, the injudicious Duke was now seen by the queen as a significant threat to her children's accession. At the same time George had resurrected an old rumour that king Edward was a bastard and not the true son of Richard Duke of York. Edward had been born in France and was known for his good looks as the 'Rose of Rouen', where idle talk said that a handsome archer had attracted the attention of his mother Cecily while the Duke was away.

All of this, in George's mind, made him the rightful heir to the throne. Louis XI further helped to promote the suggestion to Edward that George had hoped to gain the throne of England through marriage to the Burgundian heiress Mary.

In June 1477, having had enough of George's machinations and urged no doubt by his queen, who still wanted revenge for the deaths of her father and brother in 1469, Edward arrested his rebellious brother for treason and sent him to reflect on his wrongdoings in the confines of the Tower of London.

As the end of the year approached, Eleanor had overheard Richard complaining to Anne one afternoon as she was about to answer the Duchess's summons. Hearing his raised voice, she had hesitated outside the chamber.

"How can I make merry at Christmas, Anne, knowing George is in the Tower awaiting trial? He's our brother! Aye, he is headstrong and easily led but he is my father's son! He's lost his wife and child! God knows we have lost enough of our family without Edward adding to their number!" Richard's voice emanated pain and anguish.

"The Duchess of York has been speaking to Edward on George's behalf," Anne interceded.

"I doubt my mother will have any influence now. The queen has seen to that! She is behind this, I know it! She is bent on revenge for the deaths of her father and brother at Edgecoat."

"You've heard the rumours Richard. Do you think them true?"

"About Edward being a bastard? I've heard the talk, Anne, but I'm not about to shame my mother by giving it credence."

"I meant George's talk about the king's marriage not being legal."

"Again Anne," Richard sighed, "the ramifications of that contingence are fraught with danger for the unity of the country. There's no proof as far as I am aware and the queen is unlikely to give up her status without a fight! Besides, we need a strong figurehead like Edward. There are too many enemies waiting to take his place both here and in France. Of course, I wish he had made a wiser choice but it's done now and we have to live with it."

"You had better not repeat that to Edward, my Lord, or you will be joining George!" quipped Anne.

"Do not jest, Anne. George could be about to lose his life."

Eleanor's entrance cut the conversation short. She stepped back quickly as Richard brushed past without looking at her. He looked wretched. Although in recent years there had been little love lost between the brothers, Richard and George had grown up together, sharing family loyalty, banishment and reunion, fortune and misfortune. The two York brothers had married two Neville sisters. They were kin, shared blood ran in their veins, shared ancestry, shared struggles. Now one of them was in the Tower, facing a charge of treason by their elder brother the king and even the pleas of their mother Cecily, Duchess of York went unheeded.

Christmas back at court in London for Richard was a muted celebration that was less of a pleasure than an endurance. His appeals to Edward for clemency for George had fallen on deaf ears and he was in no mood for celebrating. The admiration and respect he had long held for Edward now sullied by doubt and disapproval of his brother's actions towards his own flesh and blood. Richard began to suspect the queen's unhealthy interest and controlling influence in her husband's decision making where George was concerned. There was no love lost between the outspoken Duke of Clarence and the king's conniving consort.

Richard's dour countenance was noted and commented on, as he absent-mindedly twirled his silver goblet in his long fingers, hardly raising a glance to acknowledge the guests. Taciturn and uncommunicative, he ate little from the generous platters of food presented to him, preferring instead to drain his goblet and refill it until it numbed his senses and dulled his pain. The Duke retired early, leaving the guests to enjoy the entertainment, acutely aware that not far away his brother languished alone in the Tower, reflecting on his fate, while Edward and his haughty queen laughed, danced and feasted through the winter festivities.

In January Richard attended the marriage of Edward's youngest son, Richard Duke of York, to Anne Mowbray, heiress of the wealthy Duke of Norfolk. The bride was six years old and the groom just four. There followed a great wedding feast and a week later a joust in which the queen's brother, Earl Rivers, and her eldest son by her first marriage, Thomas Grey the Marquis of Dorset, were the chief challengers. Richard took no part. He saw no point of such frivolous playacting. To him martial skills and prowess were purely for the field of battle and not to be belittled as mere entertainment.

Soon afterwards in the capital, the Duke of Clarence was tried for treason. Only Edward and George dared speak at the trial, each to give their arguments, but despite the king's best efforts to spare his brother, George was not contrite, perhaps unbelieving that his brother would actually carry out his threat. He was found guilty of treason, the sentence of death pronounced by the Duke of Buckingham. Edward delayed sentence for ten days but on 18th February 1478 George was executed privately in the Tower after being given the last rites. Edward had saved his brother from the indignity of a public execution but at the same time denied George the opportunity of airing an accusatory revelation on the scaffold. The means of dispatch was not broadcast but a rumour that George had been drowned in a vat of Malmsey persisted, which was apt, given his predilection for drink. His body was laid to rest at Tewkesbury Abbey beside the tomb of his Duchess. Another flame of the House of York snuffed out but this time not by his enemy on the battlefield but by his own kith and kin.

Subsequently, Richard's young son Edward was created the Earl of Salisbury and Richard was given back the office of Great Chamberlain which he had surrendered to George in 1472 but he gained no other lands from him. He had no wish to benefit from his brother's death and part of him resolved to exact retribution from whoever was behind his brother's untimely demise and had propelled Edward towards fratricide. Instead, for now Richard secured a license to found colleges at Middleham and Barnard Castle, where priests and choristers would pray for the souls of his family and those who had passed on.

Sickened and grieving, Richard travelled back to Middleham, tight lipped and morose, keeping to his quarters or praying alone in the chapel. He spent many solitary hours poring over his books, often avoiding mealtimes, preferring to eat alone in his chamber so as not to have to engage in meaningless conversation. Servants kept out of his way and Eleanor noticed on more than one occasion, the pages returning with food untouched. Once she glimpsed Anne embracing her husband tenderly as he wept on her shoulder and she envied their intimacy.

Although she loved Will dearly, there was always a small part of her that ached to comfort her first love. She saw Richard ride out alone, returning hours later as darkness cloaked the vale, mud-spattered and rain-sodden, the drips pouring unheeded off his hair and down his collar, his brow furrowed in a deep frown. ⚜

Chapter Sixteen

ICHARD KEPT HIMSELF BUSY. The Duke had established himself as a popular and fair-minded lord in the North, especially with the lower echelons of society, for whose benefit he often intervened. He travelled to York to settle a dispute about fishgarths in the River Ouse, which were blocking the flow, preventing good fishing further downstream. He ordered them taken down but the problem persisted and would occupy him for the next few years. York was his father's heritage and Richard was determined the city would thrive and progress under his dominion; here he gradually gained a reputation for just and unbiased arbitration, qualities no doubt derived from being instilled with the noblesse oblige of the code of chivalry that underpinned his beliefs and conduct.

Richard and Anne had travelled to the city in June of the previous year to join the prestigious Corpus Christie Guild, attend the festival and watch the mystery plays and processions, culminating at the magnificent York Minster, which had been completed a few years before. They were always warmly welcomed by dignitaries and citizens alike. York was their city and the affection of its people for their fair-minded Lord was not forced.

Richard loved life at Middleham, cocooned in the peaceful safety and slower pace of its wide valley under the moors and bluffs, its gentle country folk living a life of honest toil in fresh country air. The town's weekly market sustained its people and the community were proud to serve their resident Lord and worship with him at the parish church. They felt safe and protected under his wardenship and their loyalty was spontaneous and freely given. The Duke was happy to stay detached from the intrigues of court life in London, his travels to the capital infrequent, although as the second highest ranking magnate in the land, he was always ready to be called upon by his brother to administer justice.

George Neville, the son of John Neville, Lord Montagu, who had been killed at Barnet, had been stripped of his title as Duke of Bedford, as he was deemed of insufficient means and property to uphold the title. Richard brought him to Middleham as his ward. He had not forgotten his father's service to the House of York before he defected to Warwick's failed rebellion. Richard always rewarded loyalty and was loved all the more for it.

Eleanor was kept occupied with little William and Elizabeth, who by now was a bright ten-year-old. Bess had grown fond of her stepfather; he would play games with her and although he would tease her on occasion it was with affection. Will was engaged in training the young boys retained by Richard in hunting and hawking. Her husband was a popular master, beloved by all with a jovial sense of humour and fun. The ladies would eye him up flirtatiously but he adored Eleanor and was not tempted to be unfaithful. He got on well with Richard, the young George Neville and Thomas Scrope. The four of them would hunt together, competing for the best catch, and in the tilt yard they kept up their martial skills, battling against each other to be ready both in physical development and mental preparedness for the next call to arms.

Eleanor sometimes wondered if Will had guessed the secret of Elizabeth's paternity but, if he had, he never mentioned it. The more time he spent with Richard, however, she felt the more obvious it must have been to him. Eleanor suspected Anne had also guessed but, again, nothing was said. The year passed peacefully and life was good in the upland valleys of Yorkshire, far from the disease and death that ran in London's streets. The king had wisely moved his family out to Windsor and later Greenwich to escape the burgeoning epidemic and plague-ridden alleyways of the capital.

⚜ ⚜ ⚜

ANOTHER TWO CHRISTMASES would come and go in relatively uneventful routine for the household, although Eleanor had the private tragedy of losing a third child. The baby had arrived prematurely and did not survive more than a few hours, plunging Eleanor and especially Will into deep-seated sorrow for the loss of a much longed-for daughter and since the birth Eleanor had not conceived again. Despite this misfortune, the couple were happily content with their life but Eleanor sometimes had a sense that fate would soon disrupt the pattern of life at Middleham. She was conscious that nothing could be perfect forever and the more perfect it was, the more likely it was to alter. She had always believed destiny to be written in the stars, that it had laid down her path through life, from which there was no deviation and no amount of willing it so could alter the course that had already been mapped out for her.

In 1479 Richard had received a grant to hold fairs in the town in June and October, which was welcomed by all. Now the townsfolk would turn out twice yearly to sell their wares and entertain the many who came from miles around, thus enhancing the prestige of this Dales community, whose Lord came to be loved and respected. Eleanor would take Elizabeth to the market square to join in the dancing and celebrations with the local children and watch with young William at her feet, playing on the grass. Life seemed idyllic but as the world turned and the relentless passage of time ticked by, the ever-present shadow of change was looming, patiently waiting its chance to impact on the lives of nobleman and commoner alike.

By the Spring of 1480, encouraged by Louis XI, the Scots, having reneged on their treaty with Edward, started raiding the borders, penetrating to Bamburgh, which was burned. Richard was appointed Lieutenant General in the North and set about quelling unrest with the help of the Earl of Northumberland. He strengthened the defences and castle at Carlisle and led raiding parties into Scotland.

Edward was planning a big campaign for the summer of 1481 but after a fleet sailed into the Firth of Forth, Edward's promised support never materialised. Richard realised he would not get assistance from his brother due to the king's declining vigour and increasingly sedentary lifestyle, which had taken its toll on the once energetic and active monarch.

Richard hurried back down to Fotheringhay, where he and Edward met the exiled Duke of Albany, king James III of Scotland's brother. They agreed a truce with Albany in exchange for placing him on the Scottish throne and the return of Berwick. Middleham Castle emptied again as the Duke's retainers left for the border. Eleanor embraced her brothers, relieved that they were going North and not South to France.

Richard and Albany marched to York and by the end of July they reached Berwick with 20,000 men. The town fell and Richard's army rapidly moved North to Edinburgh, leaving Lord Stanley to besiege the castle, whose defenders still held out. In the meantime, discontented Scottish lords had captured their king and sent him to Edinburgh Castle. Richard reached the capital unopposed and the Scots requested a truce and agreed with Richard to return the dowry Edward had paid to James III for the marriage of his sister Cicely, along with the return of Berwick. The Duke then agreed to retreat peacefully to Berwick, where the castle was at last repossessed. Albany, meanwhile, was pressured to sign a truce with James and to acknowledge his brother as king, in return for a full pardon and the restitution of his estates.

Richard returned to Court to great acclaim and praise from his brother, who granted him and his heirs the permanent possession of the Wardenship of the West Marches, the city and castle of Carlisle, and control over Cumberland, amounting to a County Palatine. It had been a busy year for the Duke, keeping peace on the borders, ensuring the numerous fortresses were kept in a good state of repair, ready to repel frequent hostile insurgencies from rebellious Scottish lords, always keen to renew old hatreds with their resented neighbour. The citizens of York and beyond looked to him to settle disputes and he soon became known for his fair and just arbitration regardless of rank, title or means, treating both rich and poor with the same impartiality, meting out justice wherever warranted.

However, at Middleham, Eleanor's tranquil family life was to be shaken by further personal tragedy. Will had not gone with Richard's men to Berwick, as he was needed at the castle. On a bleak, dark February day, as a biting wind blew down from the North Pennines and the snow dusted moors stood out in stark contrast against a grey menacing sky, the hunting party crept through the woods, searching for the wily boar. Picking their way cautiously through the brittle, frost-hardened undergrowth, startled pheasants flushed from the brushwood, clucking loudly in alarm, the huntsmen crept towards a clearing where boar were known to forage. Crossbows in hand, fingers benumbed by cold despite their leather gloves, they had long since lost any feeling in their toes, when, without warning, a sow ran across their path, followed by several piglets. Thomas steadied his aim but Will grabbed his arm.

"Don't kill the sow, Tom," he whispered. "She's protecting her young. Wait..."

A few steps further on they heard rustling in the underwood and an old boar shot out from the bushes. He was a big beast, white tusked, angry and protective, standing his ground in defiance. Will raised his weapon and took a step forward, accidentally catching his boot on a protruding tree root, sending him off balance, while his arrow flew past the boar, grazing its flank. Unable to regain his footing, Will crashed to the ground, reaching frantically for his crossbow, but the boar was too quick. The enraged beast charged and thrust his tusks into Will's side, tearing into his flesh in two deep furrows and sinking its slathered jaws into the young man's torso. As their companion writhed on the ground in agony, the young huntsmen loosed three arrows which found their target, felling the boar dead.

The shocked party hurriedly slung Will over his horse and made their way back to the castle, the injured man moaning with the constant jolting, blood running down his legs, seeping into his boots. A page ran to tell Eleanor that her husband was gored and she raced to his side. He was breathing erratically and in great pain, as she hastily removed his blood-soaked clothes and tried to clean the gaping wounds and torn flesh but the blood kept coming. She ran tearfully to Anne to ask if the Duke's physician would attend Will. Several interminable hours later, he turned up and set about cleansing the lesions with wine and pouring honey into them, while Will swore in agony. With dressings bound around Will's trunk, he was carefully carried up to the bedchamber, where Eleanor tried to make him comfortable, mopping his brow and offering him wine.

He took big gulps of the rich inebriant to dull the pain before slipping into welcome unconsciousness.

For the next two weeks Eleanor nursed her husband but the loss of blood had sapped his strength and his wounds festered and would not heal. The smell of roast pig wafting up from the kitchens, usually a mouth-watering prospect, now filled Eleanor with nausea. She refused to allow a morsel of the beast who had gored her husband to touch her lips, seeing it as a betrayal should she benefit in any way from the bounty of her love's assailant. Fevered and soaked in sweat, his body inexorably weakening, dazed by delirium, Will called out in the night while Eleanor lay next to him, listening to his erratic breathing, praying for his recovery.

"Oh Will," she whispered. "Pray don't die, my love, I need you and Little William needs his papa."

Will groaned in pain and shook uncontrollably, Eleanor holding him gently, trying not to hurt him. In a brief moment of lucidity, he appeared to know he would not recover. Grabbing her arm feebly, he whispered falteringly, "Maia... set her free."

"Of course, Will," Eleanor responded as she stroked his brow, "but you *will* get better my love, you *will*," she added reassuringly.

Sadly, her belief was to prove misguided. The physician tried blood-letting, herbal poultices and cauterization, but gradually the young man's strength ebbed away, unable to fight the sepsis, until eventually merciful oblivion and death released Will from his suffering. They buried him alongside the grave of his baby daughter in a quiet corner of the churchyard. Eleanor watched in tearful disbelief as her faithful companion, confidante, friend and lover was lowered into the cold earth, snatched so cruelly from her before his time – a bright flame snuffed out so unjustly by the fickle winds of fate. She could almost have accepted it had Will been killed in battle but to lose his life to a beast of the forest, the natural world he loved and respected, seemed a cruel irony. She hugged little William to her breast, now her only living embodiment of his father's flesh and blood, while twelve-year-old Elizabeth held onto them both, trying to comfort her distraught mother. When the children's nurse came to take them from her, Eleanor sank to her knees onto the mud of the freshly filled grave, soiling the hem of her mourning dress, but she cared not. Will had gone. She was alone again. It was almost too much to bear.

Later, she walked along to the churchyard and laid a posy of early snowdrops on his grave, their delicate white blooms hanging their heads in sorrow, a sad harbinger of the approaching Spring her cherished husband would never see. She entered the empty church, knelt down and prayed to God for Will's soul, for herself and for her children. *Why has God seen fit to rob me of my husband, this good, kind man, taken too young? Am I to blame? Is this my punishment for loving two men? Oh Will, where are you? Why did you leave me?* she cried, searching for an answer but none came. As her tears fell noiselessly, a ray of pale Spring sunshine broke through the clouds and streamed through the stained-glass window, falling on her head and shoulders in a warm embrace. In the comforting glow, Eleanor was sure she could feel Will's arms around her once more, as she wept in the silent church.

A few days later she sought out the bird enclosure where the hawks were kept and, donning a thick leather falconry glove, she eased Maia gently from her perch and made her way up to the woods, stopping just short of the tree line. Eleanor whispered encouragingly stroking the bird's soft feathers, then, removing the leash and hood, she raised her arm. Maia took flight, briefly circled above her, then soared over the treetops and was gone. No more would this graceful predator respond to her master's call; now she was free as nature intended, her hunting skills and her instinct to survive would hereafter sustain her. Blinking away tears, Eleanor walked despondently back to the castle, her mind recalling the shrill sound of her husband's whistle ringing in her ears as he summoned his hawk. She turned at the postern gate, softly mouthing a final adieu, focusing her gaze on the ridgeline of the limestone escarpment, where Will's spirit would evermore run free above the valley he loved. "Fare thee well my love, God speed!"

On returning from his campaign on the borders, Richard sent for Eleanor.

"Anne told me what happened. I am deeply sorry, Eleanor," he said kindly, looking into her eyes with unfeigned sincerity. "Will was a good man, a loyal soldier and one of our best huntsmen. He will be hard to replace."

"Thank you, my Lord."

Eleanor could not look at him, tears welling in her eyes. Without Will, whose love had shielded her from her own feelings about Richard, she now faced again the constant reminder that her first love was still there, still unattainable.

"We will provide for you and your children Eleanor, you will not be left wanting," he assured her warmly.

Eleanor thanked him again and ran to her chamber, so cold and empty now without Will.

Eleanor threw herself into her work and caring for her children, as the seasons marched on. Now twice widowed, she had no interest in re-marrying, despite still being young and attractive. She felt drained of love and had no wish to become another man's possession and any approaches she received were politely rebuffed. No new man could ever come close to the two lovers fortune had already allowed her and she vowed to be content in her celibacy, her children being her sole focus of attention. Anne was concerned that her hard-working maid servant was losing her spark and becoming withdrawn, but not being in the best of health herself was unable to help.

Richard spent Christmas 1482 with Edward at court, politely socialising with the queen, her daughters and many of the Woodville family, but all the time his heart and thoughts were at his distant castle in the lush green valley of Wensleydale, with his delicate wife, his precious son, his secret daughter and her pretty widowed mother.

Chapter Seventeen

Y NOW THE KING HAD begun to succumb to the temptations of his position. Years of high living, constant feasting, carousing and intemperance had taken their toll on the once beauteous monarch, his classic features now bloated, obscured by corpulence, encouraging apathy and idleness as he luxuriated in the excesses of court life. Lethargic from lack of exercise and exertion, Edward had left his brother to deal with the Scottish threat and with Richard's increased powers, he felt he could leave the North in safe hands.

Events in Europe had taken a downturn for Edward. Louis XI had consumed much of Burgundy but as Edward was in receipt of Louis' pension, he was powerless to help his old ally, who finally capitulated to France by signing the Treaty of Arras. Mary, the heiress of Burgundy had married Maxmillian of Germany but had since died, leaving the Duchy to her son Philip and now the dauphin was to wed Maximillian's daughter. Any hopes Edward had entertained of his own daughter Elizabeth marrying the dauphin and cementing the Anglo-French alliance were now dashed. England had lost the support of Burgundy and France was threatening her shores. If Scotland allied with France, it would be devastating for England. The year 1483 was to start a chain of events that would alter the course of all their lives and plunge the country once more into chaos.

On 9th April, suddenly and unexpectedly, Edward IV died. He had caught a chill out fishing on the river Thames, to which his death had been attributed. At first Richard, back in Yorkshire, enjoying a brief respite from border unrest and happily spending time with his wife and son, was unaware of the event that had shocked the capital and would turn his life upside down. Unbeknown to him, Edward's funeral had been hastily arranged and already taken place on 20th April, his body interred in his mausoleum at St. George's chapel, Windsor. The queen, however, had failed to notify her brother-in-law of Edward's death, a patently obvious omission that she could hardly have failed to notice, that spoke volumes about her intentions.

It was not until late April that a messenger galloped up to the gates of Middleham Castle, his mount steaming as he dismounted and hurriedly approached the gatehouse.

"An urgent message... for the Duke of Gloucester... from Lord Hastings," he panted as he informed the guard. Richard looked up from his desk as his page entered the solar and handed him the sealed missive, which he hastily unrolled.

"Mon Dieu!" He exclaimed. "The king is dead!" He stood up with a shock, steadying himself on the high-backed chair, the letter shaking in his hand.

"Two weeks past! Nay, nay, this cannot be! He is too young! Why was I not informed? Anne! My brother, my brother!" he called as the words choked in his throat.

Anne rushed to her husband and held him in her arms as he shook with emotion. After a few moments, he regained his composure, his mind racing. *What will happen now? Prince Edward is too young, George is dead, I am the only senior member of the House of York still living!* The country would be left without a figurehead, vulnerable to attack and the ever-present threat of a Lancastrian uprising for at least four years until the young king came of age. Prince Edward had been brought up in the jealously guarded care of the queen's relatives, assuring that as king he would be bound to them by loyalty and influence. The avaricious Woodvilles could now seize their chance to take control.

"Lord Hastings informs me my brother has left the realm and his heir under my protection. I must go at once... but first I must go to York to pray for Edward's soul and offer my oath of loyalty to the new king." Richard paced the floor, re-reading the letter and scanning Anne's worried face before summoning his Secretary and Captain of the guard.

"Edward Prince of Wales is only 12, he cannot rule until he comes of age," he told Anne, tight-lipped.

"And yet the queen did not even see fit to inform you of Edward's death!" exclaimed the Duchess, incredulous.

"Nay Anne, she did not!" the Duke replied, stony-faced, staring at his wife bitterly as the realisation hit home. "She had no thought even to apprise me of my brother's funeral!"

The deliberate snub to the late king's only remaining brother was at the very least bad manners, if not highly suspicious. Richard sat down, reaching for parchment and quill, tapping his fingers distractedly on the desk, thoughts crowding chaotically as he searched for possible outcomes to this unforeseen catastrophe. *What was happening in London? The strange suddenness of Edward's death – The queen's failure to notify him –* Questions that would need to be answered.

As the household was gradually acquainted with the shocking news, urgent preparations for the Duke's departure began. Before he left, Richard wrote hastily to the Council, pledging his loyalty to his brother's heir but as Protector of the Realm he stipulated that nothing should be agreed which was contrary to the law and his position. He would stand as Protector for four years until the Prince was 16 and legally able to rule. Richard was determined to do his duty towards his dead brother and give the young Prince the care and guidance he would need to lead the country. A letter arrived soon afterwards from Henry Stafford, Duke of Buckingham, who was on his way from his power base at Brecknock in Wales, informing Richard that the Prince of Wales was being brought from Ludlow, where he had been under the care of his uncle, Anthony Woodville, Earl Rivers, the queen's brother.

Dressed in mourning black and with a heavy heart, Richard left Middleham for York, accompanied by a small retinue. At York Minster he said prayers for his brother's soul and swore a solemn oath of allegiance to his nephew, the soon-to-be king Edward V. The queen meanwhile had been busy in London, acting as if she were Regent, arranging with indecent haste, her son's coronation, which was set for May 4th, giving very little time for preparations. She had taken money from the Treasury, which was under the control of her son the Marquis of Dorset, the current Constable of the Tower, to fund an armed force. Sir Edward Woodville, her brother, had been appointed Commander of the Fleet and immediately began gathering ships and men, financed by the Royal coffers.

After pausing at Pontefract, Richard received another letter from Lord Hastings, urging him to secure Prince Edward without delay. The queen's family had apparently ignored his appointment as Protector and were attempting to have the young Prince crowned as soon as possible to keep control of the young monarch, rid themselves of Richard's influence and thereafter govern through the boy king to their advantage.

Arriving in Northampton on 29th April, Richard was greeted by Earl Rivers, who had brought with him a large force of 2,000 men to escort the Prince. Claiming lack of suitable lodgings, the Earl explained he had moved Edward on to Stony Stratford, 14 miles closer to London, an action which immediately sounded alarm bells with Richard, confirming Lord Hastings' warning.

The Duke of Buckingham later arrived at the inn and the three nobles dined together amicably but, after Earl Rivers had retired, Richard and Henry spoke long into the night, discussing the implications of the Earl's actions. River's blatant attempt to delay the Duke long enough to ensure the Prince was well on his way to London had failed, his plans for a hasty coronation, negating the need for a Protector, now exposed.

Henry Stafford, Richard's cousin, modest of stature, full faced, with a florid complexion and short hair curling around his ears, was the premier Duke in the land after Richard and held no love for the Woodvilles. He had been made a ward of Queen Elizabeth and, at age 11, had been forced to marry the queen's sister Katherine, who was only 7, in a marriage far below his status. He would now do everything he could to prevent this upstart family gaining control of the new king and thereby ruling the country through him. He would need to gain Richard's confidence, offer his support and guidance and persuade him to heed his counsel in order to achieve his goal. There would be no place either for Richard or Buckingham if the queen had her way, he told his cousin.

Henry Buckingham was Margaret Beaufort's nephew by marriage. Buckingham's mother, another Margaret Beaufort, was sister to the Duke of Somerset, who had been killed by Edward after the battle of Tewkesbury. His grandmother was a Neville, sister of Richard's mother Cecily. Buckingham's family had been Lancastrians until the Yorkists came to prominence but the young Duke Henry had hoped to benefit from his cousin's success, determining to stay close to the seat of power, from which he hoped to gain. However, despite his royal blood, he had been largely ignored by Edward IV and now saw his chance to influence Richard and advance his own standing. As a direct descendant of Edward III's youngest son, Thomas of Woodstock, Henry Stafford felt greater recognition was owing to him.

It was becoming increasingly clear, Henry told Richard, that he was being undermined as Protector and may even be in danger of losing his life. The Tower and Treasury were under the control of Dorset, the queen's eldest son, the fleet under the control of Sir Edward Woodville, her brother and the queen would soon have the young king under her charge. If Earl Rivers, as intended, had delayed Richard's progress into London, the king could be crowned without him and the queen's family would have complete control of the realm, conveniently ignoring Edward IV's dying wish to install Richard as Protector. Instead, Earl Rivers would fill the role and the Woodville takeover would be complete, Buckingham advised Richard. There would be no room for the late king's remaining brother and many would seek his attainder or death in order to end the influence of the House of York, in favour of that of Lancaster, followers of whom had been awaiting just such a chance as this to regain their lost dominion.

Richard, as Henry urged, would have to arrest Rivers and take the Prince into his own protection, to have any chance of carrying out his brother's wishes. With Edward dead, Richard needed all the guidance he could get and so perplexed, isolated and abruptly thrust into the position of authority his brother had bequeathed to him, he felt he was given no choice in observing his cousin's advice. He was glad of an ally whose offer of support for now at least appeared genuine.

Accordingly, early the next morning Earl Rivers, Lord Richard Grey, the queen's son from her first marriage, Sir Thomas Vaughan and his escort were taken into custody by Richard's troops and the road South blocked while Richard and Buckingham hurried to Stony Stratford to find the Prince and his entourage, already engaged in leaving for London.

Richard sank to his knees in homage to his nephew, greeting him with every respect and courtesy, informing him of his father's decision to appoint him Protector and assuring him of his patronage and safe keeping. Young Edward, tall for his age, with his father's arresting good looks, fair colouring and intense blue eyes, stared defiantly back at his uncle, confused at the proceedings. He was unaware of the improper haste and dubious intentions of his maternal family, who had kept him safely sequestered at Ludlow under the tutelage of his uncle Anthony and John Alcock, Bishop of Worcester. He had no knowledge of his family's plans to thwart his father's wishes, nor could he know uncle Richard was a man of honour, bound by his word, his motto and his faith, committed to the role his brother had entrusted to him, having sworn an oath of fealty before God to serve the new king Edward V.

Richard reassured his nephew of his good intentions, determined to ensure the Prince was correctly installed as king within the protection and guidance of the House of York until he came of age, as his father had wished. The Duke dismissed Earl Rivers' troops and returned to Northampton with the Prince under his care, while the Earl, Grey and Vaughan were sent under guard to Sheriff Hutton, Middleham and Pontefract to be held until their fate was determined.

In London, the queen, upon hearing the news of her brothers' and son's arrest, tried to canvass support to resist the Dukes of Gloucester and Buckingham, but none was forthcoming. Terrified of reprisals for her treasonable actions, she fled into sanctuary at Westminster, along with the Marquis of Dorset, her daughters and youngest son Richard, Duke of York. Since her husband's decline and indiscriminate womanising, the queen had put all her energies into preparing the way for her son's rule. If she could no longer be queen, she had decided, she would be queen regent and with her son still a minor, her influence would be absolute and unassailable. The only problem had been her late husband's choice of Richard Duke of Gloucester as Protector of the Realm, but with careful planning and the help of her brother and sons, he could be sidelined and the Prince of Wales crowned without delay. The Woodville coup had failed, however, but for now she was safe under the protection of the church and not without means, the treasure having been divided up between herself, Dorset and her brother Edward, who had sailed with the fleet. The queen had hoped her flight into sanctuary would gain her some sympathy but instead it simply served to underline her guilt. The reason for her haste to crown her son king would, however, soon become apparent.

Lord Hastings, having heard that Richard was escorting the Prince safely to London, sent word to the Chancellor, Thomas Rotherham, Archbishop of York, but the confused Chancellor immediately rushed off to the queen with the Great Seal, an action of illegality which was, however, soon rectified and the seal recovered, but not before the Archbishop's card had been marked and his dubious allegiance noted.

As Lord Chamberlain, Hastings then sent word to Richard that his actions were approved by the Council and London eagerly awaited the arrival of their new king. The Royal cavalcade entered London on 4th May to a rousing welcome, the coronation hastily prearranged by the queen having been postponed.

Now appropriate plans for Prince Edward's investiture could take place. The Prince was lodged in the Royal apartments in the Tower of London, where previous kings had awaited coronation. There was some concern over the boy's health and his doctor a frequent visitor, having been in constant attendance at Ludlow and who, along with Edward's tutor John Alcock, had accompanied the sickly Prince on his journey to London. The coronation of the young Prince of Wales was rescheduled for June 22nd; officials, dignitaries and guests were informed and new robes ordered. Richard replaced Bishop Rotherham as Chancellor with John Russell, Bishop of Lincoln, before summoning his first Council, who immediately confirmed his role as Protector and Defensor of the Realm.

Anne joined Richard in London in early June, leaving their son Edward in Middleham under the care of his nurse. She was concerned her son, a delicate child, frequently ill, would not have benefited from a long and arduous journey to the capital. The crowded, narrow streets, unhealthy air and the threat of ever-present disease would not be good for one so susceptible.

With the queen still in sanctuary after her failed plot to exclude Richard as Protector, there was still underlying unrest and distrustfulness amongst the inner core of the late king's advisors and adherents. Richard's preference for the advice and counsel of the Duke of Buckingham since his arrival on the scene at Nottingham had angered and alienated many of his late brother's supporters, including Lord Hastings. It was by his efforts Richard had been alerted to the news of his brother's death and the Woodville conspiracy. Now Hastings felt sidelined and ignored, his position at the centre of court threatened by Buckingham's meteoric rise to favour and influence.

Baron William Hastings had been Edward IV's closest advisor and confidante, enjoying the lavish and licentious lifestyle the king pursued, even to the point of sharing mistresses. Despite the late king's devotion to his younger brother, Hastings had not warmed to Richard, distrusting the young man's barely disguised distaste for their hedonistic pursuits. Richard had not approved of the Chancellor's salacious behaviour in shamelessly encouraging his brother's amorality, but since Edward's death had trusted in the Baron's continued support and assistance in carrying out his dead brother's wishes.

Unbeknown to Richard, Hastings, Lord Stanley, Bishop Rotherham and Bishop Morton of Ely, a staunch Lancastrian who had supported Marguerite of Anjou, now met in secret to discuss ways to rid themselves of the Duke of Buckingham and Richard's Protectorate in order to gain control of the new king. Hastings had used Richard to curb the power of the Woodvilles but he was loyal to Prince Edward and with Richard and Buckingham out of the way, he could see himself acting as Protector and regaining his lost influence over the new monarch.

However, Stanley with the Bishops Rotherham and Morton were at the same time, plotting to install the Lancastrian pretender Henry Tudor on the throne, plucked from relative obscurity by the schemes of his manipulative mother Margaret Beaufort, who was now Thomas Stanley's wife. Henry Tudor, exiled in France, calling himself the Earl of Richmond, was planning his bid for the English crown, bankrolled by the French, supported by Welsh rebels and disaffected Lancastrians, including Edward Woodville, who had escaped with part of the Royal treasure.

Henry Tudor had no legitimate claim to the throne and indeed no right to the self-imposed title Earl of Richmond, which had been bestowed on his father Edmund Tudor by the impressionable and easily influenced Henry VI. Edmund Tudor was one of the illegitimate children from Henry V's wife Catherine de Valois' involvement with Owen Tudor, a member of her household but not a nobleman. After his death Edmund's title had later been given to Richard Duke of Gloucester, then to George Duke of Clarence but reverted to the crown after George's death. Edmund's son Henry, then a minor, was degraded from the Earldom. Margaret Beaufort, Henry's mother had married Edmund Tudor, becoming the Countess of Richmond but she herself was descended from the illegitimate offspring produced by the mistress of John of Gaunt. Although these children had been legitimised and given the name Beaufort, they were not legally entitled to inheritance or title. Margaret had borne her son at a very young age, before her body was fully mature and subsequently was never able to produce any more children. From then on, Henry naturally became the sole focus of her attention and ambition.

To complicate the situation further, within a few days, a piece of information came to light that had far reaching consequences for Richard, the succession and indeed the stability of the country as a whole. The spectre of Edward's secret marriage to Elizabeth Woodville in 1464 now came back to haunt his heirs with a vengeance. The disclosure the queen had lived in fear of, and was at pains to conceal, now revealed itself, the reason for her deception at once becoming apparent.

Robert Stillington, Bishop of Bath and Wells, no doubt urged by his conscience and sense of duty, came forward to reveal that he had knowledge of a previous marriage contract between Edward IV and Eleanor Butler, a widow, the beautiful daughter of John Talbot, Earl of Shrewsbury. Edward had bedded Eleanor, then abandoned his obligation to her, prior to his marriage with

Elizabeth Woodville. This pre-contract rendered queen Elizabeth's marriage bigamous and all her subsequent children by Edward illegitimate. In English law, an illegitimate child could not inherit the throne. The Bishop had realised that with Edward IV dead, he was no longer forced to silence and could not stand by to watch the late king's son crowned in the light of the knowledge he possessed; knowledge that had been plaguing his conscience for almost twenty years.

Richard was in turmoil at this shocking revelation. It became clear to him now that Bishop Stillington's temporary arrest at the time of his brother George's arrest in 1477 was connected, as they both had information that would endanger the succession. This information had been suppressed by Edward and his queen successfully until now. The reasons for the clandestine nature of Edward's marriage to Elizabeth Woodvillle in 1464, now unfolded. Richard realised George's death may even have been a direct consequence of this recognition – a fact borne out now by the queen's family's haste to crown her son before this truth was uncovered.

Aghast and appalled at the dilemma facing him, Richard was now placed in the unenviable position of having no other choice than to depose his nephew. His conscience would not allow him to ignore the Bishop's words but the predicament he now found himself in was of paramount significance. If he allowed an illegitimate child to ascend the throne, he would be breaking the law but if he assumed the throne himself, as was his right as next in line, he would be breaking his vow of fealty and dishonouring his brother's children, as well as alienating much of the nobility who had supported Edward. It would not be a popular move and could exacerbate the already polarising divisions within the country but furthermore he could not be seen to be flouting the laws of succession. His motives would be questioned, scrutinised and misinterpreted by his enemies, not just in the immediate future but for generations. Despite his right as next in line, any claim he made on the throne would be interpreted as personal ambition, its premeditation assumed, the pre-contract judged an opportune and convenient argument. Nevertheless, Richard was left with no choice.

Upon sharing this shocking information with Buckingham, Duke Henry then relayed this news to Margaret Beaufort, who in turn imparted this knowledge to her husband Thomas Stanley and Bishop Morton, whose secret plans now became a matter of urgency, with the prospect of Richard Duke of Gloucester assuming the throne. Hastings saw his plan of ruling as Protector through the young king Edward V come to nothing and Morton saw his plot to crown a new Lancastrian king thwarted. They must act immediately. The plan was that at the next meeting with Richard, Hastings would have an armed guard standing by. Hastings would then ask Morton to arrange for some strawberries to be fetched from his garden, Morton would leave to give the signal and the guards would rush in and kill Richard before taking control of the young king.

However, William Catesby, Hastings' lawyer, seeing his chance to advance his own position and standing, informed on his former patron and told Richard of Hastings' plot to kill the Protector. The Duke of Buckingham, happy with the opportunity to rid himself of his rival, stood by impassively as events unfolded. Richard was incensed that his Lord Chamberlain, a man of surety, who had fought by his side at Barnet and had been his brother's closest confidant and friend, having warned him of the Woodville conspiracy had now turned against him and joined with the very plotters he had cautioned Richard against. Horrified at the betrayal but forewarned, Richard allowed the meeting to take place in the Tower on 13th June, as planned.

Richard waited for the Baron to incriminate himself with the pre-arranged request for strawberries, which duly came, upon which Richard's guard, having replaced those of the Chancellor, rushed in and, after a brief skirmish, arrested Hastings, Stanley and the Bishops Morton and Rotherham. Furious at his Chancellor's falsehood, Richard revealed the scar on his forearm, reminding him that the injury from Barnet was in his defence; incredulous as his fellow warrior, the man he thought was his friend, who had emerged a false traducer and had colluded in a plot to kill him, was led away.

Hastings knew there was no point in resisting, he knew the punishment for sedition and subversion. Morton was detained and placed under the care of Buckingham, who had requested that the bishop be placed in his custody. With the benefit of hindsight, Richard would later deplore the folly of this imprudent decision, but for now it seemed judicious. Stanley and Rotherham were later released but Hastings was immediately executed for his treachery.

Richard's anger had erupted in a tide of emotion when his faith in his Chancellor was betrayed but he had learned from his brother that swift and uncompromising retribution could halt any further disorder and show strong leadership. It was not often Richard displayed traits of the Plantagenet rage his ancestors were known for, but when faced with injustice and disloyalty, his usual quiet reticence and composure exploded into a fit of implacable fury. Richard's position as High Constable granted him by Edward IV gave him the authority to exact expeditious and just punishment for treachery, which the Duke now felt compelled to use against an attempt on his life. As Protector of the Realm, he could not be judged weak in the face of such betrayal.

Richard would not have had his brother's friend and mentor killed without good reason, although the speed at which the sentence was carried out would not be without remorse. In the aftermath, Richard treated Hastings' widow with compassion, allowing her to retain her lands which were not placed under a bill of attainder and in accordance with the late king's wishes, the Chancellor's body was buried close to Edward's in St. George's chapel, Windsor.

Also implicated in the conspiracy as a go-between was Jane Shore, former mistress of both Edward IV and Hastings and lately the Marquis of Dorset, who had escaped sanctuary and was at large somewhere in Yorkshire. Mistress Shore, buxom, blonde and beautiful, the apple of many a man's eye, witty and engaging, willing and wanton, was censured to do public penance for her sins, as much for her promiscuous lifestyle as for her involvement in the intrigue. The queen, confined to her sanctuary at Westminster, was not averse to utilising the liberty of her late husband's mistress to further her own ends, until Hastings' treachery had been unmasked.

Another Woodville plot had been discovered and foiled, but would it be the last? The Council met to assess the situation. The country was already dangerously divided internally and threatened externally by France. A strong king was a constitutional exigency England must possess, not a minor but an adult of high rank, proven military prowess and clear descent from the Plantagenet line. Prince Edward was no longer eligible to succeed his father; his coronation plans would have to be halted and a new successor appointed. There was only *one* option, the man who was unquestionably and legitimately next in line to the throne, the last remaining Plantagenet prince, the late king's younger brother, Richard Duke of Gloucester.

On 26th June at Baynard's Castle, as a throng of nobles, gentry and citizens gathered, Richard was petitioned to assume the throne, as the only person eligible through his Plantagenet ancestry to rule the country, capable of taking control of a divided nobility and disciplined enough prevent total chaos. Acceptance was the only solution open to him. His reluctance was genuine but again his motives would be distorted and pre-judged by his antagonists, intent on his opprobrium.

In recognition of Buckingham's service, Richard agreed to return the Duke's De Bohun inheritance to him, at the next Parliament, for which the Duke had long petitioned. John Howard, the Duke of Norfolk, was appointed Admiral, with further income from estates. Robert Brackenbury was made the Constable of the Tower and Keeper of the Exchange and Richard's trusted friend Francis, now Viscount Lovell, became Lord Chamberlain.

Meanwhile, some loose ends had to be tidied up. Earl Rivers, Lord Richard Grey and Sir Thomas Vaughan were brought to Pontefract, where they were tried by the Earl of Northumberland and executed for treason for their part in the failed Woodville coup.

With young Prince Edward still in the Tower apartments and his younger brother in sanctuary with the queen, Richard needed to ensure the younger Prince Richard of York was not the subject of a kidnap attempt by Lancastrians eager to reinstate the boys' legitimacy, or to use him as a spearhead for revolt. Edward, lonely and bored, feeling isolated and unwell left on his own in the Tower, requested the company of his brother, so Richard, encouraged by the Duke of Buckingham, proceeded to Westminster with the Archbishop of Canterbury to persuade the queen to allow her younger son to join his brother as a companion. Buckingham's motives at this time were clouded but would reveal themselves in time.

Richard assured the queen that her sons would be well cared for and protected, as befitting the late king's children and as his nephews. Accordingly, the two boys were reunited, although Richard's detractors would again see this action as a reason to doubt his motives and use it against him.

Chapter Eighteen

ACK AT MIDDLEHAM, THE ABRUPTNESS of the king's death had been met with bewilderment and disbelief, considering his young age. Rumours were rife that queen Elizabeth and her guileful mother Jacquetta had somehow hastened his demise, fed up with his womanising. Following Edward's chill, he had deteriorated to the point where his death had been reported but he recovered, only to succumb again a few days later, resulting in suspicions of poisoning, the first measure proving ineffective. There was no proof, however, only confusion and conjecture. The once revered charismatic military hero had allowed years of excess to take its toll on his body, rendering him languid and obese, but he was still relatively young and robust, his sudden illness both unexpected and unforeseen. The treaty with France had left a stain on Edward's reputation and his licentious behaviour had lowered the esteem in which he was held by his subjects, not least by his younger brother, but his premature death was nonetheless greeted with dismay.

The surprise and grief of Richard's hurried departure from Middleham had been replaced by uncertainty and fear, as reports of the Woodville attempt to ignore the dead king's wishes and proceed with a coronation without Richard, filtered through. Soon afterwards however, relief and joy filled the castle as news of the Prince's impending coronation and Richard's position as Protector was confirmed.

A stranger had been brought to the castle under armed guard. Eleanor learned it was the queen's younger son by her previous marriage, Lord Richard Grey, who had been with his uncle Earl Rivers hurriedly escorting Prince Edward to London, when Richard caught up with them. She caught a brief glimpse of the fair-haired young man as he was ushered in by the guards but after that there was no further sign of him. Eleanor wondered why the queen's family would engage in treasonous plotting when they had already advanced higher and gained more wealth than their lowly status afforded. Richard as Protector posed no threat to them and their positions would not have altered under his jurisdiction. Instead, they had ignored the late king's wishes and by doing so proclaimed themselves traitors, for which they knew punishment was absolute.

Eleanor helped Anne prepare to join Richard in London. The Countess was concerned that Anne's cough still persisted and worried that the journey might make her unwell, but Anne was determined to be at her husband's side. The Duchess, reluctant to leave her delicate son, had said a tearful farewell to Edward and promised to bring him back a special gift from the merchants of London.

The news of Lord Hastings' duplicity followed by his accelerated death then came as a further blow. All had assumed that the Chancellor was fully behind Richard in his position as Protector until his plot with Bishop Morton had been discovered. They understood, however, that Richard had no choice but to order the execution of his former advisor for his act of treachery, which they knew the Duke would have regretted deeply.

There was more to come. Reports of Bishop Stillington's shocking divulgence reached the household shortly afterwards, with the disclosure that king Edward's marriage had been bigamous and therefore all his children with the queen rendered illegitimate. They understood that the upshot of this astounding revelation was that Richard, as next in line, would be urged to take on the dominion himself, to try to bring some stability to a dangerously divided country. Following this, with the country in disarray, they heard the Council had met and petitioned Richard to assume the throne, which he had accepted as the only course open to him. The country could not be left without a figurehead, especially with Edward's queen still in sanctuary and the threat of a Lancastrian resurgence, backed by France, on the horizon. Edward's loyal youngest brother would now become king with Anne beside him as his queen.

Upon hearing the announcement that Richard and Anne's coronation was set for 6th July, the Duke and Duchesses' household went into a frenzy of excitement and preparation for Anne's departure. The Countess imparted the good news to her grandson Edward, who would now become Prince of Wales and would inherit the throne of England after his father.

Eleanor was in a daze. *Richard to be king? The shy youth who once loved me and fathered my child, king of England! Now he will be further from me than ever!* she reflected gloomily, the chances of him returning to Middleham any time soon now becoming increasingly unlikely. Feeling a pang of guilt that her first thought was for herself, Eleanor was at the same time gladdened at Richard's good fortune, despite the sad underpinnings. She wondered how he would feel being thrust so precipitately and unexpectedly into the most demanding role in the land, snatched from his comfortable family life in the sweeping Northern domain that had become his home. However, she knew that as king, Richard would assiduously perform the office entrusted to him and endeavour to be just and loyal, not only to his brother's memory but to his country, his people and his faith. The thought also crossed her mind that her daughter Elizabeth would never be recognised as the Princess she might have been had her birth been legitimate. Nevertheless, she concluded, a life of comfortable anonymity was preferable to the politics of monarchy, where a daughter unwittingly became a bargaining tool almost from birth and despite great wealth, personal happiness was frequently considered secondary and indeed irrelevant.

In London, Anne arrived at Baynards Castle on the banks of the Thames, where Cecily, the dowager Duchess of York, welcomed her daughter-in-law. The elderly widow, now in her late 60's, revered and respected, still radiating the ghost of her former beauty, taciturnly embodied wisdom and piety whilst mourning the unexpected death of her illustrious son – the third of her adult boys to be taken before his time. Anne commiserated with her loss and joined her mother-in-law in prayer. They discussed the unfolding situation at length with Richard and understood the dilemma that now faced him. He was the late king's only surviving brother but in assuming the throne he would have to depose his brother's children, an act which would divide the country, but a refusal would have the unwanted outcome of plunging the Realm into leaderless political chaos, a gift to England's enemies and to those planning to dislodge the House of York. Without him the country would fall back into the domestic turmoil that had preceded Edward IV.

Contrary to popular opinion and rumour promulgated by his enemies, Richard had not planned to be king, or desired it. He had no need. He had established himself as Lord of the North, benefiting from huge wealth and property and was content to control and administer the region that had become his home, surrounded by his family and the people who loved him. However, his sense of duty and protocol offered him no option but to accept responsibility, honouring the memory of his father, whose right to the throne of England, formerly approved then denied, could now be realised in his youngest son.

Edward IV had condemned his own sons by his bigamous marriage, which in law now disbarred the young Prince Edward from the throne, leaving his brother Richard as the last scion of the House of York. Richard realised he would have to accept the crown and vow to do his utmost to unite the country, win the love of his people, provide strong leadership, promote morality and clean living, whilst ensuring justice for the common man.

It would not be an easy choice but Richard was not one to shy away from duty and obligation. He knew the enormity of the task, the solemnity of the oath he would have to take, the commitment to God and country, the sanctity of kingship, the moral obligation to uphold the faith and justice invested in that highest of states. He would do what needed to be done. He owed it to his brother. The Yorkist succession so hard won, must endure. Personal persuasion did not come into it, despite appearing so to many.

Anne did not wholly welcome the news. Aside from its advantages, she considered the role of monarch to be a position of isolation, a poisoned chalice, intoxicating but fraught with danger. She imparted her fears to her mother-in-law.

"Do you not wish to be queen of England, Anne?" Cecily asked, surprised.

"Not as much as I should, I confess. I am not ungrateful but shall be sad to leave Middleham and London won't be good for Edward's health, besides Richard is well established in the North and feels at home there, where he is loved and respected."

"Richard is the *only* option, Anne," proffered the Duchess. "Edward condemned his own children by his foolish marriage. I *knew* no good would come of it! He always let his heart rule his head. Richard is more circumspect and forethoughtful, more like his father. He is the last of our bloodline. He has proved himself worthy in battle and shown good lordship and loyalty to his people, acting as a fair arbitrator and administrator. Edward appointed him Protector. It is the Council's only recourse. Who else is there? It is his birthright. The country needs a strong leader, able to guide, motivate and make judgements, not a child."

Anne could not disagree with the Yorkist matriarch but within her lurked an unstated disquiet and dread that the burden of kingship could prove too much for her diligent and faithful husband.

Richard and Anne's coronation on July 6th was the first joint investiture of a king and queen for 175 years. London was packed with nobility, clergy, merchants, soldiers and musicians; the streets thronged with spectators eager to catch a glimpse of their new king and his queen. Many commoners had not wholly understood the reasons for the rapid change of succession, despite several proclamations and sermons but accepted without question that Richard Duke of Gloucester was of Royal blood, directly descended from Edward III and as esteemed military commander and brother to the late king, was eminently worthy to succeed him.

History had shown that a boy king's rule was a recipe for chaos and destabilisation as rival factions vied for power and control. Now the cheers for Richard and Anne were spontaneous and an excuse for celebration always a welcome distraction to the everyday struggles of city life.

The procession started at the Tower and proceeded to Westminster, the priests and bishops with the jewelled cross held aloft, followed by the Duke of Northumberland holding the sword of mercy, Lord Stanley with the mace, Suffolk with the sceptre, Lincoln with the ball and cross, Surrey with the sword of state and the Duke of Norfolk with the crown.

Following the Mayor of London and Garter king of Arms, king Richard III walked, bare headed and bare footed, protected by a canopy, garbed in purple velvet, to the side of him Viscount Lovell with the sword of justice, the Bishops of Durham and Bath and Wells and the Duke of Buckingham holding the king's train. With him went his brother George's son Edward, queen Anne followed with the Earl of Huntingdon, Wiltshire and the Bishops of Exeter and Norwich, Margaret Beaufort carrying her train, followed by the Duchess of Norfolk and Elizabeth of Suffolk, Richard's sister.

Richard and Anne made a handsome couple, the two slight figures perhaps not quite embodying the once God-like perfection of his charismatic predecessor and his queen, whose ice-cold voluptuous beauty was legendary, but nevertheless they made a striking pair; Richard with his slim physique and classic noble features beside Anne's ethereal delicacy, her silky blonde hair worn loose and falling to her hips, her skin so pale it was almost transparent. To the crowds jostling to catch a glimpse of their new sovereigns, Anne appeared to them like a wraith, so fragile, the slightest puff of wind would have wafted her heavenwards but her consort's modest stature and lean frame, cloaked in royal regalia masked a hidden stalwartness, they knew this chivalrous knight had amply displayed on the battlefield.

Inside the Abbey, the king and queen, having been anointed with Holy oil, were robed in cloth of gold, the crowns placed upon their heads, *Te Deum* was sung after Mass and Communion before the procession repaired to Westminster Hall for the coronation banquet. In accordance with tradition, during the feasting, Sir Robert Dymmock, the king's champion, rode into the hall on a resplendently caparisoned charger to deliver the customary challenge, as cries of "King Richard! King Richard!" went up in acclamation.

After a brief respite at Greenwich, the king and queen set off on their royal progress on 23rd July, leaving Chancellor John Russell to carry on the Government in the king's absence. While Anne rested at Windsor for a few days, Richard travelled to Reading, Oxford, Minster Lovell, Gloucester, Tewkesbury and Worcester. With him went his brother George's son Edward, Duke of Warwick, who had been kept at the Tower under Dorset's charge. The Duke of Buckingham parted from the progress at Gloucester to convey Bishop Morton under guard to his Welsh estates. Anne then joined Richard at Warwick Castle, her childhood home, and from there they proceeded to Coventry, Leicester, Northampton, Doncaster, Pontefract and York. At Pontefract they were joined by their son Edward, who had travelled from Middleham, conveyed by chariot due to his ill health and weak constitution. The Royal family entered York at the end of August to a rousing reception and after a week of celebration, Edward of Middleham was publicly invested as Prince of Wales.

As preparations for the investiture were underway, Richard sent his Master of Henchmen, Sir James Tyrell to the Keeper of the Wardrobe at the Tower of London to procure gowns, pennons and badges for the ceremony. Richard also confided to Anne that he had arranged for the two sons of Edward IV to be clandestinely removed from the Tower and taken to a safe house, possibly Tyrell's home at Gipping Hall in Suffolk to prevent any further kidnap attempts by the Woodville family, one of which had already been foiled. Here they would be cared for until it was decided where was best for them to grow up in security and seclusion, several European destinations being a distinct possibility. Clarence's son Edward of Warwick would be placed under the care of Richard's nephew, John de la Pole, Earl of Lincoln, the son of Richard's sister, Elizabeth of York, at Sheriff Hutton.

Shortly after the Prince's investiture, an event so lavish and resplendent it served as a second coronation, the Royal family left York, Anne returning with her son to Middleham to rest, while Richard continued his progress South. The joy and exhilaration of their new-found notability, however, was short-lived. The king reached Lincoln to alarming and shocking news. The Duke of Buckingham had risen in rebellion in a plot to overthrow his newly anointed sovereign, aided by the Woodvilles, including the Marquis of Dorset, who was still at large in Yorkshire, along with disaffected Lancastrians and resentful Southerners, plotting to join forces with Henry Tudor in his bid for the English throne.

Richard was incensed and horrified. The Duke of Buckingham, his cousin, his distinguished friend and ally, lately handsomely rewarded with great riches and vast lands, had now turned traitor! 'The most untrue creature living' he railed. Upon returning to his Welsh estates with Bishop Morton in his charge, Buckingham and the cunning bishop, no longer the Duke's prisoner but instead his fellow collaborator, now conspired to join with the Lancastrian cause against Richard. Hastings had conveniently been eliminated and the king was on his royal progress without an army to protect him, buying the two schemers time to plot their treason.

To further their ends, the intriguers had allowed a rumour to circulate, that the sons of Edward IV had been killed in the Tower, thereby endorsing the rebellion in the eyes of those opposing Richard. The boys had not been seen at the Tower for some time and it was easy to fuel the inevitable gossip with supposition and presumption. If the rebels could convince enough followers that king Richard was a child murderer, it would add credence to their cause and swell their numbers.

Many who had supported Edward IV and had wished to see his son re-instated as legitimate, joined Buckingham, persuaded by the supposed murder of the Princes and the prospect of a new focus in Henry Tudor. Richard was an adopted Northerner, an unknown quantity in the eyes of the populace and had yet to gain the confidence of those in the South and West who had served and admired his charismatic brother. They, along with much of the country, were sceptical of Stillington's revelation, having accepted Edward IV once the Lancastrian claim died but now with the Yorkist king's death and the relegation of his son, that cause resurfaced.

Richard immediately raised an army and set off in pursuit of Buckingham. The Duke's progress through Wales had however been hampered by the Vaughans and Humphrey Stafford, whose troops had demolished bridges and blocked roads. A great storm and flood had then cut off the rebels advance from Wales, upon which the Duke's demoralised troops disintegrated. Henry Tudor, who had planned to join forces with Buckingham, had sailed for the West Country but his fleet had been scattered in the Channel by the same storm, forcing him to abandon his plans, retreat to safe waters and wait for another opportunity.

Having successfully persuaded the impressionable Duke to rebel, the pusillanimous Bishop Morton escaped to Flanders, leaving his accomplice to his fate. Buckingham, discarding his splendid attire, fled into hiding in Shropshire with a price on his head, but was betrayed by a profiteer, captured and brought to Salisbury for trial. The Duke pleaded with the king for an audience but Richard refused to see him. He would not face the man he had relied on, put faith in, his cousin, whom he had rewarded with great riches but who had ultimately betrayed him, accused him of nepoticide and now plotted his death, in an unlikely alliance with an ignoble Welsh upstart.

Richard was dismayed at Buckingham's falsehood. Why? Had the deceitful Duke nursed a secret agenda all the time? Had he resumed his Lancastrian family's allegiance? Was he in league with Morton from the beginning and somehow instrumental in Hasting's downfall? Was the Duke's ambition such that he aspired to the throne himself and was his outward support of Tudor simply a stepping-stone to this effect? Had Henry been encouraged in his insurrection by the cunning Bishop, who fully expected him to fail with the inevitable consequences, thereby leaving the way open for Tudor? Richard was in turmoil, his thoughts racing. He would never know nor understand what had driven his cousin to first offer his unqualified support and then turn so faithlessly against him.

For the plotters, nothing less than a heinous crime of monstrous proportions, laid at Richard's door, would suffice to persuade the masses to accept a Welsh nobody in place of an anointed king of impeccable lineage – the unknown whereabouts of Edward IV's sons being the perfect justification for their lie. For Buckingham, by fair means or foul, his regal ambitions could be realised if only he could rid himself of the present incumbent. For Bishop Morton, his Machiavellian plot, smouldering under the surface for a decade, could now seize its chance to re-ignite, selecting any convenient figurehead regardless of legitimacy, to restore Lancastrian rule. For Margaret Beaufort, quietly cultivating her husband's resentment of Richard to further her own ambitions and propel her only child to the highest seat in the realm, the pieces were conveniently falling into place. For Stanley, the lure of becoming stepfather to a king and the resulting gratitude that would, he felt sure, be coming his way, was a temptation too great to resist. To Richard, loyalty was everything and with it went trust. If that trust was betrayed, he felt it deeply and personally. To some his faith in those around him was perceived as naivety, leaving him open to manipulation but those who stood by him were rewarded with lifelong commitment and service.

Adhering to his coronation oath to rule by mercy and justice Richard did not proceed against Buckingham's followers, who were merely answering their Lord's call to arms, however, the faithless Duke was tried, sentenced and immediately beheaded for his treachery. Margaret Beaufort was implicated in the plot to assist her son Henry Tudor and was subsequently placed into her husband Stanley's custody for her role in the conspiracy, an action that in retrospect would later prove to Richard to be too lenient, given her husband's prevarications and dubious allegiance. At the same time the Duke of Norfolk had quashed an affiliated rebellion advancing on London, while Richard continued westwards, reaching Exeter unopposed, where he learned that the Marquis of Dorset had fled, along with other rebels, to Brittany.

By November, the king was back in the capital. He made Thomas Stanley Constable of England, his brother William Chief Justice of North Wales and William Herbert, the Earl of Huntingdon, Chief Justice of South Wales. He also appointed the Earl of Northumberland as Great Chamberlain. Apart from the faithful William Herbert, the trust Richard put in these men would later prove to be misplaced. He had only been king for four months and already his closest ally had risen against him, branding him a murderer and usurper and his old enemy France was plotting with a Welsh upstart to seize his throne. It was an inauspicious start to Richard's kingship and his life was not about to get any easier.

Chapter Nineteen

HE SKIES WERE DARKENING AND the hours of daylight shortening as the year drew to a close in Wensleydale. The late summer swathes of purple heather covering the moors in a cloak of vivid colour had faded into greyish brown and fierce gales were stripping trees of their shimmering autumn leaves, now falling fast into deep drifts leaving slender, naked branches finely etched in charcoal outline against pewter skies. The swollen rivers again thundered down from the high ground in a torrent of brown foam and broken branches, many entangled in the waterfalls, as the sediment ran off the moors, eroding banks, flooding fields and obliterating tracks, turning roads into impassable quagmires.

The queen had arrived home with the Prince of Wales, who looked pale and ill, but in the warmth of his chamber and with the attentions of his nurse and various physicians, he seemed to revive. Elizabeth would oft play dice games with the young Prince, or ride out with him, although since returning from York he was deemed too weak to join her. Eleanor would watch the children together, smiling to herself in the knowledge of their shared paternity. Anne watched them too, enjoying their laughter and ease of companionship. The similarity between them was not lost on her.

There was much shock and consternation in the household when they heard there had been a new uprising against Richard's kingship, initiated by, of all people, the Duke of Buckingham. Philippa had confirmed the news to Eleanor as they descended the stairwell one afternoon.

"Has the king returned to London?" Eleanor had enquired, hoping there were plans for Richard to return to Middleham.

"Aye, to start with but now he's gone West to put down a rebellion by the traitor Harry Buckingham. The king called him 'the most untrue creature living' apparently. Did you know, he and Bishop

Morton spread a rumour king Edward's sons are dead in order to gain support against king Richard?"

"Well, yes, I was shocked. I've heard the gossip. You know what people are like, always willing to believe the worst of somebody. I just thought it was mischief making. Surely people don't believe something so foul?"

"Most don't, but the Lancastrians will use any excuse to bring down a Yorkist king!"

"Why doesn't the king deny the rumours?"

"To ensure the boys' safety. If people want to believe they are dead, let them. It keeps them safe from harm or kidnap."

"So they are safe?"

"For certain they are, Eleanor," Philippa whispered, pausing on the stairs. "I overheard the queen confirm it to her mother. King Richard is no child killer. He loves his family and would not imperil his immortal soul by such a wicked and cruel act. Besides, why would he? They pose no threat to him, having already been disbarred by reason of their illegitimacy."

"Aye, he would not. I know he would ensure their welfare."

"Do not speak of it to anyone though, Eleanor. You cannot be sure who might overhear, or of their affiliation." Eleanor affirmed her silence truthfully and sincerely. She was good at keeping secrets, especially a secret charged to her by the man she loved which, she avowed, would never leave her lips.

Another young man had lately joined the household, Richard's illegitimate son, John of Gloucester, in his early teens, who had arrived with Anne from York, where he had received his knighthood from his father. He had been raised at Pontefract, where Richard had met his mother during his 4-year absence from Middleham. Eleanor immediately recognised the boy as Richard's son, the same blue/grey eyes, slight frame, classic features and quality of quiet reservation so typical of his father. Quick witted, intelligent and dexterous, skilful with weaponry, taking pride in his achievements, he was eager to earn his father's respect and the esteem of his peers. Anne's love for her husband showed in her magnanimity towards his bastard son and her acceptance of him. Eleanor knew she would in due time have to familiarise Elizabeth with the facts of her blood family, so close in proximity but so disparate in status. Eleanor saw Bess watching John in the tilt yard, with a few of the other teenage girls, whispering and giggling, eyeing up the young men, discussing their attributes. John brought to mind a younger version of Richard and despite his bastardy, would before too long be considered worthy, as the king's natural son, for the marriage market. *I will have to tell her soon*, Eleanor realised. *Bess must be apprised of their blood relationship before it's too late.*

John was not the only new arrival akin to the royal household. The queen had been accompanied on her return to Middleham by Margaret Neville, her half-sister, an illegitimate daughter of the late Earl, who was ten years older than Anne and married to Sir Richard Huddleston. Lady Margaret was pleased to act as senior lady in waiting to Anne, who valued her company and advice and likewise the dowager Countess held no resentment towards her husband's natural daughter and was happy for her to join the family. Many a nobleman would sire bastard children before committing to marriage and the Earl's courtship with Margaret's mother was long before he wed the Beauchamp heiress. As a result, Eleanor had less to do for the queen while she was at Middleham and spent more time with the old Countess.

Young Prince Edward had every care and attention and with fresh air and good food Anne felt sure his condition would improve. Reassured by his nurse that their son would lack for nothing, Anne felt it safe to return to London for the Christmas festivities with Richard, which would be their first at Court as king and queen.

The Countess, who adored her delicate Grandson, spent many hours with him, pouring over books and regaling him with tales of past Knights and glories. She commissioned for Edward, *the Beauchamp Pageant*, a lavishly illustrated history of her father, Richard Beauchamp the 13th Earl of Warwick, who had been Captain of Calais, Governor of Normandy and mentor to the young Henry VI. Each page of the illustrated volume depicting in exquisite detail a scene from the life of the Earl, which the Countess hoped would instil in her grandson a sense of pride and admiration for his illustrious ancestor.

One afternoon Eleanor found the Countess in tears, pacing the floor distractedly.

"What ails you my lady?" she enquired of her agitated mistress.

"T'is lost Eleanor, my gold locket. I rode over to Jervaulx Abbey stables to inspect a new foal for Edward but when I returned, I noticed it was gone. I still have the chain but there was a weakened link and the pendant must have slipped off as I rode. It is my fault, I *knew* I should have sent it for repair," the Countess lamented, wiping her eyes. "I sent the page back to look but he found nothing."

"Oh, I'm so sorry my Lady," Eleanor sympathised. "T'was so beautiful!"

"Aye, t'was a gift of great worth from my late husband and is very precious to me."

"I will go and look, my lady," Eleanor promised. She rode out in the late afternoon with two squires, as the winter sun hung low in the sky, searching the verges and the muddy paths for any glint of gold along the track beside the river, but to no avail.

"For certain someone will find it, my Lady," she reassured the Countess on her return, but as the weeks went by hope faded into acceptance that it was lost, despite repeated searches.

Christmas was a muted affair without the king and queen but the household did their best to entertain and cheer the sickly Prince through the dark days of winter. Snow fell on the high peaks, filling the gullies in deep drifts, while on the lower slopes sleet and rain lashed down and the cold North wind whistled over the castle ramparts, funnelling down the draughty corridors of the old stone fortress chilling the occupants to the bone. Wrapped in furs, huddled beside blazing fires the little Prince coughed and wheezed as his nurse mopped his fevered brow. Numerous physicians and herbalists were called to impart their knowledge in the hope of a cure but as the monochrome colours of winter warmed with the approach of Spring, optimism faded as Edward's health deteriorated.

In London Richard had been busy with his first Parliament, which met in late January 1484. The bill confirming Richard's right to the crown in place of his illegitimate nephew was ratified in the *Titulus Regis* and a number of reforms were put in place, including the abolition of the late king Edward's 'benevolences', changes in the bail system and refinements of legal practice, resulting in a fairer system of justice for all, regardless of rank or position, which would no longer be open to widespread abuse by those in authority. Richard created a special Council to hear complaints and requests from the poorer classes, not able to resort to legal means.

Now based in London, Richard needed to ensure his Northern power base continued to function in his absence. He established the Council of the North, covering Yorkshire, Cumberland and Westmorland, led by John De La Pole, the Earl of Lincoln. The Earl of Northumberland, who was also a member, continued to have jurisdiction over his sprawling Earldom and the Wardenship of the Scots marches. Arising from his preoccupation with chivalric ideals and aspirations, Richard also founded the College of Arms, no doubt reflecting his keen interest in heraldry and the recording of ancestral lineage, which he felt would instil pride, identity and loyalty in the many noble families that made up his realm.

After the Parliament session ended, Richard had another problem to solve. Edward's queen Elizabeth was still in sanctuary at Westminster. Parliament had deprived her of her property but allowing her to stay in sanctuary where she could secretly plot rebellion was not advisable. Richard signed an oath in public to protect and provide for her daughters and herself if they would come out; a remarkably lenient concession, considering the actions of the former queen in plotting against him and even promising the hand of her eldest daughter in marriage to Henry Tudor.

However, Elizabeth, secretly in receipt of Richard's assurance about the safety of her sons, surprisingly agreed to her brother-in-law's request and immediately wrote to her son, the Marquis of Dorset, in France, urging him to return and make peace with Richard. Dorset attempted an escape to England but was discovered and returned to the watchful care of Tudor's Lancastrian allies.

Since Buckingham's rebellion, the rumours that the sons of Edward IV were dead persisted but would not be publicly denied by Richard, as being the best way to keep them safe from kidnap, despite the damage it did to his reputation. If word got out that they were in hiding, they would immediately become a target for either a Yorkist attempt to reinstate their legitimacy, ignoring

Richard's struggle to uphold the law, or a Lancastrian backed attack on their lives. If news of their existence reached Henry Tudor, his dubitable claim to the throne through marriage to their sister Elizabeth, in seeking to gain support for his usurpation by uniting the two factions, would be nullified. Tudor needed the sons of Edward IV to be dead, in order for his unlawful claim to be seen as justifiable.

Tiring of the stifling and crowded streets of London, Richard and Anne moved North towards Nottingham, where they could find time to relax a little and Richard could enjoy the occasional hunt. The towering castle atop its prominent rock would also be more centrally sited should an invasion become imminent. Edward IV had made extensive alterations and additions to the old fortress, adding new defences and state apartments, of which the king and queen now made use. Since Buckingham's rebellion, following quickly as it did on the failed attempt on her husband's life, Anne felt safer the further North she stayed, Nottingham being only a few days journey from Middleham and the Prince of Wales. She was concerned that Richard had already faced insurrection in the South and was amazed at his calmness and determination to rule justly and fairly, come what may.

One evening as they retired, Anne shrieked in fear as a large spider descended from the bed canopy onto the sheet. Richard calmly picked up the offending creature, took it to the casement and gently laid it on the sill, where it scuttled through a crack beneath the frame.

"You're not afraid of anything, are you Richard?" Anne commented admiringly as her husband laughed.

"Not of creatures that cannot hurt me, nay, but I *am* afraid for those I love and for the duty I owe my people. I am afraid I will let them down or fail to protect them." He sat down on the bed and stared at the floor.

"You will not fail us my Lord, you are loved and respected," Anne tried to reassure him, sliding across the bed and laying her arm across his shoulder.

"Maybe in the North, yes but dissent is ever present. Look at Buckingham – who'd have thought?" his voice trailed off.

"*And* Lord Hastings!" Anne added.

"Yes, damn him! Despite what is being said, I'm not made of stone, Anne. He forced me to make an example of him so as not to appear weak but now I have to live with it. My heart tells me I acted in haste but my head argues I had no choice.

"You *had* no choice, Richard. Edward would have done the same in your shoes."

"Yes, you are right Anne, he would," Richard agreed, appreciative of his wife's support, "but he never allowed guilt to get in the way of expediency. Contrition was not in Edward's nature," Richard took a deep breath, "but it takes courage to do the right thing."

"There's a fine line between courage and recklessness, Richard."

"Hmph!," Richard nodded and smiled ruefully. "Yes, caution was not one of Edward's strong points!" As he pulled off his shirt, Anne kissed his bare shoulder before a bout of coughing rendered her breathless and she fell back exhausted onto the pillow.

Perhaps I am not so different as I would wish to be, Richard reflected, as he snuffed out the candle and lay, staring into the darkness, a comforting arm cradling his enfeebled wife.

The king and queen were just adjusting to their new elevated status and starting to enjoy the privileges of royalty when in early April their world fell apart. Tragic news reached them from Middleham, plunging the king and queen into deep and agonised mourning. Edward, Prince of Wales, Richard and Anne's only heir and hope for the future of their dynasty, had died. The Prince had made it through the long winter but his frail body was weakened and any reserves of resistance depleted. His nurse had come to rouse him from his bed one morning to find him cold and lifeless, his bloodless pallor alike to the grey, doom-laden sky cloaking the vale outside. Panic ensued and the castle descended into deep despair; the cheerless stone walls echoing with lamentation and weeping as a messenger was dispatched in urgent haste to the king and queen. The monks from nearby Coverham Abbey, the Premonstratensian monastery a short distance from Middleham, came to take the child's body away, carefully wrapping it in a shroud and placing it in a temporary resting place until a tomb could be made. The Countess was inconsolable, the Prince's carers distraught that the heir to the throne had perished under their charge.

Richard and Anne crumpled into broken hearted despair when they learned of their son's death, Nottingham's gloomy old fortress only serving to highlight their sorrow, so painful to them that a chronicler would later write: '*You might have seen his father and mother in a state almost bordering on madness by reason of their sudden grief*'. Anne was not able to bear any more children and the Realm was now without an heir. If Richard died, who would succeed him? His kingdom needed an heir. Only Edward Duke of Warwick remained as the Duke of Clarence's next in line but he was still a minor, still under his father's attainder and his mental calibre was doubtful. England did not need another Henry VI and the resulting power struggles between retainers.

In May, after a brief stop at York to offer prayers for their son, the king and queen returned to Middleham. They entered the castle quietly, as if any undue noise would disrespect their dead son, murmuring in hushed tones to the servants, rarely speaking except to enquire with the nurse how Edward had died. Eleanor glimpsed Richard briefly and was shocked at his pallor and countenance. He seemed to have aged years, his face drawn and lined, his eyes, like Anne's, red from weeping, his black mourning clothes accentuating his pale features and slight physique. Eleanor's heart went out to them, appreciating the anguish and torment of losing a child, made even more wretched by the fact he could not be replaced. Anne had been unable to conceive since her only son's birth and her failing health impacted on her fertility. All their nurturing, tutoring and preparation for England's Prince of Wales, their only hope and vision for the future of the dynasty, gone to waste. The semi-round tower on the South east corner of the castle, where Edward had played and slept, now locked and empty, cold and dark, his clothes folded neatly on the coffer, topped by a child sized coronet, his grief-stricken parents unable to enter the rooms where their precious son had lived and died.

Eleanor sank to her knees in a deep curtsey and offered her heartfelt condolences to the king and queen. She could not look at Richard directly, for fear of losing her composure, she did not want those grief-laden eyes looking back at her reaching into her soul. She still loved him and knew it would show in her face. The urge to hold him in a comforting embrace had to be repressed. She could not permit her own feelings of pity to come to the fore at a time like this and intrude into his pain, especially so now he was king of England. *King of England!* She could hardly take it in. He was so far distanced from her now, a chasm of class between them so wide that it could never again be bridged.

Richard rode over to Coverham Abbey to see his son's body and to arrange for a suitable monument and resting place. He spent many hours with the monks in prayer and discussion, searching his faith for God's will in his torment before riding back in the rain, a wretched figure in black, water dripping from his hat, mingling imperceptibly with his tears. *Is this God's judgement* he questioned himself, *for assuming my nephew's throne?* Later he rode over to Nappa Hall to speak with Thomas and James Metcalfe, who had offered their assistance in arranging for his son's burial. Richard needed to commission a tomb and settle on a final resting place befitting a Prince upon whom all their hopes for the future had been founded.

Eleanor and the ladies in waiting tried to comfort and commiserate with the queen, who seemed utterly crushed by her son's death, her sunken eyes and ghostly white countenance accentuated by her unforgiving black mourning gown. Nobody laughed or engaged in animated chatter for fear of appearing disrespectful. They tried to encourage Anne to eat, plying her with sweetmeats and delicacies but nothing tempted her. Isabella overheard Richard reflecting on the events that had turned their lives upside down, unwittingly propelling them to sovereignty and how quickly elation had turned to despair.

"It is so sad," she whispered to Eleanor as they left Anne's chamber. "I heard King Richard questioning whether their son's death was divine retribution for him assuming the throne, poor man. Who could have predicted king Edward dying so soon and his sons disentitled because of his father's bigamy?"

"The king had no choice, did he? He was the next adult in line after the Princes. What else could he have done?" Eleanor debated sadly at the thought of Richard blaming himself and the unjust aspersions that were already flying around amongst his traducers.

To distract himself, in the coming weeks Richard joined the hunting party and was gone for hours. He had imported some new birds and thoroughbred horses, which he had invited his friends to try out, competing with him for the best catch. However, on returning he appeared distracted, retiring early, not wishing to participate in social niceties. Anne and the Countess kept to themselves, sharing their grief, clinging to their faith and attempting to understand God's will in their tragedy.

Eleanor overheard the Countess repining woefully to her daughter. "It was an omen. I knew when I lost my jewel it was a portent of ill fortune." There was nothing Anne could suggest that would gainsay her mother's belief.

Eleanor noticed Richard looking at Elizabeth, now nearly 15 and on the threshold of womanhood, her rosy cheeked complexion and warm honeyed highlights in her hair reflecting her mother's genes; her soft, smoke-tinted eyes and well-proportioned features revealing her father's Plantagenet roots. Richard accepted she would not lack admirers. He spoke with her to ask after her wellbeing and happiness. She was delighted that the king had conversed and showed interest in her, commenting to her mother that he was handsome.

"He seems to like me!" Bess beamed, unknowingly firing an arrow of guilt into her mother's conscience. *I must tell her soon,* Eleanor concluded reluctantly, recognising that Bess was nearing the age she herself had been when she had first met Richard and fallen in love with him and for certain, her fair daughter would soon be attracting interest from the young men training in the tilt yard.

Richard did not have the luxury of indulging in private grief. The charge of kingship held many an obligation, regardless of personal circumstance. In May he received the Silesian ambassador of the Holy Roman Emperor Frederick III, who was duly impressed by his host's hospitality, generosity and courtesy, despite the tragedy which had so recently befallen him. The envoy enjoyed the lavish feasting laid on in his honour and was humbled by the king's gift of a golden necklace and newly pressed gold coins. Later, when attending mass at church, Richard's guest was enchanted by the angelic voices of the choir, the like of which, he wrote, surpassed anything he had ever heard. For Richard, wiping away a single tear tracking unbidden down his cheek at the sweet sound of the young boys singing he had always loved to hear, it now only served to emphasise his own loss.

The king had further business to attend to in the North. The queen, it was decided, who was herself not in the best of health, would join him later. He left Middleham and travelled to Barnard Castle, Durham, Scarborough, Pontefract, York and Sheriff Hutton, where he had established the Council of the North. Mindful of the continued French threat, Richard established a large fleet at Scarborough and by September had signed a three-year truce with Scotland, after which he returned to London, where Anne joined him for the Christmas festivities.

For the king and queen, still mourning the loss of their son, the feasting and entertainment laid on at Court were an ordeal to be endured but appearances had to be maintained. Anne, despite her worsening health, did her best to make merry and show generosity to Elizabeth, late king Edward's eldest daughter, now out of sanctuary. The twenty-one-year-old Elizabeth, beautiful like her mother, with long rose-hued blonde hair, her father's eyes and classic features, was happy to be back at her uncle's court, enjoying the feasting and finery. The queen, in her kindness to the young lady who now bore the stigma of illegitimacy, dressed her niece in a gown of the same colour and design as her own. The contrast between the two women could not have been more pronounced. Pale, delicate, grief-laden Anne, coughing into her handkerchief, painfully thin, her sunken eyes dissimulating her sorrow behind a mask of mock cheerfulness, barely eating, next to her the healthily, blossoming young girl, dancing so gracefully, her hair shimmering like spun gold, her sapphire eyes sparkling in the candlelight, her smile lighting up the room. Elizabeth, enjoying the attention, was happily aware that many young men at court desired her and many young women aspired to be like her, despite her loss of status.

Rumours, as always, were rife and the obvious admiration young Elizabeth had for her uncle the king set tongues wagging that

Richard would hasten his wife's demise in order to marry her. Richard sat gloomily beside his ailing queen, his mind full of the endless problems and threats he still had to face, not the least of which was the Welsh nonentity Henry Tudor waiting just across the sea to snatch the throne of England, and with it the hand of his niece, now smiling provocatively at him.

Distractedly fidgeting with the rings on his slim fingers, pausing only to take a long draught of wine from his golden goblet, the music and pageantry of the scene before him fading into a blur of sound and colour, Richard felt numb, his mind wandering back to the soft green valley and fresh Yorkshire air of his home, where his son, his passport for the future of the House of York, now lay cold and silent in eternal darkness. Beside him his frail wife, gaunt and ghostly white, attempting unsuccessfully to disguise her grief and failing health with a feigned smile. Richard knew it may not be long before this gentle lady joined her sister in an early grave.

As the new year dawned, the king was kept busy preparing for an invasion which, he had just heard from his spies in France, was confirmed for late summer. With the spectre of war again hanging over him, Richard was before long confronted with the tragedy he had lately feared, the not wholly unexpected death of his stricken queen. Anne's mortally contagious condition had deteriorated rapidly since Christmas and the doctors forbade Richard to share her chamber. In March 1485, on the day of an eclipse as the sun went dark, Anne died and with her the last remaining light out of Richard's life. The second fragile daughter of the Earl of Warwick had joined her sister and her only child in Heaven. Richard was alone. His father, his three brothers, his only legitimate son and now his wife, all dead.

Richard's grief was there for all to see. At Anne's funeral in Westminster Abbey he wept openly, unable to hold back the agony of his loss from the eyes of the congregation. *How has it come to this? Why has God decreed this wretchedness for me?* He wondered desolately. *How have I gained the highest estate in the land, yet have lost everything?*

Immediately the rumour mill began again with the resurrection of the story that Richard would now wed his niece Elizabeth to prevent Henry Tudor from marrying her. Although Richard would have been gratified to thwart Tudor's plans by such a charade, in truth he had no wish to marry the girl and the prospect of the resulting scandal so soon after his wife's death forced him to issue a public denial and send his niece off to Sheriff Hutton to be out of the limelight. Instead, Richard had begun negotiations with Portugal for a marriage between himself and the king's older sister, Princess Joanna, who was herself a great granddaughter of John of Gaunt.

Richard needed an heir to replace his son and an alliance with the Portuguese Princess would unite the houses of Lancaster and York, which was precisely Henry Tudor's aim. Richard was satisfied the safety of his nephews was secured with a plan to send them to the Low Countries, although Edward's state of health was a pressing concern as despite his doctor's repeated administrations his condition had deteriorated. He would need to be cared for and it may be prudent to separate the boys. Firstly, however, Richard had to deal with the imminent threat from the Lancastrian pretender.

A forlorn and solitary figure, hunched disconsolately over his desk awash with the documents of State, bereft of the comfort of his family, the young king reflected on his life and the misfortune that had dogged his short reign, his prayers to God for guidance so far unheeded.

Would his troubles never cease?

Chapter Twenty

ICHARD COULD NOT BE SEEN to succumb to private despair. He was the king, his Realm was under threat of invasion, yet internally a deep-seated schism still dissected the nobility, dividing loyalties and families. His people now more than ever needed strong leadership and direction but whether he could count on the faithfulness of the peerage with their disparate agendas would remain to be seen. Nevertheless, he *had* to believe he could. Basing himself once more at Nottingham, in order to have a more central position from which to operate, Richard busied himself with preparations, securing loans and sending out letters to all commissioners of array to ensure troops were equipped and ready at short notice. Wherever Tudor would decide to invade, as invade he would before the end of the coming year, the kingdom needed to be watchful, alert and united in a common cause to protect her shores from foreign violation.

In tranquil Wensleydale, the news of Anne's death came as another terrible blow to the household. The Countess shut herself away to pray and grieve alone. The loss of both her daughters, her husband, her grandchild, together with her inheritance, which had been divided up between her sons-in-law, had left her heartbroken and destitute. By Richard's kindness she was able to stay at Middleham, but he was now king, far from home and unlikely to return any time soon. The threat of war was looming and more young men would die. *If the worst happened and Richard was deposed, what would happen to her?* the Countess worried. Her grandson Edward, Earl of Warwick was living at Sheriff Hutton under the care of John de la Pole, the Earl of Lincoln, Richard's nephew. However, George's son was slow witted, still under his father's attainder and therefore not considered eligible or able enough to inherit the throne after Richard.

Eleanor's brothers had already left Middleham to join the king. They had seemed upbeat as she bid them adieu, confident that a small force of French mercenaries was no match for Richard's superior numbers. They were both married now. Edward, who had inherited his Aunt Mabel's farm, had a young son and James's wife was carrying their first child. Eleanor and her sisters-in-law were able to share their concerns and joys in mutual understanding of the love they held for their brothers and husbands. As always, when soldiers were summoned to fight, was the nagging fear that they would in all probability not return. Battle was ferocious, cruel and bloody and even if you survived, your injuries may only be a precursor to unavoidable death. Many a young wife was propelled into widowhood before her time, as Eleanor well knew.

Eleanor did her best to help the Countess come to terms with her bereavement. They packed away Anne's clothes and jewels, ready for Richard when he returned. Eleanor listened to the Countess describing her daughters in their youth, all the plans and hopes she had cherished for them and how in the end she could not protect them from God's will. She thanked Eleanor too for Elizabeth's friendship with her grandson as he succumbed to his illness and surprised her with a revelation.

"Anne knew, Eleanor," the Countess remarked casually when they were alone. Eleanor looked up startled and stopped folding a silk gown into a capacious wooden coffer.

"Knew? My lady?"

"She knew Elizabeth was Richard's. I think she had known for a long time."

"Oh… I am so sorry my lady," Eleanor attempted to recall a time when Anne might have guessed, or perhaps heard it from Richard. "She ne'er spoke of it." Eleanor said sadly, remembering Anne's kindness and regretting her own deception.

"Nay, that wasn't her way," The Countess assured her. "She did not begrudge you, Eleanor. She knew Richard had fathered his two natural children, John and Katherine, before they were wed, for whom he cared and provided and she was pleased he could see Elizabeth grow up at Middleham. Anne liked you, Eleanor, she understood. Richard was a good-looking youth and many a young maid would have been tempted."

"I hope she could forgive me, my lady," Eleanor replied sorrowfully, humiliated that Anne had known all along and now she could not apologise to her or ask her forgiveness. Poor sweet Anne, she must have loved Richard so much!

"For certain, she would have forgiven you both, Eleanor. Anne never held a grudge, even when her father bade her marry Eduard of Lancaster and the Duke of Clarence hid her from Richard."

Eleanor found herself thinking about love and how it manifested itself in diverse ways. Most intense was the all-encompassing love she had tasted with Richard, that physical attraction, adoration of character, obsession, blindness to faults and togetherness of soul she knew she would not feel again. She had felt pure animal lust, the compelling magnetic attraction and unquenchable desire she had experienced with Phillipe, but meaningless when contrasted with the fondness, tender companionship and contentment of the gentle love she felt for Will. Above all ranked the most spiritual, pure, enduring, unconditional love – the unbreakable bond of motherhood she had with her children, Elizabeth, William and her deceased infant daughter. She concluded she was fortunate to have sampled love in its many guises and bade herself be content with her lot and not want for more.

That night Eleanor prayed for Anne, for the Countess, for herself, her children and for Richard. This noble family's fortunes were perpetually linked with hers, not only through her livelihood but through the father of her child, who's blood was his and she would join with their laughter, tears and ultimately their destiny, suffering their losses or delighting in their joy.

The Countess decided that the beautifully illustrated book about her father Richard Beauchamp that she had commissioned for the Prince of Wales should now go to her grandson Edward of Warwick, Isobel's son, who was still at Sheriff Hutton, along with his sister. She wrote to the Earl to ask if she could pay him a visit and was delighted to receive an invitation.

"I have had an invitation from the Earl and Countess of Lincoln at Sheriff Hutton to visit my grandson. I wonder if you would like to accompany me Eleanor?" Anne Beauchamp asked Eleanor one afternoon as she re-read the letter. She had decided that her hard-working maidservant would benefit from a change of scene to lift her spirits.

"You may bring Elizabeth and William too, of course. There are other Royal children there," she added.

"Oh, aye my Lady, I should like that very much, thank you," Eleanor beamed. She eagerly packed for herself, the children and the Countess. Despite her 31 years, Eleanor had never left Wensleydale and, together with her daughter and little William, was excited at the prospect of seeing Sheriff Hutton Castle and journeying away from Middleham.

A few days later, on a bright clear mid-June day, the party set out for Ripon, with a small group of attendants, a baggage cart and several guards, stopping for the night at Markenfield Hall, the home of Sir Thomas Markenfield, High Sheriff of Yorkshire and his wife Lady Eleanor. They spent a pleasant evening at the Hall, dining informally with their hosts, before resuming their journey to Sheriff Hutton the next morning.

Sheriff Hutton Castle, built by John Neville at the end of the 14th Century, a square stone edifice of Yorkshire stone with four substantial towers dominating each corner, stood on high ground surrounded by wooded parkland, its prominent position affording far reaching views over the Vale of York. As they approached, a grand gatehouse opened into a large courtyard overlooked by the Great Hall, Chapel and guest accommodation. Richard's Council of the North, which occasionally met here, was presided over by John de la Pole, under whose care several Royal children were safely harboured a good distance from the capital. On their arrival the visitors were welcomed by their hosts who after directing them to the guest quarters, accompanied them on a tour of the castle and its extensive grounds.

Eleanor caught sight of king Edward's 19-year-old daughter Elizabeth, as she played a game in the gardens, with her cousin Edward of Warwick. She had recently come up from Court to be removed from the spotlight and focus of rumour mongers who had tried to insinuate a scandalous union between herself and Richard.

Eleanor could quite see how this beautiful vivacious maiden with her shining blue eyes and rose gold hair could turn any man's head, like her mother before her. Eleanor wondered how she must feel, plunged into the indignity of illegitimacy, no longer entitled to be called Princess, most eligible female in the land. She learned that Richard was negotiating a possible marriage for Elizabeth to Manuel, Duke of Beja, a far superior match than her status now warranted, if for no other reason than to prevent Henry Tudor from benefitting from her hand, should his invasion be successful. *Pray God that will never happen* thought Eleanor, as a spontaneous shudder convulsed her. Should Tudor succeed, Richard's death was a certainty.

Since Anne's death, Richard had sent his natural son John to Sheriff Hutton to join the other Royal children domiciled there but Eleanor learned he had recently left to take up his first position as Captain of Calais. Eleanor wondered about Richard's younger bastard daughter Katherine and if she resembled her own Elizabeth and what their mothers were like, although she tried to put out of her mind, images that would arouse her jealousy. Eleanor had to admit Richard was a young man when he left Middleham, all those years ago and it was inevitable he would be tempted to explore his sexuality with the young ladies of Court, who would have been flattered by the attentions of this prepossessing young Duke.

THEY HAD NOT been at Sheriff Hutton for more than a couple of days when Richard arrived unexpectedly from Nottingham on a brief visit to the Council of the North. Eleanor's heart leapt as she saw him dismount in the yard, enter the castle and climb the steps to his apartments, his black mourning attire contrasting starkly against his pale skin. He looked pained, drawn and mentally fatigued, his brow creased with care, his shoulders hunched wearisomely and he appeared to be in some discomfort from his ride. Eleanor wondered if the weakness in his back had worsened, however if it had, he masked his impairment well, as he arose refreshed the next morning and she saw him in the bailey wielding a heavy battle axe quickly and skilfully. She watched him with admiration, tinged with a sadness and fear for what he would shortly need to face, the fate of England resting on his agile young shoulders. *How can he bear this burden?* she pondered sorrowfully.

The young squires stopped their sword play to watch him, the accomplished soldier and leader they admired, now their king, his lean figure belying the strength within. The king offered to spar with one of the older youths, who readily agreed at the opportunity to learn from him as they clashed and parried, sweat dripping off their faces, until a blow from Richard knocked the weapon from the youth's hand, the point of the king's blade hovering inches from the lad's neck. Richard congratulated his young opponent on his swordplay, gripping his shoulder in an encouraging grasp prompting smiles and applause all round, their joviality concealing the dread within. They all knew it may not be long before their skills would be put to the ultimate test in deadly combat on the battlefield but with their fearless warrior king to lead them, they felt cheered, emboldened and inspired. Thoughts of defeat were dispelled by their king's approval and at this moment victory appeared beyond doubt for these novice soldiers.

The meal in the great hall that evening was a more lavish affair now that the king was amongst them. The Earl and Countess of Lincoln sat at the top table next to Richard, who listened politely to his hosts' conversation but his eyes were blank and he did not smile. Eleanor noticed Elizabeth of York glancing up at him admiringly trying to catch his eye but he avoided his niece's gaze. It could not be noted that he offered her any encouragement no matter how innocent, scandalmongers being quick to seize on any look or word which could be made to add up to more than its worth. The talk at table had been all about the coming invasion, the number of loyal retainers they could rely on from the North and the likely landing place the aggressor would choose. Amongst the guests was the Duke of Northumberland, having been summoned to attend the Council. He appeared sullen and brooding, occasionally surveying Richard contemptuously, his dispassionate expression barely disguising a desire to be elsewhere, his disgruntlement at having relinquished much of his Northern jurisdiction to Richard, never having diminished.

Later that evening, after the tables had been cleared away and the guests retired, Eleanor glimpsed Richard sitting, lost in thought, staring vacantly through the open casement, where the warm summer sky held the twilight in timeless suspension. *He looks so alone,* she thought. He was the last of his line, all his brothers dead, his wife and his only legitimate son dead. He must have thought God was punishing him for something. *How could one person shoulder all this grief?* Eleanor wondered sadly. The Earl and Countess tried to cheer him but his melancholy seemed to drain the life and soul out of their disconsolate guest.

When Eleanor took a supper of wine and bread to her hosts, Richard was pouring over dispatches. He spoke to the Earl and Countess to answer briefly but otherwise appeared remote and detached. Eleanor noticed them exchanging anxious glances as he gazed despondently into space, their attempts at polite intercourse unheeded. She longed to hold him close, offer words of solace, feel again the warmth of his body next to hers, that familiarity she had missed so much. Her chance was to come sooner than expected.

The following evening sat alone after the household had retired, Richard appeared to relax a little. A summer storm had cooled the air and a fire had been lit to warm the night-time chill. Informally dressed in a loose white silk shirt and hose, seated at a desk absorbed in papers Richard looked up and smiled warmly when Eleanor entered the chamber.

"Eleanor, how are you? Pray stay with me a while. I should be glad of your company."

"Of course, your Grace. I am quite well, thank you." Eleanor curtsied and stood waiting for his command. As she took in his pleasing classical profile, slim figure and toned physique, that surge of attraction she had first felt for this enigmatic nobleman so long ago, came flooding back. His shirt falling open at the neck down to his chest and close-fitting hose hugging his lower body, gave him an undertone of dormant sensuality of which he was quite unaware but which now reawakened Eleanor's long suppressed craving for him. Far from diminishing his appeal, maturity had sculpted his features and physique, enhancing his masculinity to the point where Eleanor had to steel herself not to want to throw herself at him. Silently possessing him with her eyes it was as much as she could do to register his words. He read her hesitancy as courtesy for his status.

"Pray be seated Eleanor, no need to address me formally." He wanted her to treat him as an equal and not be in his thrall. As she sat down on the settle, he handed her a goblet of rich Claret.

"How are you enjoying your stay here at Sheriff Hutton?" he asked politely.

"Very much, thank you," Eleanor smiled, "and Elizabeth loves it here," she added.

"She has grown into an alluring young woman, Eleanor. How old is she now?" he enquired somewhat sadly, as he twisted the stem of his bejewelled wine glass in his fingers, the flickering fire glare reflecting off the rings he wore, dancing in shafts of light shimmering like stars.

"She has just turned 16, your Gr... er, Richard," Eleanor corrected herself, uncomfortably aware of his position and unsure of the familiarity of her address.

"We should find her a husband. There are plenty of young men who would be glad to wed her," Richard commented. He seemed distracted and distant.

"Aye, I am sure of it," Eleanor paused, equally unfocused, not quite knowing what else to say. Somehow though, it mattered not. They had a bond of familiarity that had never quite been forgotten. The king and his one-time lover sat silently for a few minutes, as the cinders fizzed in the grate and the liquor numbed their senses. Richard broke the silence, gazing into the glowing embers, speaking his thoughts out loud.

"I am so alone, Eleanor," he sighed. Eleanor's heart skipped a beat that he should be so candid with her.

"The burden of kingship is hard enough but to carry on without..." his voice trailed off as the words choked in his throat. He raised his hand to cover his face as tears sprang in his eyes.

"I am truly sorry, Richard. I understand..." Eleanor struggled to find words of solace but he continued as if she had not spoken.

"I've lost everyone I love, my wife, my child, my father, all my brothers; I have no heir and now my enemies are snapping at my heels. Have I been so wicked that God punishes me so?" he gave voice to his thoughts with rising anger, slamming the goblet down, spattering red droplets over a pile of letters on the desk.

"Oh Richard, you are not wicked, your people love you… I love…" she stopped, remembering her place but he seemed not to notice.

He got up and rested his head on his arm against the chimney breast, staring into the smouldering remains of the fire, shaking with emotion, words too long held back spilling from him in a tide of repressed suffering.

"I've tried to do everything expected of me, keep the country together, address injustice, reward loyalty, punish treachery, protect the innocent but *still* good fortune eludes me. Men in whom I put my faith and fealty have betrayed me. I have been falsely accused of the most-foul murder, labelled a usurper, my good intentions misrepresented, all my motives misconstrued." He took a laboured breath, his voice cracking with emotion.

"If I show weakness, I will be crushed, if I show strength, I will be condemned for it. Is it not enough that my enemies are at the door, my family lost, my kingdom imperilled, everything I cherished trampled in the dust? What more does God want of me? Mon Dieu! How has it come to this?"

He started to weep quietly at first but then yielding to suppressed despair, his tears, so long held back burst forth in a torrent, his shoulders shaking as deep sobs consumed his body. Eleanor could not bear to see him in such distress. She stood up and moved closer, unsure if she should be so familiar with her sovereign but yearning to comfort him.

"Richard…" she whispered, laying her hand gently on his arm.

He turned abruptly at her touch, grabbing her zealously around the waist, pulling her to him, enfolding his arms around her like a young boy craving succour. Catching her breath, surprised at his impulsive response, she nevertheless returned his embrace readily, part of her desperately wanting to absorb his pain, to expunge it willingly, to do her duty of love for her king and part of her aching to show her love for the man she adored. He clung to her, burying his head on her shoulder and cried like a child, pouring out all the hurt and anger of his pent-up grief. Eleanor wept too, the joy of holding him close once again tempered with the wretchedness of his despair was almost more than her heart could withstand, as the tide of repressed feelings came flooding back.

"Oh Richard, my love, I am here, let me help you," she entreated, struggling to contain her own emotion.

She held him tenderly until his sobs subsided and he raised his face to hers, his vision blurred, his lips salty with tears, now pressed hard onto her mouth in a kiss of impassioned yearning. Trembling with the fervency of her desire, Eleanor responded readily, her long withheld devotion liberated once more, as she was instantly transported back to that evening on the hill. At last, she was a teenager again, melting in the arms of her young man, full of the first exuberance of innocent youth, as the years of unrequited love fell away. This was no fantasy, no intangible dream. This man was real, palpable and corporeal. He was warm, sentient and responsive and he was here with her. How she had hungered for this moment!

"Lie with me Eleanor and comfort me tonight," he breathed ardently as he clung to her, "I need you". Her heart leapt. *Did he really need to ask? Did he not know she had spent every waking moment reliving their union?*

She followed him into his bedchamber, holding him close as they lay on the bed, his head resting on her breast, as fresh tears ran down his cheeks. Soon he slept while she lay awake, listening to his breathing as she had done with Will, stroking his hair, watching his chest rise and fall, his noble features for once relaxed, serene, lit by the palest glow of moonlight filtering through the casement. She lay quite still, holding the man she loved, had loved for half a lifetime, would always love until her dying day, fearful lest this longed-for union was just an illusion and any sudden movement would dispel the mirage and shatter the dream.

Later, in the dark and still of the night, Richard awoke and started to kiss her again, intensely and more ardently as she reciprocated, their mouths devouring each other hungrily; the years of pain and anguish dropping away as Eleanor gave herself to him, body and soul, entwining her limbs with his, trembling with the ecstasy of total submission. At last, here was her chance to show him how much she loved him. Not as a naïve maiden, unsullied, unsure of herself; no, now she was a woman, a woman who knew the power of her charms and how to use them to please a man, not just any man but the man who had lived in her heart for 16 long years. The fire within her burned so intense it took her breath away and she was lost, consumed by him, fused into one being. No longer sovereign and subject, simply a man and a woman, flesh against flesh, he was hers and hers alone in this moment. Nobody could take that from her.

"My beautiful Eleanor," he breathed, his face deep in her hair.

"Oh, Richard you are my one true love. I am yours, only ever yours," she gasped.

Gone was the clumsy fresh-faced youth of 16, here was a grown man, mature, strong and sensuous, an exemplar of knighthood, dutiful, courageous and constant, an embodiment of rugged masculinity, handsome and virile, desirable and responsive yet also deep and discerning. Eleanor knew that despite his physical presence, she could not quite reach to the inner recesses of this impenetrable man's psyche; part of his inner self would always be hidden from her but the fact he was here with her in the flesh was enough. Her fingers stroked the taut muscles on his neck and forearms, expanded and sculpted by years of wielding heavy weaponry, reminding her of the conflict he had faced and what he would still have to face. Every nerve in her body ached for his touch, responded to his every move as they made love.

From the urgency of his passion, she sensed he had not lain with a woman for some time. She thought of poor frail Anne, slipping away without him beside her, forbidden by doctors to share his bed, as her illness took hold. She envisaged him sitting alone amongst the deeds and rolls of State, the burden of his position weighing heavily, as his wife was dying. She pictured his solitary figure weeping at her tomb in the Abbey, a broken man weighed down by obligation and duty, enduring relentless physical pain, utterly desolate, forsaken by all except his God and even *He* seemed to be looking the other way.

When he slept again, Eleanor lay awake, her whole being alert, bathed in the euphoria of their shared union, reliving the rapture of requited love, although her joy was fleeting, ethereal and bittersweet. A nagging dread told her this may be the last night she would share with him, the thought of which was almost too painful to contemplate. Richard was in the prime of life, the most marriageable widower in Europe with the crown of England poised to adorn the head of its new queen. Eleanor knew he would have to marry again, to provide an heir but without his beloved family around him, the loneliness of his position would be burdensome. She kissed his forehead tenderly, gently brushing his hair from across his face, luxuriating in his body warmth, delighting in the thrill of his skin against hers and willing time to stand still. She wanted these treasured moments to last forever.

Laying her head gently against his chest, she could hear his heartbeat, feel his blood coursing through his veins; blood that had percolated down from the great Plantagenet kings, blood now giving their daughter life, blood that could shortly be spilled in the butchery of battle. Her lips moving soundlessly in prayer, she beseeched God to comfort this brave guardian of England, to give him strength and courage to bear the trials of what was to come, his enemies circling like vultures, keen-eyed for any sign of weakness. She prayed he would find happiness and love once more and that his enduring faith and devotion would at long last be rewarded. *Had he not suffered enough? Surely the good Lord would not desert him in his hour of need?*

In the morning when she awoke, he was gone. She lay hugging the sheets where he had slept, burying her face in the pillow, where his head had rested, breathing in the essence of him, reliving the passion they had shared, his touch, his kiss, his firm muscular frame, the familiar curve of his misaligned spine as she ran her fingers down his back, the imperfection in no way, detracting from his magnetic appeal, indeed only serving to increase her admiration for his fortitude and resolution. *Was it a dream?* Had she imagined him in the half light of dawn standing above her, whispering "*Adieu my lovely Eleanor*" and kissing her tenderly, taking one last look at her curvaceous figure, fresh complexion, soft lips, long eyelashes and silken copper tresses cascading over the pillow?

Later when Eleanor arose, she learned from the page with a sinking heart that the king had left for Nottingham again, accompanied by the Earl and his retainers. On the lid of an oak coffer at the foot of the bed lay a small silver badge cast in the image of a wild boar and a remnant of parchment. On it in Richard's neat hand was written: *'Thank you Eleanor, think of me, pray for me, R'*. Eleanor gazed at the totem. Would the fearless creature that had slain her gentle Will, now shield her first love from mortal peril?

Grasping the cherished symbol devotedly, she sank down on her knees beside the bed and prayed fervently, her tears running down her clenched fingers, dampening the coverlet, Richard's emblem digging into her palm, the pain in her heart eclipsing the stab of the angular metal. *Will I ever see him again?* she shuddered, quickly dismissing a thought too terrible to entertain. She knew, however, that no man would ever reach into her soul that way again. He had taken her to the gates of heaven and now his departure sent her crashing back to earth once more. *Why oh why, did he have to be king?* The cavernous gulf between them so exquisitely banished in the heat of the night, was once more in place; the door between them so invitingly opened, now firmly slammed shut.

Later that day Elizabeth came to show her mother a gift that had been left for her. A small prayer book, beautifully illustrated, wrapped in a parchment, on which was written *'For Elizabeth, may the Lord keep you.' Signed Ricardus Rex.' Loyaulte me lie.'*

"A gift from the king!" she exclaimed in astonishment.

"Keep it safe Bess," Eleanor wrestled with her conscience. Should I tell her? Nay, not yet. A better time will come. When Richard has defeated the invader and the Realm is at peace, then I will tell her she is her king's natural daughter.

"I will treasure it!" Elizabeth vowed, holding the book to her breast.

She sat down to read the prayers within but the Latin text was unfamiliar, so she hurried off to ask the priest to translate some of the devotions for her. Her mother watched her go with a heavy heart, knowing she must soon reveal the truth *but not just yet!* The secret she had jealously guarded for sixteen years could surely wait a little longer; a precious jewel hidden in the inner sanctum of her subconscious, away from prying eyes and the cold light of day.

Chapter Twenty One

N HIS RETURN TO NOTTINGHAM Castle Richard ordered the Great Seal to be brought to him. He sent Viscount Lovell to guard the port of Southampton against potential enemy incursions on the South Coast. Lord Stanley, meanwhile, had asked the king if he could return to his Lancastrian lands, to which Richard reluctantly agreed, providing he left his son, Lord Strange, as surety for his father's allegiance. A casual observer would surely have seen the prevaricating Stanley's motives as covertly suspect but Richard took his Constable at his word. Should Stanley turn traitor, however, they both knew his son would pay the price.

Richard had signed a treaty with Brittany to provide 1,000 archers in return for Henry Tudor and other rebels, but he had since learned that Henry Tudor had evaded captivity and escaped to France, no doubt tipped off by Bishop Morton, who was in touch with Henry's mother, Margaret Beaufort. She would have heard about the agreement from her husband, Lord Stanley, who was on Richard's Council. Tudor, now with French backing, was joined by John De Vere, Earl of Oxford, eager to settle his personal score with Richard, having himself escaped from Hammes Castle. This highly experienced soldier and commander, along with Henry and his mercenaries, sailed from Harfleur to England on 1st August 1485.

Six days later, Tudor's invasion force, numbering in the region of 5,000 men, landed at Milford Haven on the coast of Wales, marched North and then East. Sir Rhys ap Thomas, who had been tasked with guarding the coast against such a threat, betrayed his king and country by allowing the invader's armies to proceed unhindered through Wales, over the border towards the centre of England and the road to London. Many zealous Welshmen saw Henry Tudor as their new hope for a Welsh ruler, a new king Arthur, come to rid them of the oppression imposed on them by these warring English noblemen, and gladly swelled the invader's ranks along the way.

Richard had invited Lord Stanley to join him in Leicester, but the equivocal response that Stanley was 'suffering from sweating sickness' and could not attend heightened the king's suspicions as he spoke with his secretary.

"God's teeth, that man has shown his true colours!" Richard fumed, angrily banging the table with his fist. "Fetch Lord Strange John! We will see if he can vouch for his father's fidelity."

As his secretary bowed and left, Richard paced the floor, before seating himself dejectedly at the desk, absorbed in thought, turning his rings distractedly. When Kendall returned a short time later, he ushered in a terrified Lord Strange, supported by two guards.

"He has attempted an escape, your Grace," Kendall spoke tersely, barely masking his contempt as Lord Strange fell on his knees.

Richard observed the young man broodily for a moment, tapping his fingers on the table.

"Your life is apparently of as little worth to your father, as his king is to him," he snapped bitterly.

"Sire, my father has assured me of his fealty!" pleaded Strange pathetically, as Richard scoffed acerbically.

"Huh! I hear your Uncle William has gone over to Tudor!"

"I fear so, your Grace... b...b... but I assure you Sire, my father remains your true Lord."

"Mmm... That remains to be seen. Pray he does so, young man, for he wagers your life upon it."

Richard dismissed the trembling youth with a derisive gesture. As the guards left with their charge, Richard sat back in his seat, deflated and despondent, his anger dissipating at the sight of the forlorn young nobleman, so undervalued by his father.

"So Stanley reveals himself for the conniving snake he is," Richard sighed to himself as much as to his secretary. "The man cares so little for the life of his son that even a command from his king cannot divert his devious purpose," he muttered in disbelief, marvelling at this unfeeling lord's indifference to his offspring.

"Aye Sire, Lord Stanley has ever tacked to the prevailing wind."

"Hmm," Richard smiled wanly at the analogy "and when the storm hits, he scuttles to the nearest port!" He took a deep breath. "Indeed John, I've been a fool to trust him." Kendall silently agreed but would never admit so to his king.

"You cannot know the secrets of men's hearts, Sire," he supported.

"Would that I did though, John," Richard exhaled dismally. "T'would have saved much trouble."

Part of Richard could not help but entertain the vague hope that with Stanley's support the outcome could be decisive. Would this unscrupulous Northern baron really sacrifice his son, his own flesh and blood, for that of his undeserving stepson? Was the promise of advancement and accolades under a new king more than he could resist? This time Richard was not entirely convinced of the answer. It was an even wager but not one that he could afford to ignore. Fate would decide.

The king arrived in Leicester on 19th August, where he was joined by the Duke of Norfolk and, at the last minute, by the lagging Earl of Northumberland. Richard took with him a combined force of 10,000 men, outnumbering Tudor two to one, moving out of Leicester on 21st August to intercept the enemy forces before they joined the road South to London. However, the Stanleys had another 5,000 men, which would even the odds for Tudor if they changed sides. William Stanley had already been declared a traitor by Richard, so his choice to fight for Tudor was predetermined. Remaining doubtful of his own judgement, Richard surmised that, as he held his son, Thomas Stanley could not commit himself openly. It was not the first time Richard's trust had been his undoing.

The Royal army camped near Sutton Cheney, while Henry's forces advanced from Atherstone. Richard and his knights attended mass in the village church, where prayers were said for victory and for England. As night fell on the eve of battle, the two armies could see their enemy's fires glowing in the darkness, both sides dreadfully aware of the only two possible outcomes, defeat or victory, death or glory. Which would be their fate? Whatever the outcome, one thing was certain, many would lie dead or dying on this field before the sun dipped below the Western horizon once more.

Sleep deserted Richard. The feeling of dread lying like a lead weight in the pit of his stomach would not go away. He had felt it before on the eve of battle but with his revered brother at his side, victory had been all but assured. Now he faced his enemy alone and despite his loyal knights, the rank and file who made up the mass of his army were unseasoned and untried. He and his knights would have to lead by example, to turn the battle in their favour to ensure his troops were not discouraged. The fate of the nation hung on tomorrow's outcome; his own destiny resting in God's hands.

Richard scanned the pages of his Book of Hours, reciting the prayers he now knew by heart: *"I ask thee O most gentle Christ Jesus, to keep me and defend me from all evil and from my evil enemy and from all danger present, past and to come."* Pacing his tent distractedly, he stepped out into the cool summer night, staring up at the dark sky filled with a million stars, everlasting and eternal symbols of hope, the infinite wisdom of God, the insignificance of man and the promise of immortality. He prayed for his kingdom, his life, his faithful followers, his children, the souls of his departed family and that, in the hours to come, his courage and his God would not fail him.

Images flashed before him; his father Richard, Duke of York, whose head, together with that of his brother Edmund, had adorned the gates of York; his larger than life brother Edward, the *'Sunne in Splendour'*; incarnate, obdurate tragic George, whose ambition and jealousy cost him his life; their proud mother; gentle Anne, his frail, delicate wife; his cherished son; his brother's son, whose throne he had been compelled to take; the women he had loved, the children he had fathered. He saw the lush green pastures of Yorkshire, the high limestone crags of Wensleydale, the tumbling waterfalls, the forests where he hunted, the distant fells of Cumberland, the quiet meadows of Fotheringhay; places that would always be in his heart and soul; corners of blessed England that had shaped and nurtured him.

The faces of men who had died at his command haunted him, Rivers, Hastings, Buckingham, traitors who had forced his hand through their duplicity, men he had trusted and relied upon. He thought of his brother's children plucked from the highest estate to the ignominy of illegitimacy, his attempts to protect them, the lies of his enemies determined to bring him down and brand him a murderer and usurper, all his motives distorted and falsified. Rumours from the ranks that some of his own men had turned traitor clouded his thoughts. Would Thomas Stanley's dubitable fidelity stand the ultimate test and ensure the life of his son Lord Strange, held hostage as surety? Only tomorrow would tell.

Richard felt completely alone, clinging tenuously to the one constant in his life, his faith. Whatever tomorrow would bring, Richard avowed he would face it head on, sword in hand, with God by his side in defence of his Realm, the fate of the Plantagenet dynasty resting heavily upon this beleaguered young monarch.

ON THE MORNING of 22nd August 1485, as dawn broke over Redemore plain, the king awoke from a short, fitful sleep and summoned his chaplains for a brief Mass. He spoke with his knights, positioned his guns and archers along the ridge of Ambion Hill, erected his array of banners and standards, and was helped into his precision crafted armour, moulded closely to his slight figure, the padded breastplate and backplate expertly fashioned to support and conceal his biflected spine, together with an individually shaped saddle which afforded a degree of comfort for the ordeal ahead. Finally, clad for battle, his surcoat resplendent with his coat of arms, Richard donned his helmet encircled by its golden coronet. His nobles questioned the wisdom of their king identifying himself as a prime target but Richard, determined to lead from the front and by example, would show both friend and foe who wore the crown and was proud to serve his people as the rightful king of England. He would defend this right until death if need be and if God decreed otherwise he would accept his fate with dignity.

A note, found pinned to the Duke of Norfolk's tent, had been brought to Richard that morning. The cryptic message read: *'Jockey of Norfolk, be not bold, for Dickon thy master is bought and sold.'* Richard crushed the note angrily in his fist, unwilling to accredit the unknown source as anything but enemy propaganda. He knew he must steel himself for the coming onslaught and not permit any lingering doubt to erode his courage. He knew now he could not count on the support of the Stanleys but with superior numbers and with right on his side, he must win the day! He *must*! The alternative was unthinkable.

Dismissing any nagging negativity for the job now in hand and mounting his redoubtable battle-trained destrier, Richard addressed his troops, confirmed his attack plan; standing in the stirrups, his voice echoing down the ranks, this youthful warrior king galvanised his men. Beneath him restless and wilful, his majestic grey stallion, his mane the colour of sea spume, eyes wide, nostrils flared, sensing the tension in the air, stamping and rearing impatiently as Richard's squires sprang away from the prancing hooves. Richard steadied his steed, stroking the animal's neck reassuringly and, as White Surrey's agitation soothed to his master's calming voice, he gave his orders.

Sir Robert Brackenbury would open hostilities with the guns, having brought them from the Tower, then the archers would unleash their storm of arrows, before John Howard, the faithful Duke of Norfolk, would lead the vanguard into the fray. The king's mounted knights would follow before the foot soldiers and lastly the Earl of Northumberland's troops would bring up the rear. If they were victorious, as he assured his troops they undoubtedly would be, Richard avowed it would mean the crushing of all traitors, an outcome that would remain the same whichever side prevailed. With victory would come unity and strength and he would lead the country to a new golden age of justice, faith and loyalty, God willing.

Opposite them across the wide-open expanse of scrub and heathland sloping Westwards, Tudor's forces were lining up; a collection of Welsh dissidents, French mercenaries and pikemen. These were experienced soldiers, schooled in battle and familiar with the continental style of fighting utilising tightly packed phalanxes of foot soldiers with 18ft long pikes, unfamiliar to English forces. Apart from the skilled knights of the nobility, Richard's army of relatively inexperienced and hastily recruited men were at a disadvantage, despite their superior numbers. Tudor had as his commander the seasoned Earl of Oxford, veteran of the battle of Barnet, determined to keep his men in close formation after the debacle of Warwick's defeat. He held a personal grudge against Norfolk, who had benefited from the redistribution of the rebellious Earl's lands after Barnet and was out for revenge on the second Yorkist king he had faced in battle, *only this time he would win*, he avowed purposefully, as he organised his troops.

Richard had at his side knights devoted and steadfast; his stalwart supporters, his advisors, his friends, true to the House of York, names that would forever be linked with his, their loyalty unquestioned; John Howard, Thomas Howard, Robert Percy, Robert Brackenbury, John Kendall, William Catesby, John Conyers, Walter Deveraux, John De La Pole, James and Robert Harrington, Richard Ratcliffe, Lords John and Thomas Scrope, Richard Huddleston, Ralph Ashton, Marmaduke Constable, Thomas Pilkington, George Talbot, Thomas Metcalfe, Lord Dynham, Thomas Broughton, Thomas Markenfield, John Neville, Humphrey Stafford, John Grey, Thomas Babbington, the Mauleverers; men of courage and honour, ready to lay down their lives in defence of their king and country.

Those masters of prevarication, the self-serving Stanley brothers Thomas and William, stationed themselves to the side of the two armies, on a hill to the South, confirming to Richard that relying on their support was a fruitless endeavour, a foolish expectation of loyalty where there was none. Richard surveyed the scene. He had the advantage of the high ground and the enemy would have the sun in their eyes but as the ground fell away in a gentle slope to the West, a hollow of marshy ground between the two armies presented an obstacle which, as battle progressed, could hamper movement and would eventually prove to be conclusive.

The sun was high in the sky and beat down relentlessly as engagement commenced with a volley of gunfire and archery from both sides before the Duke of Norfolk's vanguard charged down the hill to engage in hand-to-hand fighting. Engaging with Oxford's vanguard of well commanded forces, the lion-hearted Duke was soon overpowered and slain, John De Vere brandishing his sword exultantly as his rival died; a final payback for his defeat at Barnet and subsequent years of exile. As brave Norfolk fell, anger rose in Richard's breast; a deep visceral rage against the Lancastrian defectors toadying to that cowardly opportunist, that unworthy usurper, that vainglorious Welsh status seeker, who colluded with traitors and self-serving manipulators, who had dared to invade his realm and spill the blood of true-hearted men.

Espying Tudor with a small band of men moving in the direction of Thomas Stanley's forces, Richard, filled with ire and a compulsion to settle the score once and for all, made the courageous but impetuous decision to charge. If he could reach Tudor and cut him down before the challengers had time to react, the enemy threat would evaporate like the morning mist, and victory would be his. *Tudor was in his sights. Now! Carpe Diem!*

The King raised his arm, battle-axe in hand, and spurred his restless mount into action, galvanised by his previous victories at Barnet and Tewkesbury, any thoughts of defeat banished by the fierce confidence of youth and the driving force of resolve.

Charging down the hill in an unstoppable gallop, his visor snapped shut, his armour glinting in the morning sun, a golden crown encircling his helmet, his valiant destrier thundering towards his foe, his faithful knights at his side cutting a swathe through the enemy troops, his standard of the white boar streaming out in proud defiance behind its bearer, Richard III, king of England made his way relentlessly towards the red dragon of Wales, towards destiny and death.

Not death by the glory of hand-to-hand combat with a skilled adversary, not death by Henry Tudor, who shrank, paralysed with fear behind his troops as Richard hacked his way towards him; no, death came to Richard by treachery, by falsehood and deceit.

This brave young knight of slight build, wracked by the debilitating fatigue of scoliosis, fought ferociously through the ranks with extraordinary courage, bringing down Sir John Cheyney, a giant of a man, before slaying Tudor's standard bearer William Brandon just yards from Tudor himself. Richard and his knights had been pushed towards the marshy ground near Fenn Lane and, floundering in the mud, Richard's stout-hearted warhorse had unwittingly unseated the king, who continued to fight valiantly on foot. At one point he was urged to flee, as many of his rank and file were doing, seeing him thus surrounded, but Richard refused, vowing to stand his ground or die king of England.

Victory was almost within his grasp, Tudor, his horrified foe tantalisingly close, when immediately Richard and his small band of followers were overwhelmed by the cavalry of William Stanley's 3,000 troops bearing down on them, acting on the instructions of his older brother Thomas, watching from the hill. The slippery Stanleys had finally abandoned their king, turned traitor and come down on the side of Henry Tudor, who now cowered in mortal terror behind a bristling wall of French pikemen. Richard III, king of England, was brought down by sheer weight of numbers, his helmet hacked away, his desperate cries of "Treason, treason!" carried off by the summer breeze to be lost in the haze and clamour of battle. As blow after blow rained down on the stricken king, Richard gave up the fight and accepted his destiny. *Thy will be done O Lord*, he yielded. It was almost a relief, an emancipation. Soon he would be reunited with his beloved son, wife, brothers and father. He could see their faces, hear Anne's voice calling him. Death was the release he now longed for. Fear and pain were no more. *"Sweet Jesus, receive my soul,"* he prayed as the world went dark and the uproar fell away into silence, before a last shuddering breath escaped from his broken body.

All this time the Earl of Northumberland had not stirred from his position on the hill. He watched impassively as Richard was surrounded, watched as he was hewn down in the mud, watched as his king's life expired, his trusted knights dying around him but still Percy held his ground. No doubt fuelled by years of resentment for the loss of his power in the North and the promise of increased supremacy should Richard perish, the self-motivated Earl did nothing. He looked on unmoved and motionless as his sovereign's battered and bloody corpse was stripped naked and slung unceremoniously over the back of a horse like a common criminal, his banner of the white boar wrested triumphantly out of the mire by one of Tudor's trophy bagging men.

After being borne to Leicester in this degrading state, Richard's body was put on display for two days before being hastily placed, without ceremony, tomb or memorial, in a short shallow grave, by the monks of the Greyfriars church. He was 32 years old.

Richard's royal army fled for their lives in shock and confusion when they saw their king slain and Thomas Stanley exultantly placing the circlet of gold onto Henry Tudor's head. The battle was won, they were vanquished. Any knights left standing would now be hunted down and executed for treason against the new monarch, any blood affinity of Richard would be killed and any known followers proclaimed traitor. A new age of tyranny and terror had begun. The white rose of York had been trampled underfoot, crushed, stained red with the blood of steadfast allegiant men, the Plantagenet flame all but extinguished, their great dynasty dying with the setting sun.

Chapter Twenty Two

EWS OF THE BATTLE AT Bosworth took several days to filter through to Middleham but when it did it was met with stunned disbelief. The king dead! Their beloved Lord of the North country, their brave champion, a young man in the prime of life, slain unmercifully on the battlefield, his bloody, mud-spattered, twisted, beaten body paraded through the streets of Leicester, naked for all to see; his followers killed or hunted down to face trial and a traitor's death; the crown of England snatched by a pretender of dubious descent, aided by treacherous Welshmen, greedy Frenchmen and English traitors of the lowest calibre.

Lies were already being broadcast that Richard was a murderous tyrant and Henry Tudor the valiant liberator, lies manufactured by greed and cowardice, lies that would bury the truth in the fickle memory of the populace, lies that would last forever.

The messenger described the battle, as the household rushed to hear the news. He told how the Duke of Norfolk was brought down, before Robert Brackenbury, Richard Ratcliffe and faithful John Kendall, amongst many others, were all slain as the king charged into the melee, his battle axe whirling, cutting, slashing, edging ever closer to Tudor, who stood rooted to the spot in terror behind his pikemen. But for the treachery of the Stanley's, awaiting their moment, and the inaction of Northumberland, Richard may have reached his goal, courageously refusing a fresh horse on which to escape before he was overwhelmed by sheer weight of numbers, cut down mercilessly by a dozen blows from halberd, sword, dagger and mace, to sink into oblivion, his helmet wrenched off, a slice to the back of his head spilling his blood and brains into the rich soil of Bosworth field.

Eleanor, lately returned from Sheriff Hutton, her senses awakened, her passions re-kindled since her liaison with Richard, had felt a sense of foreboding that she had tried to dismiss. Now, standing on the edge of the anxious crowd, she knew why. She listened horrified, unable to take in what she heard, desperately wishing she could cover her ears in denial. *Nay, nay, nay, merciful Jesus, oh pray God not this! Not Richard! Not Richard! This cannot be! I will not believe it! I cannot!* Gathering her skirts, she fled from the castle, away from those cruel words she had prayed never to hear, away from the sword of despair that pierced her heart, away from the unbearable truth, the nightmare she had long dreaded now realised, her throat choking with every gasp, until she was barely able to breathe. Up the hill she ran, stumbling over her skirts, wracking sobs enveloping her body, the pain in her chest overwhelming her, the pounding in her heart refusing to accept what in her head she knew she must, as she flung herself down on the grassy slope at the spot where he had first loved her.

"Oh, dear Lord, how can this be? My brave Richard, my one true lord and master, my king, my valiant prince, my lover, my life! You are gone from me forever, never again will I look into those soft sad eyes, hear your gentle voice, feel the warmth of your caress, the vigour of your kiss, your mouth fusing into one with mine! How can I endure this loss for all eternity? Your love for your family, for England, for your people, your faith, your loyalty and piety, the tragedies you had to bear, your pain, your loneliness, your courage in the face of shameful treachery. Why, oh why did God allow this to happen? What will befall us all now?

Eleanor's thoughts raced. She felt sick at the thought of his lean, unclad body, abused, violated, blood and mud-smeared, callously pitched over a horse's back, hands and feet bound, like so much baggage, paraded through the streets of Leicester like a common felon, defiled and dumped unceremoniously in a hurriedly prepared grave – what manner of man would do that? she wondered, appalled at the lack of respect. This was a king of England, a brave warrior, a man of honour, faith and principle, so unlike those who succeeded him, who usurped his crown and seized his kingdom.

Only two days earlier the people of this same city had cheered spontaneously as their king marched off in pomp and splendour to defend his people from a foreign invader. Now they welcomed the victor in a shameful show of fickle appeasement and disloyalty.

Oh Richard, you deserved so much better than this! Eleanor wept, trying desperately to see God's purpose in this tragedy. *Merciful Lord why did you desert him in the hour of his most urgent need?* she cried searching for an answer but none would come, no solace, save the whispering sough of the summer breeze as it whipped her hair around her face and wafted away into the haze like a long drawn out exhalation of breath.

Eleanor thought of Elizabeth, a beautiful young maiden, now sixteen, with her father's eyes and slender lissom frame. Wracked with guilt for withholding the secret of her daughter's birth, for denying her child the chance to know and love the man who gave her life, Eleanor pictured the hurt in her daughter's eyes when she realised the truth her mother has kept from her. Never again would Bess see her father, have occasion to laugh with him, throw her arms around him in affectionate joy or know of his love for her. *Oh Bess, I should have told you! Forgive me!* The Plantagenet gene surging through her daughter's veins must never be disclosed for fear of her life, as England would have to re-adjust and re-group under a new tyranny, determined to expunge every last drop of Yorkist lifeblood from its people.

Doubled up with grief, unable or unwilling to move, she knew not how long she lay there, but the sun was low in the West when Eleanor raised herself, wiping her tear-stained cheeks on her sleeve. Shivering involuntarily as a freshening gust of wind cooled her skin, she closed her eyes and took a deep breath of the sweet ambrosial air of this lush green valley; the same air that once *he* breathed, filled his lungs as he rode his courser, blew his hair across his face as he followed the hunt, stole his voice away over the crags, fed his smile, fuelled his kiss. Never more would Richard savour the fragrant morning scent of a wildflower meadow, shade his eyes from the midday sun, or tremble in the gathering dusk of a Wensleydale evening, as Eleanor would have to without him.

Somehow her life would go on, the relentless march of time stretching ahead as each page of history turns, regardless of the fortunes of those caught up in the flow. Somehow, this young woman would have to endure the loss of the man who had first captured her heart, stolen her soul, penetrated her subconscious, pervaded every waking hour and force herself to come to terms with the tragedy of his untimely death. She knew memories of him would invade her sleep, a fleeting joy only to be cruelly crushed as reality dawned, when the pain of her loss would revisit her time and again, as if for the first time. She already knew she would see him everywhere, a shadow in every dark corner, a footstep on every stair, an echo in every corridor, a ghost in every dream, a spirit unable or unwilling to leave the people and places he loved.

She thought about her life at Middleham castle, the old Countess, now alone and bereft of her family; her own fair daughter, about to reach womanhood, not yet aware of her royal blood, her young son, who was so like his gentle father. In a few years she would no longer be needed by them; what would she do? Where would she go? A religious order perhaps? Somehow, Eleanor knew she had to survive, sustained by God's love and the precious memories that resided within her, shut away, secret, eternal. Time would tell. Time would write her a new chapter. In a thousand years, this maid of Middleham's life would be as distant as the faintest star in the universe. Who would know or care that this lowly maiden had once aroused the ardour of a king of England?

The church bell rang out, it was time to go. Eleanor stood up stiffly, brushing grass strands and clover leaves off her skirt, when glancing downwards, her attention was suddenly caught by a tiny blue butterfly fluttering up from her feet. As she stepped aside to avoid it, something else in the long grass caught her eye as it reflected the sun's rays, nestled between the twisted stalks of buttercups and meadow foxtail. She bent down and picked it up – part of a silver belt buckle, well weathered but unmistakable.

"Oh Richard, Richard!" a sob of recognition caught in her throat, remembering his frantic fumblings and teenage passion of their first union. Closing her eyes and pressing the worn fragment gently to her lips, she made her way slowly down the verdant greensward, clutching the precious memento of her fallen lover tightly against her leaden heart, fresh tears blurring her vision as she returned to her life, her children, her future stretching before her, empty and desolate, without the men she had loved.

High overhead, as the tiny figure of a young woman trudged forlornly homeward, a lone buzzard soared effortlessly into the golden sky, wheeling gracefully over the moorland heights, away from this tranquil valley, away from the rich pastures of clover, lady's smocks and meadowsweet, oblivious of the everyday lives of those below and the dawning of a strange and terrifying dark age, searching, searching for its prey, as new life waited for its parent's return.

The End

Author's Conclusion

LEANOR'S STORY IS A WORK of fiction. There is no evidence to suggest there was ever a maid of Middleham of this description, or that she had a child by Richard Duke of Gloucester. However, the events of Richard's life and death described here are based on fact. He lived at Middleham in his youth, returning later when he married Anne Neville. He was known to have had several illegitimate children before his marriage, the exact number of which remains uncertain.

530 YEARS LATER, I stood outside Leicester Cathedral on a clear, crisp Sunday in March 2015, awaiting the funeral procession of our last Plantagenet king. I waited for six hours, unwilling to move for fear of losing my place amongst the throngs of citizens flocking in ever increasing numbers to the city streets and beyond. Finally, just before 6pm, the funeral cortege approached. The mortal remains of king Richard III, borne past in a simple oak coffin, were preceded by mounted knights in full armour, followed by clergymen and dignitaries while thousands of white roses thrown by the crowd littered the city streets. My rose landed on the bier and my heart went out to this most brave and chivalrous knight, who had lain ignominiously under a car park, lost for half a millennium. As the Cathedral bell tolled, the crowds went quiet. Shouts of 'God bless you Richard, rest in peace', broke the silence, while the coffin was carried slowly into the church, watched by thousands along the route and at home on television screens.

Draped in its embroidered pall and topped by a beautifully crafted golden crown, the coffin was displayed for five days before being lowered into its final resting place. Long queues of visitors snaked back through the city streets, waiting for hours to file past

Richard's coffin and pay their respects. Respect long overdue. A service of re-interment took place on the Thursday, attended by HRH the Duke of Gloucester, the Archbishop of Canterbury, many other dignitaries and specially invited guests. At last, I thought, this would be a more fitting farewell for a king of England who died so young, so bravely and so tragically, slain by the treachery of those who should have been most loyal.

Richard's last hours after the Battle of Bosworth on 22nd August 1485 were, in my opinion, one of the most abhorrent and disrespectful episodes in our long history, as the king's naked body was callously thrown over a horse and paraded through the streets of Leicester, before being cast into a hastily dug grave, which was too small for him. This heinous offence, this shameful disrespect to a brave warrior, an anointed king of England, would forever cast a black shadow of moral turpitude on the perpetrators of such a vile and pitiless act.

Now, as I watched and waited outside the Cathedral, I hoped the ceremonies of this day would go some way towards atoning for his treatment in 1485. I felt a personal shame as a citizen of my country who had allowed history to stand unchallenged. This courageous young man who tried to save England from the tyranny of the Tudors, who believed in justice for the common man, who tragically lost everyone he loved and yet was vilified and branded a tyrant, murderer and usurper by his successors, eager to establish a firmer footing for themselves and divert attention away from the shadow of their doubtful lineage.

Henry Tudor's subsequent efforts to suppress his double illegitimacy from the public perception, would result in the contemptible and ignoble defamation of his predecessor, whose bravery, loyalty and chivalric ideals he strove to uphold lay trampled in the mud that fateful day on Bosworth field.

In fact, the Tudors tried so hard to write themselves into the history books as the saviours of England they almost succeeded and to this day many still believe Richard III to be the monstrous caricature of a man, who murdered his way to the throne, portrayed so vividly by Shakespeare, over a hundred years later. They ignore the fact our esteemed playwright's witty portrayal of Richard III clearly alluded to Elizabeth I's Lord Privy Seal, Robert Cecil, her unpopular spymaster, who was hunchbacked and small of stature. Shakespeare, with his eye for the dramatic, would make use of as many devices as possible in order to present his subject as a degenerate villain, a crowd-pleasing anti-hero, in an effort to amuse the queen and represent her grandfather as the conquering hero who rid England of a tyrant. If gossip and lies painted a blacker picture, all the better for it. Tudor England was not about to gainsay him. Henry VII and his spin doctors could lay as many murders as they wished at Richard's feet without fear of rebuttal.

Many of his detractors conveniently forget that Richard III was a devoutly religious man, brought up in the strict traditions of the Catholic church, unswervingly loyal to his brother king Edward IV, whose children, I and many others, fervently believe, he would never have considered harming and who was praised by his subjects in his lifetime for his fairness, generosity and concern for the common good. I submit that not for one moment would he have ever entertained the needless murder of two children, his own kin, thus condemning his soul to eternal damnation – there was no need, their succession was already invalidated by their father's profligacy. Richard's strong belief in moral integrity, honour and probity ensured he attempted to uphold these qualities in everything he did. His enduring Christian faith underpinned his life and purpose and the tragedy of this was his spinal condition, which in the beliefs of his time, was equated with wickedness and moral degeneracy, the absolute opposite of Richard's character.

He strove to be the best he could be, ignoring his physical pain, disguising what must have been a constant cause of discomfort and sadness to him, given the perfect physique of his older brother, which makes his prowess on the battlefield all the more remarkable. He was thrust into the highest position in the land, not from vaulting ambition or greed, as Tudor propaganda would have us believe, but from necessity, by virtue of his Plantagenet ancestry and the need to unite a divided country.

In his short reign Richard strove to reverse injustice, create a fairer legal system, unite warring factions and lead his people into a life of piety and faith, adhering to their Christian beliefs, traditions and family values.

Despite history singling out Richard III as a usurper, why does it seem to be overlooked that William I, Stephen, Henry IV, Edward IV and Henry VII all usurped the throne, whereas Richard III was proclaimed king by an act of parliament, rendering him the only one of them lawfully crowned? The answer lies with the Tudors and their wish to legitimise their dynasty in the eyes of posterity.

'One who deceives will always find those who allow themselves to be deceived.' Niccolo Machiavelli

Contrary to public perception, Richard had neither a hunchback, *nor* a withered arm, *nor* walk with a limp. Yes, he did have scoliosis, which must have been a painful and debilitating hindrance to him in battle and throughout his life, but despite his slight frame he proved to be a skilled, courageous fighter and consummate horseman. During his lifetime, his physical abnormality was not apparent, seen only by those who knew him intimately; the only contemporary description of him being that he was small of stature. Only after death when his naked body was on show did his crooked spine reveal itself – a gift to the Tudor propagandists who greedily seized upon this abnormality to malign an honourable man. Richard III, the last of the Plantagenets, the only king of England to die in battle since 1066, who all his life aspired to the code of chivalry and strove to uphold morality, was denied in death the very protocol he lived by. Richard's outstanding bravery at Bosworth is no less astounding than the treachery that brought him down.

I strongly believe that if Richard III had been victorious at Bosworth, he would have led England into a new golden age of honour, truth, mercy and justice – instead we were thrust into the dark and troubled Tudor dynasty of lies, greed, destruction, fear and cruelty, far more damaging than the Plantagenet dynasty that preceded it.

Interestingly and perhaps gratifyingly for Richard's supporters, the Earl of Northumberland, Henry Percy, was slain in 1489 by an angry mob near Thirsk, for his failure to support Richard at

Bosworth and William Stanley was later executed by Henry Tudor in 1495. Small recompense, however, for the loss of a man of such valour and integrity.

Now, as befits a former king of England, Richard III rests forever at Leicester Cathedral, in a simple tomb of finest York stone and, as a committed Ricardian, I hope one day we can clear the name of this most loyal and steadfast knight, whose like we will not see again.

Our eternal gratitude will never be enough to thank Philippa Langley and the late Dr John Ashdown Hill for their tireless efforts in searching for, discovering and identifying Richard III's mortal remains, without which the last of our great Plantagenet kings may have lain undiscovered for many years to come, perhaps forever.

Postscript

The Middleham Jewel

In September 1985, a beautiful jewel was found to the south east of Middleham castle beside a path which would have led to Jervaulx Abbey. This Medieval jewel in the form of a diamond-shaped locket was crafted in gold, engraved with images of the Trinity, the Nativity and a richly enamelled inscription, topped by a huge dark blue sapphire, possibly originally bordered with pearls. It would have been made for a lady of great wealth and piety, worn as a token of faith, protection against illness and the rigours of childbirth. This story suggests this jewel belonged to Anne Beauchamp, the Countess of Warwick in the latter half of the fifteenth century but this is merely the author's notion, rather than established fact. There are several ladies of wealth and position who may have owned the jewel and lived at some time at Middleham Castle. The jewel is currently on display at the Yorkshire Museum in York.

Middleham Castle

Middleham Castle still stands proudly on its hill above the town, now ruined, open to the skies, roofless, all internal structures long perished, save for sturdy stone skeleton walls, now serving as roosting perches for rooks, starlings and pigeons, outcrops of wild thyme and harebells sprouting from the crevices. Stairways crumbling, gaping holes where windows once held fast, echoes of past magnificence, footprints of lives once lived. It is not hard to imagine the castle full of life, servants coming and going, guards at the gates, nobles dining in the Great Hall, relaxing in the solar or praying in the chapel. Visitors can still climb up to the topmost turret and look out across Wensleydale, towards the site of the old Norman motte and bailey fortification and up to the moor beyond.

Every year Richard III's banner flies from the flagpole on his birthday (2nd October) and other notable dates and Ricardian summer fairs are occasionally held in the castle precincts in July. The castle is maintained by English Heritage and the ticket office and gift shop is within the grounds.

THE RICHARD III SOCIETY

READERS INTERESTED IN joining the Richard III Society, whose aim is to promote research into the life and times of Richard III, secure a reassessment and raise awareness, may do so through their website online at www.richardiii.net The annual membership fee includes the Society's annual publication *The Ricardian* journal and a quarterly *Ricardian Bulletin* magazine, packed with informative articles, photographs, letters, book reviews, details of forthcoming events and merchandise for sale. There are numerous affiliated local Richard III Society Groups and Branches around the UK and internationally, where members can meet regularly for talks, discussions and social occasions.

SUGGESTED NON-FICTION READING

The Maligned King by Annette Carson, History Press.
Richard the Third by Paul Murray Kendall, Norton & Co.
Richard III, Loyalty Binds Me by Matthew Lewis, Amberley.
The Betrayal of Richard III by V.B. Lamb, History Press.
The Search for Richard III by Philippa Langley & Michael Jones, John Murray Publishing.

ACKNOWLEDGEMENT

WITH GRATEFUL THANKS to the artist P.J. Lynch, who kindly granted me permission to use his beautiful illustration on the cover of this book.

Go, soul, the body's guest,
Upon a thankless errand;
Fear not to touch the best;
The truth shall be thy warrant.
Go, since I needs must die,
And give the world the lie.

Sir Walter Ralegh c.1592

Artist's impression of King Richard III.